A Hint of Seduction

"Witty dialogue, a gamble, a horse race, a hunt for three noblemen, and a gossip columnist whose titillating tidbits have the *ton*'s ear all combine in this delightful Regency romance that showcases Grey's ability to bring the wit of the era to life. A charmer for sure!"   —*Romantic Times*

"Each new Amelia Grey tale is a diamond. This story is wonderfully fast-paced with delightful surprises and many laughs. Ms. Grey has proven once again she is a master storyteller."   —*Affaire de Coeur*

"Pure delight . . . This story is so much fun to read, it will keep you entertained until the last page is turned. Treat yourself to this pleasurable, captivating story. You'll find yourself as besotted to this story as John is to Catherine."
    —*The Best Reviews*

A Little Mischief

"A wonderful adventure story with lots of twists and turns."
    —*Rendezvous*

"Filled with witty banter . . . that kept me laughing out loud . . . For anyone who loves romances rich with laughter, *A Little Mischief* is not to be missed."
    —*Romance Reviews Today*

continued . . .

A Dash of Scandal

Never a Bride

"Will keep you up all night—praying for a wedding. Fresh and original and destined to be a keeper. Charming and delightful—a must-read." —Joan Johnston

"A delightful Regency romp. You'll have lots of fun with this one." —Kat Martin, author of *Perfect Sin*

"An uplifting, wonderfully sensual story. I hated for it to end." —Meryl Sawyer, author of *Trust No One*

"Readers will be quickly drawn in by the lively pace, the appealing protagonists, and the sexual chemistry that almost visibly shimmers between them in this charming, light-hearted, and well-done Regency." —*Library Journal*

"Witty dialogue and clever schemes . . . Both of Grey's vivid characters will charm readers." —*Booklist*

A TASTE OF TEMPTATION

Amelia Grey

BERKLEY SENSATION, NEW YORK

THE BERKLEY PUBLISHING GROUP
Published by the Penguin Group
Penguin Group (USA) Inc.
375 Hudson Street, New York, New York 10014, USA
Penguin Group (Canada), 90 Eglinton Avenue East, Suite 700, Toronto, Ontario M4P 2Y3, Canada
(a division of Pearson Penguin Canada Inc.)
Penguin Books Ltd., 80 Strand, London WC2R 0RL, England
Penguin Group Ireland, 25 St. Stephen's Green, Dublin 2, Ireland (a division of Penguin Books Ltd.)
Penguin Group (Australia), 250 Camberwell Road, Camberwell, Victoria 3124, Australia
(a division of Pearson Australia Group Pty. Ltd.)
Penguin Books India Pvt. Ltd., 11 Community Centre, Panchsheel Park, New Delhi—110 017, India
Penguin Group (NZ), Cnr. Airborne and Rosedale Roads, Albany, Auckland 1310, New Zealand
(a division of Pearson New Zealand Ltd.)
Penguin Books (South Africa) (Pty.) Ltd., 24 Sturdee Avenue, Rosebank, Johannesburg 2196, South
Africa

Penguin Books Ltd., Registered Offices: 80 Strand, London WC2R 0RL, England

This is a work of fiction. Names, characters, places, and incidents either are the product of the author's imagination or are used fictitiously, and any resemblance to actual persons, living or dead, business establishments, events, or locales is entirely coincidental. The publisher does not have any control over and does not assume any responsibility for author or third-party websites or their content.

A TASTE OF TEMPTATION

A Berkley Sensation Book / published by arrangement with the author

PRINTING HISTORY
Berkley Sensation edition / December 2005

Copyright © 2005 by Gloria Dale Skinner.
Cover art by Leslie Peck.
Cover design by George Long.

ISBN: 0-425-20721-8

BERKLEY® SENSATION
Berkley Sensation Books are published by The Berkley Publishing Group,
a division of Penguin Group (USA) Inc.,
375 Hudson Street, New York, New York 10014.
BERKLEY SENSATION and the "B" design are trademarks belonging to Penguin Group (USA) Inc.

PRINTED IN THE UNITED STATES OF AMERICA

10 9 8 7 6 5 4 3 2 1

One

"It is with true love as it is with a ghost; everyone talks about it but few have seen it." As the new Season begins, many lovely young ladies will be looking for love among the *ton*'s of unattached gentlemen. And none will be more sought after than the last remaining bachelor of the once famous Terrible Threesome. Andrew Terwillger, the Earl of Dugdale, is back in Town, but is he looking to make a match?

Lord Truefitt
Society's Daily Column

OLIVIA BANNING FOLDED the week-old edition of the *Daily Reader* and handed it back to her aunt. "Lord Truefitt is colorful with his tittle-tattle, Auntie. I wonder if anyone in London's Society ever tries to find out who he is."

Agatha Loudermilk laid the paper on the bed beside her and looked up at Olivia. "I'm sure there have been hundreds over the years who would like to know, but not me. If his identity were discovered, he would no longer have access to the *ton* and couldn't write any more columns. He's so clever with his quotes and so delicious with his gossip that I don't want him to stop."

Olivia smiled down at her great aunt, who was propped against fluffy pillows having her morning chocolate and toast in bed.

"He does have a way with openings. Remember, last Season he started every column with a quote that had something to do with horses."

"Yes, I do. And the year before that every column of gossip started with a quote from Shakespeare. It looks as if this Season he is starting each daily with a quote about ghosts."

Olivia gave her aunt an indulgent smile. "You are looking much better today. It must be because spring is in the air."

Her aunt's lively green eyes sparkled as she said, "I am much better indeed, but the reason is not the sunshine or the passing of winter. Come and sit beside me, Livy." She patted the bed. "I've been making plans for us and it's time to tell you about them."

Intrigued by the excitement showing on her aunt's aged face, Olivia pushed the news paper aside and sat down. If Agatha was making plans for a party, it was a sure sign she was over the serious illness that had gripped her for most of the winter.

"I must go to London soon and I need you to go with me."

Surprised by this statement, Olivia said, "Auntie, you were in bed with that terrible cough for weeks. You're not well enough to take a trip to London. Besides that, I'm sure the roads are still boggy and treacherous. It's best you forget about traveling for a while."

"I say nonsense to both your concerns, Livy. I'm feeling better than I have in years, and as far as the condition of roads, they should be in passable shape by the time we're packed and ready to leave."

Olivia knitted her brows together in bewilderment. "I don't understand. You haven't been back to London since you came to live in Kent and take care of me a dozen years ago. You've always said there is nothing for you in London anymore. Why do you suddenly need to go now?"

Her aunt leaned forward and in a whispery voice said, "Lord Pinkwater wants me to come to him. He has something to tell me."

Obviously her aunt wasn't as healthy in mind as she was in body if she was talking to someone from the afterlife. Olivia eyed her aunt with concern, for Lord Pinkwater had been dead for years.

"I think you're confused about something, Auntie," she said softly, hoping not to upset her aunt's delicate hold on reality. "You do remember that Lord Pinkwater died more than thirty years ago, don't you?"

Agatha laughed softly. Her bright eyes danced with intrigue. She suddenly looked very mischievous for a lady well past her prime.

"Of course he did, my dear. How good of you to point that out. I should have said that *his ghost* is beckoning me to come to him."

At first Olivia didn't know how to respond to that shocking revelation, so she merely repeated her aunt's words in the form of a question. "A ghost is summoning you to London?"

"Yes." Agatha picked up her warm chocolate and sipped it.

There wasn't even a hint of a tremble or a shake in the blue-veined hand that held the delicate china cup, but something was wrong. Her aunt appeared as lucid as Olivia, but there was no way Agatha could be.

Concern quickly turned to apprehension and a shiver of disquiet stole over Olivia. She wouldn't allow herself to panic—yet. There had to be a logical reason for Agatha to think a ghost had visited her. Perhaps she was taking the opening of Lord Truefitt's column a little too seriously.

Agatha looked better and stronger than she had in months. The luster had returned to her long, silver hair. Her appetite was adequate, and she was taking long walks in the garden each day. Her face, while showing lines of age around her eyes and mouth, was glowing with good health.

But what could have happened to her sound mind?

Olivia cleared her throat and rearranged the folds of her pale blue morning dress while she thought about what to say. She certainly didn't want to upset Agatha, so a calm approach was in order.

"I don't think you're feeling well, Auntie. Perhaps I should take your tray and let you nap. We can continue our conversation later in the day."

"Oh, heaven's angels, Livy, don't make me sound like I'm on my death bed. My cough is gone, my strength has returned. I've been going downstairs for a month now. I am not sick in body nor am I weak in my mind."

Not knowing what else to do, Olivia rose from the bed and plumped the goose feather pillows behind her aunt. If molly-coddling wasn't going to pacify Agatha's fragile hold on reality she'd pursue a different approach and take charge of the situation.

Firmly she said, "And apparently your activities of the past four weeks have been too much of a strain on you. Clearly you are not yourself. You just said a ghost told you he wants you to come to London."

"He does," Agatha said without a hint of embarrassment or doubt. "And my pillows are fine, thank you very much.

Listen to me, Livy. I'm not going insane. I know Lord Pinkwater is calling to me and I must go to him."

Olivia let her arms drop to the sides of her muslin skirt. Not willing to give in to Agatha's pronouncement, she said, "But that's absurd, Auntie. Even if Lord Pinkwater's ghost is alive—I mean, if he is real or present or whatever ghosts are—why would he be summoning you to London?"

A faraway expression settled on Agatha's face. Her eyes held an unusual glimmer and her thin lips settled into a wistful smile. Olivia had the feeling her aunt was looking into the past, at days long gone but often remembered.

"You know that Lord Pinkwater was the man who broke my heart all those years ago, and that he is the reason I never married."

"Yes," Olivia answered, wondering what could have happened to trigger Agatha's reflective mood on the past.

"I never gave up hope. I always felt he would come back to me some day. And now he has."

Olivia's breath caught in her throat at the sadness she heard in her aunt's voice. She'd always known that Agatha had never married because the legendary Lord Pinkwater jilted her when she was eighteen and ran off with another young lady more than forty years ago.

In the twelve years Agatha had lived with Olivia she'd seldom mentioned the man. Olivia had assumed that after all these years her aunt had finally gotten over him, but apparently her heartache had only deepened.

"But you knew he was a rogue who had many lovers before you agreed to the betrothal. He didn't even marry the woman he left you for. I don't think he ever loved anyone but himself. Why did you wait for him?"

"I had to. It didn't matter that he never really loved me. I loved him and that was enough. It still is." She turned her gaze to Olivia. "At last, he wants me to come to him."

Suddenly Olivia reached over and put the palm of her hand to her aunt's forehead. Agatha brushed it aside.

"Stop that, silly girl. Don't fuss or worry about me. I don't have a fever, and I've not suddenly gone mad."

"I don't think you're crazy," Olivia said, wondering if she really believed that. "Perhaps you've had too much tonic and you are imagining him calling to you in your dreams."

Olivia needed a logical explanation for her aunt's sudden revelation.

"I haven't had any laudanum in weeks. Ask Susan, she will tell you."

"The maid will say whatever you tell her to," Olivia insisted.

"Then take all the tonics and elixirs in this house and throw them away if you don't believe me." She reached up and took hold of Olivia's hand. Agatha's skin was warm and her grip was as steady and firm as her eyes. "I'm not imagining this. Lord Pinkwater's spirit is as real as you and I. This is very important to me, Livy. I must go to London and find him."

Olivia was moved by her aunt's passion, but all that did was fuel her unease about Agatha's state of mind. Olivia wasn't even sure she believed in ghosts. She'd never had serious reason to think about it. She'd read about them in any number of books and heard stories, but she'd never seen one.

And even putting all that aside, this wasn't a time in her life when she wanted to leave Kent and travel to London. She was looking forward to the spring dances, house parties, and the continued attention of a certain young gentleman who had recently caught her eye.

"If Lord Pinkwater has a ghost, I mean if he is a spirit or

whatever he is, why doesn't he just fly through the air and come to you?"

Agatha let go of Olivia's hand. "I don't know the answer to that yet," she said with all conviction. "I suppose he can't. Or, perhaps it's because London is where we met and where we last saw each other. Maybe he wants to tell me why he left me for Lady Veronica. Maybe that's why his soul is not at rest. It doesn't matter. I'll ask him when we find him."

An anxious feeling shimmered down Olivia's spine. "When *we* find him?"

"Yes. I know he resides at a house in London but not which one."

"Auntie, surely you aren't suggesting we go searching homes for a ghost."

Agatha smiled as sweetly as if she were talking to their minister after Sunday morning worship. "That's exactly what we're going to do. I have it all worked out. I've decided to give you a Season in London. That way we will be invited to all the best parties in private homes in Mayfair."

"You know he's in a house in Mayfair but not which one? How do you know that?"

Her aunt looked aghast that Olivia could even ask such a silly question. "Lord Pinkwater wouldn't dream of staying in any other section of London, dead or alive."

Olivia felt sufficiently rebuked. "All right, but how will you determine which house he is in?"

"I'll know when we enter the house whether or not he resides in it. I'm not sure if I will sense his presence or if he will show me a sign. But I will know when I reach the house he inhabits."

Olivia lifted her skirts and knelt down beside the bed. "Auntie, you know I would do anything for you, but how can I help you find a ghost? I'm not even sure I believe in them. And you know I have no desire for a Season in London. I'm hoping to get to know Mr. Yost better when the spring assemblies begin."

Agatha patted Olivia's cheek with her warm, soft hand and smiled at her with affection. "I know you think this young man pleases you, and perhaps in certain ways he does, but I think he is much too weak for you. You need a stronger, more prosperous gentleman."

"Nonsense. Look where my mother ended up with a strong, prosperous man. She spent all her days alone in the quiet countryside while her husband maintained a full social life in London. I'd rather have a country gentleman for a husband who will love me and live with me than an absent titled lord."

"And perhaps you will have such a country gentleman. But in the meantime, it will be good for you to spend the Season in London with me and meet gentlemen more fitting to your station in life than Mr. Yost. You might even catch the eye of a viscount or an earl."

It was obvious her aunt wasn't listening to her. Attracting some peer was the last thing Olivia wanted. Her mother had married the youngest son of an earl but the union hadn't brought her happiness.

"I'm pleased to have caught the eye of Mr. Yost, Auntie, and you know that."

"Oh, heaven's angels, Livy, I'm not asking you to choose a husband in London, but why would you want to settle for a common man in Kent before you at least look over the available gentlemen in London? I'm only asking that you go with me and help me search for Lord Pinkwater's ghost, and then you can come home and marry Mr. Yost or whomever may catch your attention—if that is still what your heart desires. I don't want to go without you, but

I will. I must settle this part of my past which has haunted me for years."

Her aunt was serious. She would go alone.

As a young child, Olivia remembered hearing many stories from her mother about how well-respected her Aunt Agatha was in London and what an exciting life she lived. Agatha Loudermilk, twice removed cousin to the powerful Duke of Norfolk, had sat at the tables of kings and at the feet of queens, but she'd only given her heart to one man.

The undeserving Lord Pinkwater.

Agatha had left her active life in London to come to the country and take care of her grandniece Olivia after Olivia's mother died and her father didn't want the responsibility of seeing that an eight-year-old girl had the proper upbringing. It was just as well since her father, whom she never really knew, died a year after her mother.

Olivia couldn't bear the thought that Agatha would return to London and be seen as a batty old woman no longer in her right mind looking for a ghost. She didn't want that for her aunt. Olivia owed her. Agatha came to her aid when she needed it and now Olivia would help her. She would go to London and protect Agatha's exceptional reputation.

"Of course, Auntie," she said with a resigned smile. "I will go with you, but I have one request."

The sparkle returned to her aunt's eyes instantly. "Anything."

"Let's not tell anyone we're searching for Lord Pinkwater's ghost. I think it will be best if we keep this between us."

Agatha patted Olivia's hand. "I won't say a word to anyone but you, my dear."

𝒯HE LOW RUMBLE of chatter filled the club room at White's as Andrew Terwillger, the fifth Earl of Dugdale, looked across the table at his two friends. A bottle of the best port money could buy stood in front of them. The first pour was still in their glasses and already Andrew sensed Chandler and John were restless and eager for the evening to be over.

At the far side of the room a warming fire crackled and hissed, taking the chill out of the air. The gentlemen's club was filled with men Andrew had known for years. Some played billiards in the next room; others participated in heated games of Whist or some other card game, while a few were just drinking, talking, and laughing. Everyone seemed to be having an enjoyable time, except the two at Andrew's table.

Andrew was trying to figure out why he hardly recognized the men who'd been his best friends for over fifteen years. They hadn't changed in appearance but were both different in demeanor.

He'd just returned from having been gone almost a year and he was ready to give in to some well-deserved debauchery. But his friends couldn't be less interested in drinking, gambling, or seeking the bed of a shapely young woman.

Andrew asked, "Why do I get the feeling that I'm keeping the two of you from something?"

Chandler Prestwick, the Earl of Dunraven, and John Wickenham-Thickenham-Fines, the Earl of Chatwin, glanced quickly at each other before looking back to Andrew.

"I don't know," Chandler said. "It's not me. How about you, John?"

"Certainly not me," John answered cautiously and

picked up his glass of port and raised it in salute to Andrew. "I have plenty of time. It's good to have you back in Town."

"I'll drink to that and add it was good news to hear your financial troubles were settled once you learned the problem was that your estate manager was stealing from you," Chandler added.

Andrew picked up his port and clicked it against his friends' glasses. "Right. I should have checked up on Willard Hawkins long before I did."

"All that matters is that you got to the bottom of this mess. Though, too bad he took a shot at you and escaped before you could turn him over to the local magistrate."

"Yes, the bloody criminal needs to be chained to the walls of Newgate," John said.

Andrew had made light of the fact that Hawkins had shot at him. He didn't want his friends to know the bullet had grazed his arm. It hadn't occurred to Andrew that his estate manger might carry a pistol, so he hadn't been prepared to be shot at.

"He will be caught soon enough," Andrew assured them. "I met with a Runner from Bow Street today. He's heading to Derbyshire first thing tomorrow to find him. Hawkins has relatives in that area so I'm thinking he's hiding out somewhere around there."

"Sounds reasonable," John agreed.

Chandler laughed suddenly. "In our younger days, we wouldn't have even thought to ask for help from a Runner, the Thames Police, or anyone else to find the thief."

"We would have gotten on our best horses and ridden after the bastard ourselves," John added.

"And we wouldn't have stopped until we found him," Andrew said.

"I still have my pearl-handled rapier. That would put a scare in him."

"I was always better with a pistol. He wouldn't get past a shot from me."

"Well, if you both remember I'm pretty good with sword and pistol," Andrew bragged good-naturedly.

Chandler gave him a friendly punch on one shoulder while John gave him a thump on the other.

They all laughed and tipped their glasses together again before taking another drink. For a moment Andrew felt like his old friends were back at the table with him. They were having a good time, bragging and drinking just like they used to. There was the possibility of an adventure in the air.

The year Andrew had spent at his country estate had been good for him. Instead of spending his nights drinking and gambling and his days sleeping he'd taken the opportunity to study and learn about his lands. He spent time with his tenants, helping them break horses and tend fields during the day and was so exhausted in the evenings he'd had no trouble sleeping. His body was firmer, stronger, and healthier.

His mind was sharper, too.

Doing physical labor was uncommon for anyone of the gentry or the peerage, but Andrew was glad he'd done it. Being with the farmers and seeing what they produced helped him know that the figures in Willard Hawkins's books had to be wrong.

"You know, we can still do that," Andrew said when he put his glass down.

"What?" Chandler asked.

"Go to Derbyshire and find Willard Hawkins ourselves. I wouldn't need the Runner if I had the two of you helping me."

"Are you serious?" John asked, the smile fading from his face.

"Why not? No one rides, hunts, or fights better than we do. As I recall, there was a time when we set our minds to it, we could do anything we wanted. That hasn't changed, has it?"

Chandler and John glanced at each other again and Andrew felt the excitement that was between them just moments before ebb away.

"No, we haven't changed, but our lives have," John said.

"You know we'd love to do it, Andrew, but we have responsibilities now. Best you let the Runner handle it for you this time," Chandler said.

In that moment Andrew knew what it was that stood between him and his friends.

Their wives.

John and Chandler were no longer carefree bachelors who could take off at a moment's notice. And Andrew was also getting the feeling they were both quite pleased with their new lives as husbands rather than rogues. The Terrible Threesome, the name they had each worn with honor, was a distant memory to them.

He looked at his friends in a whole new light. They looked happy, and Andrew didn't understand that. He couldn't imagine loving one woman enough that he'd rather be with her than out gaming, drinking, and carousing with his friends.

Andrew might not like the change in their relationship, but he had to accept it, not that he was going to let them know that.

He leaned back in his chair, lifting the front legs off the floor and chuckling low in his throat. "You're both unbelievable."

"In what way?" Chandler asked, lifting a brow.

"Marriage has made weak-kneed sops out of the both of you."

John's dark eyes narrowed and he scowled at Andrew. "That's going a bit too far, even for a best friend."

"Really?" Andrew challenged again, a hint of a smile lurking at the corners of his mouth. "How so? You're not interested in adventure anymore. Now that I have money in my pockets neither of you are willing to gamble the night away with me. And I think it's safe to say you've both given up your mistresses since marriage."

Chandler answered, "That doesn't make us sops. We're both quite happy with our wives. We were actually thinking that maybe you had come back to Town to tell us you were ready to consider making a match."

Andrew laughed again and let the legs of his chair hit the floor with a thud. He was content with his life. He was free of any responsibility and he had no hankering for married life and all the chains it put on a man.

"Not a chance in hell. Look at you two. You're both squirming like worms in hot ashes. You can't wait for our conversation to be over so you can go back to your quiet homes with your beautiful wives. No thank you. I'd rather chase the likes of Hawkins."

"And what do you think is wrong with being happily married?" John asked.

"Boring comes to mind. So tell me what's right with it?" Andrew asked. He spread his arms wide and looked around the room.

"Are you suggesting we don't have a good time when we are with our wives?" Chandler said.

"If so, nothing could be further from the truth," John added.

John and Chandler gave each other that now familiar quick glance. Andrew threw up his hands and said, "I give up. I'm completely uninterested in spending the rest of the night watching you two with these ridiculous happy home expressions you keep giving each other."

Andrew pushed back his chair, ready to rise and seek his pleasure elsewhere.

"Hold up, we're not leaving yet and neither are you." Chandler picked up the bottle and added port to all three glasses on the table. "When you fall in love you'll come around to appreciating the simple pleasures of married life just like we have."

"God save me from such a dull state. I'd just as soon be in prison."

"That's a lie," John said with a laugh.

"You're right. Maybe that is going a bit too far." Andrew grinned. "But I'm glad to know what took the starch out of the two of you. I'm definitely staying away from love and marriage."

"To do that you will have to stay away from all the young ladies."

"That's right. John and I certainly weren't looking for love."

"It found us. So, are you ready to swear off all women but your mistress?"

"Hell no. I'll just have to prove to you both that I can enjoy the young ladies without getting caught by one of them."

John and Chandler laughed.

"What's so funny?" Andrew asked, still not knowing if he was ready to forgive his friends for getting married and leaving him to his own devices every evening.

"You, thinking you can run away from love," John said.

"I managed to outwit fate and not marry when I was down to mere coins in my pockets. I think I can dodge Cupid's arrow for a few more years." Andrew picked up his glass and saluted them. "So I won't become a squeeze like you two, victims living under the cat's paw."

"You are cock-sure tonight," John replied, not the least offended by his friend's accusations.

"I have reason to be. When I left London last year I didn't know if I would ever have enough money to return. But I'm back, I have money, my estates are prospering better than ever. In fact, I intend to see about finding an agreeable mistress."

"With your attitude a mistress is just what you need. A wife would never put up with you."

Andrew smiled. "Yes, but I need the parties, too, and I'm ready for them to begin. In fact, my Aunt Claude has planned an evening at my house the first week of the Season."

"A party? You don't say," Chandler said.

"Naturally, I want to have a first look at all the young ladies who are making their débuts."

"There's nothing wrong with that," John told him.

"And I'll add: May love always be chasing you," Chandler added with a grin.

"But never catch up to me," Andrew said.

John and Chandler picked up their glasses and drank to Andrew's proclamation.

Two

OLIVIA CONSIDERED THE receiving line at the Earl of Dugdale's house ridiculously long. In the two previous nights that she and her aunt had attended parties in London they had not had to queue like this at anyone else's home. Thank goodness it was a warm night.

The inconsiderate earl had obviously invited entirely too many guests and as far as Olivia was concerned, Lord Dugdale was taking too much time greeting each person presented to him as he stood at the rear of the vestibule.

She and Agatha had quietly arrived in London a month ago. But before they were unpacked and settled into their leased town house in Mayfair, word of Agatha's arrival had spread throughout the city and invitations to parties, the opera, and teas were being delivered at the rate of three and four a day.

It might have been more than a dozen years since Agatha Loudermilk had been in London, but obviously no one had forgotten the well-liked woman who had commanded the ear of every member of the *ton*. Word had spread quickly that the once grand spinster was back in Town.

Agatha had been careful in her selection of parties they would attend. She was mainly interested in the smaller soirées that were given in private homes rather than the larger ones held in magnificent places like the Great Hall.

During the prior two evenings Olivia had met several handsome gentlemen and three of them had asked to call on her. But she had declined them all. She had settled in her mind that she wanted to marry a man like the quiet-spoken Mr. Yost, and she wasn't going to be persuaded from that goal by a handsome young Londoner with a title connected to his name. Neither her aunt nor her mother had found happiness with their choices of men from among the *ton,* so Olivia had concluded long ago that she wouldn't either.

The night was unbelievably beautiful and unseasonably warm for so early in the spring. There wasn't even a hint of a breeze in the thick, unusually mild air.

A small slice of moon offered the dark sky little light, but the walkway in front of the house was well lit with street lamps and lanterns from the half dozen or so carriages that waited to deposit their passengers. Music could be heard coming from inside the house and it mingled with the rumble of constant chattering and occasional laughter that could be heard up and down the queue.

Aunt Agatha didn't seem to mind the long line that inched its way up to the front steps flanked by an iron arch that had been decorated with fresh flowers. She chatted happily with the lady in front of them. Olivia found herself moving slightly to the side of the line, which happened to put her in a perfect place to observe the earl, who stood in the foyer of his house.

A thread of unexpected anticipation wove through Olivia as she watched the handsome man smile and heard him flatter each lady who reached him. He bowed, kissed hands, and laughed with all the self-confidence of a wealthy, titled gentleman.

She couldn't help but notice the earl was the complete opposite from Mr. Yost in appearance and manner. The man from Kent was much shorter and fairer than the tall earl, but perhaps his face was bit more handsome than Lord Dugdale's. She had never seen Mr. Yost greet anyone with the self-assurance of their host for the evening's party.

There was no doubt Lord Dugdale was a likeable fellow judging from the faces of those he greeted, and he was far from shy. He stood tall and powerful looking with his black evening coat cut perfectly to fit across his straight shoulders and broad chest. The fabric of his royal blue waistcoat and expertly tied neckcloth spoke of prosperity and privilege, and he wore both of them well.

The style of his fine, medium-brown hair was straight and attractive with the sides barely covering his ears while the back went past his nape. It fell in feathery wisps across his forehead and made him look a little roguish, a little daring, but also extremely dashing, and that made Olivia's heartbeat speed up a little.

His face was strong, masculine, and cleanly shaven. His lips appeared full and his mouth wide and manly. The narrow bridge of his nose heightened his well-defined cheekbones.

Olivia continued to peruse the powerful-looking man at her leisure when suddenly she realized that the man was looking back at her, his gaze studying her face. Her heart fluttered and her stomach quickened deliciously, unexpectedly, when their eyes met.

Olivia watched his gaze skim down her face, over her breasts, which were tastefully exposed by a low-cut ivory gown, before he glanced back up to her green eyes again. His obvious scrutiny made her tingle with awareness way down in the pit of her stomach.

Unlike her usual well-controlled self, she felt her face flush. She lifted her chin a notch to counter his arrogance, though the thought that he looked her over as intently as she assessed him flattered her.

Because of the distance between them she couldn't read the expression in his eyes very well, but she had the distinct feeling that he approved of her inspection of him and that he enjoyed his evaluation of her.

"What do you think of the earl?"

Olivia's attention snapped back to her aunt when she realized she'd been spoken to. She was a bit uncomfortable that Agatha had caught her staring at the man.

In a voice much huskier than she intended, Olivia said, "I haven't even met him yet. How can I know what I think of him?"

"Well, you've certainly stared at him long enough," her aunt bantered lightly with a teasing smile playing about her lips. "Do you think him handsome?"

How like her aunt not to let her evade a question. "I suppose he could be called handsome—by some."

"Some? My dear, I'm certain every young lady in London would consider him one of the finest-looking men in all of England."

Olivia turned her back on the earl so she wouldn't be tempted to cut her eyes around to look at him. "There should be more to attract a young lady's attention than mere appearance."

"Yes," Agatha said. "Wealth and titles are always nice additions."

"I was talking about things like character, kindness, and whether or not he's benevolent."

"I'm sure the earl is filled to overflowing with all those worthy traits and more."

"Are you? I'm not. Don't you remember the things we heard about him just last evening?"

"You mean that he was once a member of a trio called the Terrible Threesome? But we've known that from years of reading Lord Truefitt's tittle-tattle in the *Daily Reader*."

"Yes, and we also know that he has shamefully trampled on hopeful young ladies' affections for years."

"Nonsense. He is merely a young man who's having difficulty finding the right lady to be his wife," her aunt said, looking up the line to where the earl stood. "Waiting to be sure you ask the right one is not such a bad thing. I do believe he's the only one of the Terrible Threesome who isn't married."

"That must mean he is the worst of the lot."

Her aunt laughed with such freedom that Olivia had to laugh, too, even though she'd never been more serious about what she'd said.

And a moment later added, "The very kind Mr. Yost hasn't broken any young lady's heart that I'm aware of, and his standing in the community is sterling."

"He's also a bore," Agatha quickly countered. "Don't you find Lord Dugdale's reputation the least bit intriguing or tempting, or perhaps a little dangerous?"

Olivia squared her shoulders. "A rogue who gives no thought to how many hearts he breaks? Absolutely not.

Who would want to marry a rake, even if he is young, handsome, and titled?"

"Obviously everyone but you, my dear," Agatha said with a hint of merriment in her eyes. "I dare say Lord Dugdale is considered the most eligible bachelor in London this Season."

Olivia wasn't surprised or daunted by her aunt's words. The earl was a splendid-looking specimen. But he was not the kind of man Olivia would ever trust with her heart.

Olivia smiled at her great aunt, whom she loved dearly. From what she'd heard about Lord Dugdale, he must be much like her aunt's Lord Pinkwater. It was no wonder that Agatha was drawn to a man who resembled her past love.

What Olivia couldn't understand was how Agatha could still be controlled by the ghost of a beau who had stolen her heart and then left her to a long life of heartache and loneliness. Olivia wouldn't let that happen to her. She felt sure she would be safe from such heartbreaks with a kind man like Mr. Yost.

Feeling confident in that thought, Olivia said, "Well, when I meet the earl, Auntie, I shall be sure to give him wide space and leave plenty of room for all the ladies who want his attention, because the only man whom I want to claim my attention is back in Kent."

"Agatha Loudermilk, by all the saints in heaven, why have you waited so long to return to London?"

Olivia glanced up to see a petite lady rushing toward them as they made it to the bottom step of the doorway. Her silver hair was arranged high on top of her head and threaded with tiny ribbons and flowers. The woman's dark eyes jumped with excitement and a big smile stretched across her aged face.

Agatha reached out her arms and engulfed the petite woman in an affectionate but delicate hug. "I finally had a reason to return."

"Yes, I heard you're sponsoring your grandniece for the Season, but I also hope you came to see old friends like me."

"Without a doubt."

"I'm so happy you could attend my grandnephew's party tonight, but we must get together just the two of us so we can remember old times. Why haven't you set a date for us to get together?"

"You know I've been trying to get settled. We will get together soon, Claudette, and thank you for the invitation for tonight's soirée. My, but you are as youthful as when you were presented at court."

"Thank you, my dear friend. I'm always trying new creams from this wonderful new apothecary that hasn't been in London very long. This shop has a potion for everything. Perhaps one of them has finally started working."

The two ladies laughed for a few moments before Aunt Agatha said, "I have someone I want you to meet. This is my niece, Olivia Banning. Olivia, this is one of my dearest friends for many years, the dowager Viscountess Collingsworth."

"How do you do, Viscountess?" Olivia curtsied. "It's a pleasure to meet you. I've often heard Aunt Agatha speak of you."

"And I'll wager not a word of it was good."

Olivia laughed lightly. "On the contrary, all of it was good, and I'm sure all of it was true."

"In that case, I'll mind my manners and try not to disappoint you."

Suddenly there was a loud crash of something breaking.

Olivia, Agatha, and the Viscountess looked inside the house and saw a shattered china urn on the floor, perilously close to the feet of the earl.

Shocked gasps, shrieks, and ohs continued to rumble throughout the crowd like a wave rushing to the shore.

"Did you see that?" someone said. "Blasted thing almost hit Dugdale."

"How did it fall? There's no one on the landing," another person offered.

"Merciful heavens," the Viscountess said in a breathless voice as she flipped open her fan and started patting her chest with it. "How could this be? Excuse me, I must check on what happened."

Olivia, her aunt, and several others stepped up closer to look inside the house. A horseshoe landing rose above the foyer and a decorative shelf extended out from the railing. On one side of the ledge sat an urn that matched the broken one on the floor.

As the Viscountess hurried inside, Olivia heard her aunt whisper, "It's Lord Pinkwater's ghost. He's trying to tell me he's here in this house."

"Auntie, not so loud," Olivia admonished quietly. But it was too late. Someone had heard her aunt's whispered words.

"A ghost knocked over the urn?" a lady cried out into the hushed crowd.

"Did someone say there's a ghost?" another person asked.

Stunned gasps raced throughout the crowd again and suddenly Lord Dugdale was surrounded by people clamoring with concern.

Olivia couldn't see him over the chattering group, but she heard him when he spoke reassuringly and said, "Quiet everyone. Listen to me. There is no cause for alarm. I'm sure a few of you would like to believe it was a ghost who made the urn fall, but—"

"What else could have caused it?" someone from inside interrupted him.

"Look for yourself, my lord. It's clear there's nobody up on the landing," another person said.

"This incident was only an accident caused by an employee who failed to place the urn securely on the shelf," Lord Dugdale assured the man. "Let's all get something to eat and drink. The dancing will begin shortly."

Olivia watched the crowd follow the earl into his front room before looking back at her aunt, who seemed wide-eyed and frozen by the mishap.

"See, Auntie, a careless servant put the urn too close to the edge and it fell off," she spoke softly and calmingly. "It was not a ghost."

Agatha stared into Olivia's eyes. "No, it wasn't an accident. It was Lord Pinkwater's ghost. I'm sure of it. You heard someone say there was no one on the landing who could have pushed the urn off. He's here, Livy. This is the house. I must go inside and find him."

Where a few minutes before Olivia was uncomfortably warm, now she felt suddenly chilled. "What exactly do you mean, find him?"

"I told you I would know when I felt his presence. That urn was a sign to me that he's here. I'm going to search every room in that house until he makes himself known to me."

Olivia stopped her aunt. "But what makes you so sure Lord Dugdale will allow you to look through his rooms?"

Her aunt took a step back and looked at her as if she were mad. "I don't plan to ask for permission."

Olivia was startled by Agatha's statement and her unease grew. "What do you plan to do? There are close to one hundred people in there."

"Oh, I won't let them bother me. Besides, I think most ghosts live in bedchambers or perhaps in the attic. I'll search both."

A strong feeling of protectiveness overcame Olivia. She was afraid Agatha would do something imprudent and get herself thrown out of the party, out of the *ton,* and out of London.

Olivia had to do something quickly.

"You can't search this man's bedchambers and his attic."

"Of course I can. What I must *not* do is get caught doing it."

Suddenly Olivia could see her aunt's irreproachable reputation changing to that of a mad old lady searching private homes for a ghost. Except for Olivia, all Agatha had was her spotless reputation. Olivia wouldn't let that be tainted if she could help it. She wouldn't let her aunt be rejected by a Society that had once and obviously still thought so highly of her.

"I'll do it for you, Auntie," she said, fearing what she might be getting into but knowing she had no choice if she wanted to keep everyone from learning that Agatha was searching for a ghost.

"What?"

"I'll search the house for you."

Her aunt's eyes widened. "You can't. I won't hear of it. Your reputation would be ruined if you were caught snooping through the earl's house."

"I won't get caught. I move faster than you do. Besides, if I'm seen, I'll merely say I was looking for the retiring room and lost my way."

Her aunt looked at her as if she had gone mad. "That still won't work, Livy. Lord Pinkwater wants to talk to me, not you. He won't show himself to you."

"He will know that I'm acting as your emissary. He will sense that in me," Olivia said, making up her thoughts as she talked. "I don't know how it all works, but ghosts can read our minds and they know about these kinds of things."

Maybe I am the one who is batty!

Agatha's brow lifted. "They do?"

"Yes, I read about it in a book," Olivia said, stretching the truth a little further than she probably needed to, considering the confused expression on her aunt's face.

"Which book? I don't recall it?"

"I don't remember exactly, as there are so many books that have information about ghosts in them, and it's not important right now anyway." Olivia took a deep calming breath and then said, "It's just better for me to do this than you. I'm the one who will go upstairs and search all the rooms. I will let you know if I feel his presence."

Her aunt smiled sweetly at her. "You would do that for me?"

Olivia nodded and gave her an affectionate smile. "Of course. Now, you've been standing too long. Let's go inside. I'll get you something to drink and see you to a chair where you can listen to the music and then"—she paused as she needed to swallow the lump in her throat—"and then I will search the house for Lord Pinkwater's ghost."

An hour later, a runner of fine carpet muffled Olivia's steps as she left the ladies' retiring room and tiptoed down the brightly lit corridor. Her heart pounded with uncertainties in her chest, but she forced herself to remain collected. The area seemed to stretch forever toward the closed door at the end of the corridor.

Olivia was not looking forward to walking down it because she was invading her host's privacy, not a very honorable thing to do.

The room set aside for the ladies to refresh themselves was one of the bedchambers. From her quick assessment of the vicinity it appeared there was only one other room on the floor. She had reason to believe that what lay behind the door at the other end was also a sleeping room.

Olivia wondered why she'd told her aunt she would search the house for a ghost. It was insane. Why had she even agreed to come to London on this ill-fated mission? She should be in her own hometown waiting for the shy Mr. Yost to ask her to dance. Instead she was in a handsome earl's house searching for a phantom that probably didn't exist.

She had no fear of actually finding a ghost, but had to glance in each room. That way she could look Aunt Agatha in the eyes and in all good faith say that Lord Pinkwater's ghost was not in this house.

When Olivia made it to the end of the corridor she glanced back. All was quiet, but it wouldn't be for long, as ladies were continuously coming and going from their designated room.

She took a deep breath and placed her hand on the door knob and slowly turned, then pushed the door open just a crack and listened. No noise came from inside the room. She looked behind her again and then opened the door a little farther so that she could stick her head around the door and sneak a quick peek inside.

Light from the corridor sliced into the room, shooting a beam of brightness across the floor. A tall tester bed stood against the far wall. The draperies, canopy, and coverlet were a rich burgundy-colored fabric trimmed with short, gold bullion fringe. Her gaze darted past the luxuriously appointed bed to a tall, mahogany dressing table where a lamp burned low. Glowing embers smoldered in the fireplace along the back wall.

There was a warmth in the room that called to her until Olivia heard voices coming up the stairs behind her. A chill flew down her spine and her heart jumped to her throat. For an instant she was panic-stricken. If she was caught she could never explain this rude intrusion.

Did she have time to shut the door and get down the hallway to the retiring room? If she didn't make it she could say she was confused about which room was for the ladies.

Moments seemed to tick by while she considered what to do. The voices grew closer.

With no time for further thought, she quickly dashed inside the bedchamber and quietly shut the door. She leaned against it, closing her eyes, not daring to breathe, and waited for the voices to fade away while she calmed her racing heart.

When the corridor was quiet once more she took a deep breath, opened her eyes, and stepped away from the door. Her gaze scanned the handsomely decorated room. It appeared to be the sleeping quarters of the master of the house.

A shiver of curiosity raced through her.

Olivia knew she should leave at once, but she suddenly felt no inclination to do so. She was fairly certain she didn't believe in ghosts, but something strange, something she didn't understand, was pulling her farther into the room, beckoning her to take a closer look at the forbidden.

Perhaps it was mere curiosity because she'd never been in a man's private chamber before. All she knew was that now she was inside, she couldn't resist the temptation to admire the earl's room.

She slowly made her way over to the bed and placed her hand on the burgundy fabric of the coverlet. It was cool to her touch and the grade of cloth so fine it felt almost silky. The pillows at the head of the bed were large and inviting to slumber.

Feeling more at ease the longer she stayed, she walked over to the pillowy-stuffed wing chair that was upholstered in linen. It looked so comfortable that she sat down and lifted her feet off the floor, swinging them as if she were dipping them into a cold stream on a hot afternoon.

Olivia laid her head against the soft cushion and her mind drifted back to when the earl's gaze caught hers as she stood in line. Her breasts tightened as she remembered how his intrusive stare had sent unexpected tremors of awareness low in her abdomen.

Shaking off those unwanted feelings, she rose and walked over to the exquisitely carved dresser with a square looking glass. In the center of the marble top a copper basin glimmered appealingly, glowing like alabaster in the soft light from the low-burning oil lamp.

To one side of the basin lay an ivory-handled hair brush, a short fat bottle filled with liquid, and a small saucer holding some coins. On the other side rested a china dish with a block of soap lying in it and a stand that held a shaving brush.

Olivia picked up the bottle and inhaled. It smelled of musky, mint-scented water. She smiled. It was masculine, yet heavenly pleasing to her senses.

Is this how the earl smells?

She put the bottle down and picked up the soap. Cupping it with both hands, she put it to her nose. It held the same fresh, clean scent of mint. She closed her eyes and breathed in heavily again.

"What the devil are you doing?"

Startled, Olivia jumped and dropped the bar of soap onto the dresser. It hit the copper basin with a loud clanging noise that seemed to reverberate throughout the room.

"Oh, heavens above, you startled the living daylights out of me," she said as she fumbled for the soap and quickly put it back into its proper place before looking back at the earl.

Leaving the door ajar, he walked farther into the room. "You're startled? Imagine how I feel finding a young lady in my bedchamber."

She felt her cheeks flame red. Oh why had she let the urge to explore his room overcome her? A quick peek was all she needed to satisfy her aunt. What madness, what folly had controlled her? The worst possible thing had happened. She had been caught.

"I was just—" She stopped. What could she tell him? The truth?

No. He'll think I'm doddering or insane. And maybe I am for not leaving when I had the chance.

She had made her aunt promise not to mention their mission to anyone and she couldn't either. Could she?

"Go on. You were what? Looking over my things? Perhaps planning to steal a few items?"

His implication was clear and she didn't like it.

"Of course not," she said indignantly, trying not to be frightened by his accusation or the dangerous way he advanced on her.

His hard gaze strayed to the items on the dresser before settling on her face once again. "Were you looking for jewelry or some coins to hide in your handkerchief?"

"I'm not a thief!"

As soon as she said that she realized how laughable that sounded considering the fact she was in his private chamber looking over his intimate belongings. What else could he possibly think?

He lifted a skeptical brow. "Then why are you in here?"

Which would she rather he believe, that she was looking over the items in his room hoping to steal something from him or that she had taken leave of her good senses?

Suddenly Olivia blurted, "If you must know, I was looking for a ghost."

Three

OLIVIA CRINGED INWARDLY. Right now she wished she were a ghost so she could vanish through the walls and never be seen again.

She couldn't recall a time in her life when she had ever been flustered, but this man had her close to it, and in less than two minutes of being in his presence.

How was she going to get out of this with some of her dignity intact?

His dark, honey-colored eyes narrowed just enough to show his disapproval as his gaze swept up and down her body. A chilling expression eased over his face and Olivia knew she was in real trouble for the first time in her life.

Taking a deep breath, she knew she must remain strong and not cower or all was lost.

His posture was proud and erect as he walked closer to her and asked, "You were looking for *what*?"

Olivia wasn't sure she liked the way his gaze took in

every detail of her face as he quickly closed the short distance between them. He was too close. The intensity of his expression did confounding things to the throbbing of her heartbeat.

She had no choice but to follow through now that she had unexpectedly divulged the truth. She just had to keep her aunt's name out of her confession.

"I was looking for Lord Pinkwater's ghost."

His voice was as chilling as his expression when in a husky whisper he asked, "In my bedchamber?"

"It is the place most ghosts reside, isn't it?" she challenged him and wondered why she did so when she was in a perilously difficult position.

She was a sensible woman. Why didn't she just ask his pardon and make a hasty retreat all the way back to Kent? And pray she never saw the handsome earl again?

"I wouldn't have an idea about where ghosts dwell. I've never looked for one."

Olivia wanted to fend off his deliberate stare with one of her own but his physical presence in the room prevented her from doing so. His tall body used up the space, filling the softly lit area, and making her knees uncommonly weak.

A shivery awareness stole over her. Her body and her mind were completely responsive to Andrew Terwillger, the Earl of Dugdale.

She clasped her hands together in front of her, hoping to remain strong and conceal her true emotions. She couldn't allow him to frustrate or intimidate her, but most of all she wouldn't permit him to stir up her womanly senses any more than he already had.

It was unlike her to be so attracted to a man that all her senses went on alert.

"I know it sounds preposterous, but most ghosts seem to visit people in bedchambers," she managed to say in an even tone, but knew she must have sounded like a deranged idiot.

"You're right, it does." He picked up the soap. "Did you expect to find Lord Pinkwater's ghost in this?"

A flush blazed up her neck. She felt her cheeks flame red for the second time. He was intentionally mocking her.

She wouldn't let his behavior affect her.

"Of course not."

She straightened her shoulders and huffed, and then got even more perturbed when she saw the faint trace of a smile curve the corners of his lips.

He thought this humorous? Knowing he was amused made her more determined than ever to stay in control and find an acceptable way out of this predicament.

"Are you sure you weren't after the coins on my dressing table?"

She pierced him with what she considered her most firm and resolute expression. "I held your soap in my hands, not your money. I am not destitute. I have no need of your possessions, my lord."

Shadowed lamplight made his face seem sinister as he regarded her with half-closed eyes, all signs of a smile gone from his lips. Still, he studied her.

"I'm afraid your answer as to why you are in my private rooms has not been adequately answered. You're not explaining yourself very well, Miss—"

"Banning," she said, lifting her chin and doing her best to remain composed. "Miss Olivia Banning, and how can I possibly explain myself well at all, sir, when you barge in here without knocking, scare me out of my wits, and then have the audacity to accuse me of being a thief. It's shameful."

He cocked his head and asked, "Scare you? Audacity? Shameful? This is *my* room. I often barge into it, and always without knocking."

"Perhaps from now on you won't be so hasty."

"To enter my own bedchamber? That's an unbelievable statement, Miss Banning."

"Surely when you have guests in your home there can be a more civilized approach to finding someone in your private chamber other than assuming they want to steal from you."

Her mind was racing and she was coming up with crazy answers but it was the best she could do under the circumstances. If she didn't stay on the offensive he would overcome her.

"There is a very logical conclusion I could draw from finding a beautiful young lady in my room, but I'm not convinced you want my thoughts going in the direction of thinking you have designs on me and you want a passionate rendezvous."

She gasped. He was outrageous.

"Does your ego have no boundaries, sir? How dare you suggest such a thing? I don't even know you."

"True, but you were definitely looking me over when you were in the receiving line."

Olivia felt a guilty flush creep into her cheeks again. This man was maddening, fascinating, and invigorating.

"This is a large residence, my lord. It would be very easy for someone to get lost among the many rooms."

"I suppose one could get lost, Miss Banning. But right now all of my guests except you are downstairs finding their pleasure in my food, my wine, and my music. You are the only one up here in my private chamber sniffing my shaving soap."

Olivia cringed again. What she had done sounded so improper when he said it that way.

She needed to leave. She should be begging his forgiveness and heading for the door. Instead she was standing here trying to match wits with him and her efforts were futile. It was clear he was not going to be appeased by anything she said.

Taking a calming breath she answered, "You are quite right, my lord. I should be downstairs enjoying the party, so if you'll excuse me, I'll take my leave."

She started to walk past him but was stopped when he grabbed hold of her gloved wrist. Olivia glanced down at his strong, capable hand. She felt power beneath the commanding grip of his masculine fingers. She lifted her lashes and their eyes met and held. Suddenly, she experienced that same strange sensation low in the pit of her stomach as when she first noticed him staring at her on the walkway, that same strange sensation that pulled her into his chamber.

"Not so fast, Miss Banning," he said, his tone sounding as stormy as his dark honey eyes. "No proper young lady would be caught prowling in my rooms."

"Prowling? What strong words you use, sir."

"Would you prefer *pilfering* or *snooping*? Do those words better suit you?"

"Of course not. I was merely—" She stopped.

"You were prowling through my private chambers looking for something. Tell me the truth. Who are you and what are you after?"

She had told him the truth, or as close to it as she dared. She had to search the house for Agatha, but she had no excuse for stopping to smell his soap. Other than it was as if she'd been incapable of leaving before she looked around his room.

There was no way she could tell him that she had to hunt for a ghost because she couldn't bear the thought of her aunt's flawless reputation being ruined by the scandal of everyone thinking she'd gone mad, thinking a beau who'd jilted her over forty years ago was now calling to her from the afterlife.

It wouldn't matter if Olivia's reputation was ruined in London. No one knew her. Besides, she planned to return to Kent. But her aunt would forever be remembered as a foolish old woman thinking the man who had jilted her had returned from the grave to claim her.

Olivia wouldn't allow that to happen.

She had no choice but to stick with the truth, though at all cost she had to keep Agatha's name out of it.

"Truly, I'm searching for Lord Pinkwater's ghost. I've heard he's in London and I thought I sensed his presence when the vase fell from your foyer landing. I only meant to peek inside this room, not enter it."

"To see if you could find a ghost among my belongings."

Once again she thought she saw a flicker of a smile playing about the corners of his lips, but he was remaining so stoic, she couldn't be sure.

One thing she was sure of. She would never forget the scent of his soap or those strange sensations that developed low in her abdomen.

She swallowed hard. There was no way she could appear any more foolish, so she answered, "No, that was mere curiosity once I found myself inside. What I meant to say is that I never intended to actually enter your chambers. I heard someone coming up the stairs, and I didn't want to get caught at your doorway so I stepped inside, and then—" She stopped again.

He lifted a skeptical brow. "And then what?"

She hesitated, searching for the right words. "I've never been in a gentleman's rooms before, and I must admit my curiosity got the better of me. There, now are you happy that I've admitted to such inquisitiveness?"

"I accept that curiosity led you to my dressing table, but if a ghost led you into my rooms, either you should be committed to Bedlam or you are a good actress. Either way, I still see no reason why I shouldn't call the magistrate and have you taken straight to Newgate."

She tried to pull her wrist from his grasp but he was too strong. His hard gaze remained firmly on her face, searching her eyes. Then, suddenly, without warning, he let go of her.

Keeping her voice level, she said, "By all means call the magistrate if you wish, my lord. I have told the truth and even you should know that sometimes people stray into the wrong rooms at private parties."

Without giving clear thought to what she was doing next, Olivia suddenly held her arms out wide and said, "I did not come in here to steal anything from you. Search my person. You will find that I have nothing of yours on me."

"You would really let me search you?"

His tone, the light of intrigue in his honey-colored eyes, made her stomach quiver deliciously. Teasing warmth tingled across her breasts. She sensed an unusual quickening between her legs. What was she doing challenging this man to touch her?

Maybe I have gone mad.

She slowly returned her arms to her sides. She took a step back and found her hips pressed against the dresser. There was no escape. She was trapped but strangely not frightened.

She looked into his eyes again and suddenly she felt hot, breathless, and excited.

"I only meant that I want you to be sure that I have taken nothing from your room, nor do I want anything from you."

He advanced on her, imprisoning her with his powerful body, near enough to touch her. His voice was low and suggestive as he whispered, "So you said. But perhaps, I will search you. Just to be sure. Do you have anything hidden in your hair?"

The earl leaned his body closer to hers. She sensed his strength, she felt his heat. He reached up and placed one hand to the side of her head. Warmth flooded her at his touch.

He lightly threaded his fingers through the side of her hair, making a few strands of her dark blonde curls tumble from the chignon at her nape. The gentleness of his caress was strangely soothing when it should have been egregiously shocking.

A small puff of breath was all that escaped her lips. She knew she should push him away, or scream, or at least slap his face. But she had no desire to do any of those things. She stood there, barely breathing, and allowed him to mesmerize her with his compelling touch and provocative words.

"How about your ears? Have you hidden something behind them, Miss Banning?"

His hand softly, confidently slipped down to her ear. With his fingertips he outlined its shape, very slowly, before slipping his fingers behind her ear to tenderly caress the soft skin there with the pads of his fingers. His caress stimulated her more than anything she'd ever experienced.

Olivia was glad the dresser offered support, because at the moment she feared her legs were too weak to hold her.

She didn't understand why it felt so good to have this man touch her.

"Perhaps it's in your mouth," he said in the same husky, enticing voice.

His fingertips never left her skin as they fluttered from behind her ear and over her jaw line until his thumb rested at the corner of her lips. His palm lay against her neck and she knew he could feel her pulse beating out of control.

He leaned in closer and still she didn't object. Heat from his body and his breath fanned on her cheek. The musky mint scent of his soap stirred the air. Was it coming from him or wafting up from the block that lay on the dresser behind her?

With his mouth no more than an inch from hers, his eyes locked on hers, she was attuned to his every breath. And her heart thudded wildly against her chest.

He traced the curve of her upper lip with his thumb. The warmth of his touch sizzled through her. For a moment, she was afraid he was going to kiss her, and then just as suddenly she realized she was afraid he would not.

Her lips parted and her tongue lightly wiped across the pad of his thumb. She heard the quick intake of his breath.

Olivia trembled with a need for something she didn't understand.

"You are very tempting, Miss Banning, very tempting indeed. Do you realize how easy it would be for me to take advantage of you right now?"

She nodded.

"Are you frightened?"

She had no breath to speak so shook her head.

"I didn't think so."

His lips came down to hers, lightly brushing across them. The contact was delicate, feathery, and enticing. Olivia's stomach quivered, but she didn't back away from his intimate touch.

Lord Dugdale raised his head and looked down into her eyes. She felt her heart flutter in her chest just as her lashes fluttered against his beckoning stare. She knew he was questioning her, asking with the lift of his eyebrows if he should try his luck and kiss her again or should he step away.

Kiss me again, she wanted to say. Her lips parted but she couldn't seem to find the words on her tongue.

He placed the tips of his fingers under her chin and lifted it ever so slightly while his thumb caressed her bottom lip. The lace from the cuff of his sleeve brushed her neck as the back of his arm rested softly, innocently, against her breasts.

"Your mouth is beautiful, Miss Banning. Made for kissing."

Slowly he bent his head and kissed her again, moving his lips seductively over hers. His lips feathered down her chin, over to her cheek.

She felt his breath on her ear before she heard his whispered words, "You're heavenly."

Slow curls of unexpected pleasure came alive inside her, and without conscious effort her chest lifted to feel more of the weight of his arm upon her. The warmth of his touch seeped inside her and she gave herself up to these new, unexplained feelings of desire.

All of a sudden the bedchamber door swung open with a clatter. Andrew lifted his head and stepped away from Olivia. Glaring light from the corridor shone brightly in her eyes.

She heard gasps of outrage. She saw three ladies in the doorway, but the only faces she recognized were her Aunt Agatha's and that of the Viscountess Collingsworth.

"Livy! By the holy saints above, what are you doing in here and what is that man doing to you?"

"Nothing," Olivia said, horrified. "We aren't doing anything."

"That's not how it looks," the Viscountess said. "Andrew, my heavens, what is she doing in your room and in your arms?"

"Was he kissing you?" Aunt Agatha asked.

"No, of course not," Olivia exclaimed and winced at the prevarication.

He was most certainly kissing her, but how could she admit that to the three ladies staring at her with shocked expressions on their faces. The questions were coming so fast and she didn't have time to think, but instinct told her the truth was the last thing she should admit to.

She would never live down this folly.

Never.

How could she have been so tempted by this man? To enter his room? To allow him to kiss her? What strange enchantment had come over her?

Olivia turned to the earl. "Tell them we weren't doing anything," she whispered huskily.

With a grim expression on his face, softly he murmured so only she could hear, "I want nothing more than to assure them of that, but it's a bit difficult to do when three ladies saw you backed against the dresser and my hands on your face."

"You must try."

"Oh, I intend to try, Miss Banning."

Squaring his shoulders and looking at the small gathering, he placed a smile on his lips and seeming in total control said, "No matter what you are thinking right now, ladies, this is not what it looks like. I was merely trying to help Miss Banning get something out of her eye."

The ladies in the doorway started talking among themselves. Olivia held her breath. Would her aunt believe such an unlikely story?

"Can't you be any more convincing than that?" she whispered.

Lord Dugdale turned back to Olivia. "What else would you like me to say?"

Animosity emanated from him. His honey-colored eyes suddenly appeared to be dark amber. She felt chilled beneath their cold stare.

"This is your fault," Olivia whispered, wishing she'd never stepped a foot inside this house.

He gave her a questioning look as he folded his arms across his chest. "Mine? Did you not demand I search your person?"

"No. I mean, yes, but I never expected you to take me up on it. I never expected you to kiss me and touch me in such an intimate fashion. You are supposed to be a gentleman."

"When a woman offers herself to me, I am only a man, Miss Banning."

Olivia gasped in outrage and quickly glanced at the chattering ladies in the doorway to see if they were listening to her and the earl. They were too busy talking about what they saw among themselves at the moment.

She glared at the earl and whispered back to him, "I did no such thing."

In a low voice that continued to be more of a growl, the earl muttered, "You planned this, didn't you?"

"What are you talking about?" she whispered, a shiver of apprehension racing down her back.

She saw something in his face that she hadn't seen before—mistrust. It struck her like a sharp knife to the chest. "I am not a cunning woman. I planned nothing but a quick peek inside your room. You are the one who came in and made it much more than that."

"The innocent act is over, Miss Banning. I now know what you were after."

"What?"

"My name."

She couldn't believe what he was implying. How dare he think she wanted to trick him into marriage? The very idea was so foreign to her that it was almost laughable. How could what started out as a simple search of the house to help her aunt turn into such a disaster?

"No. I wouldn't do that," she said with all the earnestness she was feeling. "You can't believe me capable of such deception."

"Yes, Miss Banning, I do. You planned this little rendezvous to trick me into marriage."

Four

WAS IT ANGER or surprise that stirred inside him at being manipulated?

All eyes in the room were on him. That had never bothered him before now. But this was different. He didn't like the feeling of being backed into a corner, especially by a mischievous miss.

Andrew moved a step away from the lovely but devious young lady. He should have known immediately what the golden-haired beauty with the shining blue eyes was up to when he found her in his room, but he'd let his attraction to her rule the head in his trousers rather than the one housing his good common sense.

He should have escorted her out immediately, but she'd tempted him to linger.

Not only was his great aunt looking at him with accusing eyes, but there was also a rather tall, regal lady who he assumed was Miss Banning's aunt looking straight at him with a gaze that looked like it could pierce steel. And if that wasn't enough to turn an already disturbing evening into a hellish nightmare, the Lord Mayor's robust, loud-speaking wife, Dorothy Farebrother, was eyeing him as if he were a dirty lecher ready to pounce on an innocent girl.

That might not have been too far from the truth only minutes ago. But not anymore. His hot arousal had vanished as quickly as warm breath hitting the air on a freezing day.

Andrew was too much of a gentleman to tell the three older ladies that the beautiful miss standing beside him was most likely a deranged young woman who first told him she was looking for a ghost and later admitted she was merely curious as to the contents of his bedchamber. And he would like to inform them all that this entire situation had been staged by her in hopes of tricking him into marriage.

But instead of the truth, he stated, "There has been a great misunderstanding here. This is not a rendezvous or any kind of affair of the heart. She and I don't even know each other."

"That's not what it looked like to me," the Lord Mayor's wife said.

Ignoring her interrupting remark, Andrew continued calmly, "I came up here to get a handkerchief and she was peering in the looking glass. I believe there might have been something in her eye."

Andrew had no compunction about lying to cover the reputation of a young lady no matter how designing she might be. It was especially easy when the lie would benefit him as well.

"He's right, Auntie," Miss Banning said as she immediately started blinking rapidly and rubbing one of her eyes. "He did not invite me in here, nor had I any idea he would come in here. We've never spoken, nor have we met until just now."

"And I don't believe we've met, my lord," her aunt said, walking closer to him while keeping a stern expression on her face.

"That's right, Agatha," his petite Aunt Claude said. "You didn't meet my grandnephew earlier. The receiving line was halted when the vase fell from the landing. Andrew, may I present one of my oldest and dearest friends, Miss Agatha Loudermilk. I believe you have already met her grandniece, Miss Olivia Banning."

Oh, yes, indeed he had met her. He had touched her. He had tasted her, and despite her cunning, he wanted to taste her again.

It was a little late for formal introductions, but Andrew allowed his aunt to have her way, so he suffered through them, including the bows and curtseys.

"What I would like to know is how you missed the retiring room?" Mrs. Farebrother asked Miss Banning as soon as the pleasantries were finished. "There would have been any number of ladies in there who could have seen to your eye."

Miss Loudermilk glared at the Lord Mayor's wife and said, "She is my niece, Dorothy, and I will be the one to question her about this, thank you very much, and if you don't mind, stay quiet."

Dorothy sniffed, raised her thick eyebrows in disdain, and said, "Of course not. I just don't understand why she didn't leave these rooms the second she realized she was in the master of the house's bedchamber?"

"I knew as soon as I entered it was not the retiring room," Miss Banning said, "but I had no way of knowing this was Lord Dugdale's private chamber."

"With these grand furnishings?" the brash Mrs. Fare-brother asked, stretching her arms wide.

Andrew noticed how Miss Banning defended herself as she unobtrusively moved away from him and closer to her aunt.

This was beginning to feel like a drunken, madcap masquerade ball, except he could see all the faces. Andrew knew he had to take control of this situation before things got worse. He'd had enough of these women sniping at each other.

"Ladies, there has been no harm done here. Let's forget this happened and go back downstairs for something to eat and drink."

"Not so quick, my lord. I am not willing to concede that there has been no harm to my niece. That has yet to be determined. However, I will be happy to entertain you and your solicitor tomorrow afternoon to hear what you have to say for yourself concerning this turn of events."

"Auntie, what are you talking about? We've explained what happened. It's completely unnecessary for you to summon the earl for such an insignificant matter."

"This is not an inconsequential matter, my dear girl. The fact is there are witnesses to you being alone with this man in his bedchamber."

Andrew had to give the young lady credit for knowing how to play the part of the innocent victim with conviction. Before she'd stepped away from him her eyes seemed to be pleading with him to do something, but he'd felt little sorrow for her, considering she brought this unpleasantness on herself.

He'd fully expected her to demand marriage on the spot. He could only thank his lucky stars that hadn't happened—yet.

Since the introductions, he'd forced himself not to look at Miss Banning for fear her aunt might think he was trying to send her some kind of secret message, but suddenly across the space between them their gazes met.

Andrew was instantly reminded of how good she felt in his arms, how wonderful the softness of her mouth felt beneath his lips, how sweet and innocent she'd tasted on his tongue.

"In my day, if a man disgraced a young lady he was made to marry her as soon as the proper bans could be posted," the Lord Mayor's wife blurted out.

"I don't want to marry him," Miss Banning said firmly, her eyes darting from him, to the Lord Mayor's wife, to her aunt. "He did not disgrace me. You don't know what you are talking about."

"His hands were on your face. I saw it," Mrs. Farebrother insisted.

"Dorothy, please be quiet and let me handle this."

"By all means, Agatha, you should be the one to find out what was going on in here. But I'm certain they were touching."

"Might I ask who was touching whom?"

Gasps echoed like a lonesome whisper around the suddenly silent room.

Andrew's gaze flew to the doorway just in time to see the buxom Lady Lynette Knightington stepping from behind his short Aunt Claudette to get a good look at what was going on inside.

Bloody hell!

"You may ask, but you might get snapped at for doing so," Mrs. Farebrother said in an annoyed tone.

"I heard voices and came to investigate. What's going on in here?" Lady Lynette asked.

"We don't know yet," Mrs. Farebrother answered before anyone else found their breath. "The three of us were on our way to the retiring room when Claudette noticed Lord Dugdale's bedchamber's door ajar. We walked over to close it and found the two of them in here in what possibly could have been an embrace."

Heaven help him. What next? This was worse than any poorly acted comedy he'd seen at the Lyceum. He had to get all of the ladies out of his rooms before anyone else showed up.

"Mrs. Farebrother is speaking out of turn," Miss Banning remarked, stepping forward as color fled up the column of her slender, beautiful neck and settled in the softness of her cheeks.

"Yes, she is, and that's enough from you, Dorothy." His Aunt Claude spoke up for the first time in quite a while.

"Indeed," Miss Loudermilk reprimanded. "How dare you continue to insert yourself into this very private matter when you've been asked repeatedly to stay quiet?"

"I'd hardly call it private when the three of us witnessed their embrace. Just because we have been friends for more than thirty years, Agatha, you have no cause to speak to me in such a tone."

"I do when you continue to offer an opinion that is neither wanted, nor is it needed. I insist on handling this delicate concern without your help."

"I know what I saw," Mrs. Farebrother insisted and folded her arms across her chest defiantly.

"But nobody is asking you about it," Miss Banning said in a composed tone.

"That's not true," the Lord Mayor's wife complained. "Lady Lynette asked."

Andrew was ready to throw them all out.

"Ladies," Andrew said tightly as he walked past them and to the door. "I really must insist that you go back downstairs and rejoin the party. As Miss Loudermilk suggested, anything that needs attention can be dealt with by the two families tomorrow."

"So true, Andrew," his aunt said and joined him by the door. "It's time we all returned to the party."

"I trust that all knowledge of this incident will stay in this room," Andrew said, though he knew it was too much to ask. "I wouldn't like to see Miss Banning's reputation tarnished over something that was of no consequence whatsoever."

"Of course you can trust me to never breathe a word of this to anyone," Mrs. Farebrother said.

She might have been the first to declare the vow, but Andrew saw exhilaration in her eyes that told him she couldn't wait to get downstairs and tell others what she had seen. He wouldn't be at all surprised to find out that the stout, loud-speaking woman was one of the ladies who constantly fed information to the writers of the scandal sheets.

Even Lady Lynette, who was known to be one of the kindest of the spinsters in the *ton,* had a compassionate smile on her face, but an unusually bright gleam of excitement in her eyes.

It was uncommon for a duke's daughter to remain unwed past her twenty-first birthday, but as far as he knew, Lady Lynette, who was nearing, if not past, thirty, had never been seriously courted. She'd been born with a dark red birthmark on the side of one cheek. It wasn't hideous, but most people would consider it unsightly the first time they saw her. She was also taller than most men, which unfortunately added another strike against her marriageable prospects.

To her credit, she had lovely green eyes and a full womanly figure, and she was always cheerful. She'd never let her quite noticeable birthmark keep her in hiding. She attended most of the parties each Season and occasionally she was asked to dance.

Andrew had no doubt that when this incident got out, it would be the Lord Mayor's wife who tattled to the gossips, and not the duke's daughter. He was certain the story would be all over the party within the hour, and highly embellished to boot.

"Please, ladies," he said again. "I must insist you go belowstairs."

Miss Loudermilk lifted her chin. "I'll expect you tomorrow afternoon before tea." She then took hold of her niece's arm just above the elbow and almost herded her out of the room with Dorothy, Lady Lynette, and his aunt following them.

His last glance at Miss Banning caused his stomach to tighten. She was a good actress. She had a convincingly distraught expression on her face, but he was sure the entire evening had gone according to her plan.

But he would take over from here.

Andrew had no intention to alter his bachelor lifestyle and take on the responsibilities of a wife. And a beautiful chit with tempting lips wasn't going to change his mind about that.

As soon as the ladies were gone Andrew shut the door behind them. He took a deep breath and ran both hands through his hair.

What an evening.

First, a priceless urn had fallen from the shelf where it

had been sitting for the better part of fifty years. It landed only inches from him. If it had landed on his head he could have been killed. And now a very appealing miss was trying to leg-shackle him.

What nerve she had to enter his room, pilfer through his things, and set a plan to become his countess.

He'd come close to being forced to marry once before and had managed to escape. He'd find a way to cheat Cupid once again.

The only thing he could do right now was to go downstairs and act as if nothing had happened. And on his way down, he would take a vow to never again host a party in his home.

As soon as he entered the crowded room he found a servant and asked that he be brought a brandy. Champagne and wine were not strong enough to get him through the rest of this evening.

The music sounded uncommonly loud and the chattering of his guests was more of a resounding roar in his ears. Light from the hundreds of candles seemed harsh and brassy rather than soft and golden. The strong smells of perfumes, liquor, and flowers mixed heavily in the unseasonably warm air.

He would have liked nothing better than to clear his house of all the richly dressed women and impeccably clothed gentlemen and have the time to reflect on the possible consequences of the past few minutes, but he couldn't do that. He had to make the best of what was surely to be a long night.

Over the next couple of hours, Andrew made a point of walking from room to room, talking with everyone in attendance. All his guests were having a marvelous time. He discussed horses with the Marquis of Westerland, hunting with Lord Colebrook, and politics with the Duke of Knightington and two other members of Parliament.

Andrew had already danced with three different young ladies who were enjoying their first Season in Society. And he was gliding across the crowded dance floor with the fourth, but he really didn't see the lady's face in front of him at all. His thoughts were on another female—one standing by his dresser, her golden-colored hair bathed in lamplight. He would never forget the look of pure, innocent pleasure on her face as she held his soap to her nose.

Her delicate skin didn't have the milky white look of so many young ladies he'd admired over the years. Her complexion had more the color found in a piece of expensive parchment.

When she'd offered him permission to search her body he hadn't been able to deny himself the pleasure of touching her, breathing in her scent, and tasting her lips and mouth. Once his fingertips caressed her silky soft skin it was as if nothing else mattered. He had to kiss her and that had made him want to lay her on his big bed and sink deeply into her.

At the time it didn't seem so unusual that she was more than willing to allow his forward advance, never once trying to stop him. He should have known she had her own designs when she didn't admonish him for his forward behavior in any way. He'd been too enchanted by her beauty, her boldness, and her body.

How could he have passed on the challenge she threw out to search her person to prove her innocence?

He couldn't.

And she knew it.

That thought tightened his stomach with anger. He

wasn't used to being outmaneuvered by a bewitching young lady.

The problem was that he'd been captivated by her before he ever opened his mouth to say a word. Obviously that had been part of her plan.

And it had worked.

Otherwise she would have screamed for help when he touched her or at least slapped his face. Yet, all she had done was melt into his arms as if she had been waiting a lifetime for him to come and awaken her to the wonderful, sensual pleasures of kissing.

She could claim all she wanted that she was really looking for a ghost or merely curious about the contents of his room, but he was convinced what she really wanted was to be the wife of an earl.

He'd stepped right into the middle of her plan.

Andrew shook his head as the young lady he was dancing with twirled under his arm. He couldn't think about Miss Banning as looking like an angel and feeling like a long-lost lover in his arms, especially when he was in the company of a young lady who was trying desperately to charm him with her smile.

He must remember Miss Banning as the sprite who entered his private chamber without invitation and made herself at home. He must remember her glaring at him with seeming outrage when he had accused her of being a thief. He must remember she had laid the blame for their being caught on him.

Yes, that was the image of Miss Banning he must remember.

She was obviously drawn to his title and fortune, his connections to London's most prestigious families, and maybe even his looks. Most young ladies considered him the handsome sort.

She had remained adamant that there was nothing between the two of them during the conversation in his room with the older ladies. But he was sure that was all part of her innocent act to get her way eventually.

Andrew escorted the young lady off the dance floor and returned her to her mother who was bent on regaling him with her daughter's attributes. She was lovely, with dark hair and light brown eyes. Any other night he might have been tempted to spend more time with her.

But not tonight.

He bid his farewells to the ladies and was heading to get another drink when he saw his good friends John and Chandler standing by the courtyard door. Both were motioning for him to follow them outside.

He had no doubt as to why they wanted to see him alone.

For a moment, he was tempted to ignore them and not to go, but realized he would have to face them sooner or later.

Glancing at the hall clock, he saw it had taken more than two hours for them hear about his misfortune with Miss Banning. That surprised him. If this entire incident hadn't been so serious, he would have laughed.

Andrew stepped outside into warm night air. It was a clear night, free of fog, clouds, or mist, but only a small slice of a bright moon broke the blackness of the sky. Andrew couldn't help but think the endless canopy of darkness matched his mood. He spoke to several people who were also enjoying the nighttime atmosphere before reaching his friends who stood at the far end of the portico.

"What the devil is this we hear about you and a young

lady being caught in your bedchamber?" John asked as soon as Andrew was close enough to hear them.

"If it's true, it's one hell of a story," Chandler added.

"No kidding," Andrew said after taking a deep breath.

"You look like you need a drink," John said, offering Andrew the glass he held in his hand.

He needed more than just a drink. A beautiful enchantress was trying to upset the contented balance he'd just achieved in his life. He feared it would be a battle of wills between the two of them.

"My finest brandy hasn't begun to dull my senses to-night."

"Maybe that's just as well. Tell us what happened."

Andrew gazed out over his garden. The greenery was lush from rain and dotted with splashes of color from the spring blossoms. The entire back area glowed from lamps that lit the limestone walkways.

He shook his head and laughed. "It is so unbelievable, my friends, that it's downright laughable."

"Speak, man. Tell us, what were you thinking to arrange an interlude with a young lady in your room?"

"And while you had one hundred guests in your house? It's absurd." John added.

"You've done some wild things, Andrew, we all have, but this goes beyond them all."

Andrew looked from one friend to the other. He knew they thought him mad. "That's the hell of it, fellows. I didn't arrange to meet her. I had never even met her. I went up to my room and there she was."

"Who?" John questioned.

"The lady's name is Miss Olivia Banning."

"You'll have to point her out to us."

"I've looked the house over," Andrew answered. "She's already left the party."

"So who is this Miss Olivia Banning?" John asked. "And what was she doing in your room if you didn't invite her?"

Andrew hesitated. He hadn't kept much from them in all the years they'd been friends, but he didn't want to tell them how Miss Banning had looked shadowed by lamplight, standing by his dressing table, holding his shaving soap to her nose, eyes closed and inhaling the scent.

Even now the remembrance did strange things to his insides.

"I'm not sure. She was just standing near the looking glass."

"Well, surely you asked her. What did she have to say for herself?"

Should he tell them what she said? That she was looking for a ghost and became curious once she entered his room? He was tempted, but no, that, too, he would keep to himself, for now anyway. He would stay with the story that she found his room by accident and she had something in her eye.

"Not much," he lied without compunction. She'd had plenty to say and she wasn't shy about it, but his friends would never know that, either. "I thought at first maybe she was going to steal something. I had some coins on the dressing table."

"How did she get into your bedchamber? It wasn't locked?"

"No. I—she said something about getting lost while going to the ladies' retiring room. While I was trying to find out who she was and what she was doing there Aunt Claude, the young lady's aunt, and the Lord Mayor's wife saw the door to my room ajar and came to investigate. Before I could get everyone out, Lady Lynette came in asking questions."

"Damnation," Chandler whispered. "That many people saw her in your room? What a hell of a mess."

Andrew took a deep breath and shook his head as he remembered the bickering of the three older ladies. God save him from a scene like that again.

"It was lunacy," Andrew said.

"Bloody hell. It sounds like it," John said.

A short unexpected laugh escaped past Andrew's lips. "This party has been a disaster right from the beginning of the evening."

"Yes, we heard about the urn falling from the landing at the top of the stairs before we arrived. How the hell did something like that happen?"

"I don't know, but I'm beginning to think fate has decided to play a few cruel jokes on me."

"So what happens with the young lady now?" Chandler asked.

"I'm going to call on Miss Banning and her aunt tomorrow afternoon and settle this. No doubt it will get out and the tittle-tattle sheets will chew on it for a few days, but with a little luck it will eventually die away as all scandals do."

"Yes, but how will you settle it? Marriage could be demanded of you."

Not in this lifetime.

"Don't worry, my dear friends. I have a few ideas. After all these years of spurning the pushy mamas and irate fathers, not even giving in to marriage when a financial match would have been so easy and welcomed, I'm not about to be caught in parson's mousetrap now."

"For your sake, I hope it will be as easy for you to ditch the fortune seeker as you think."

"I don't foresee a problem. I can be very persuasive. Now, I'm going back to the party."

"We're here, if you need us," Chandler said and clapped Andrew on the arm.

"I know that."

It was strangely comforting to know that his friends, who had made it clear that they preferred their wives' company to his, were still there for him when trouble came knocking.

Andrew turned and walked away.

Immediately his thoughts went deep. Perhaps all he had to do was mention to Miss Loudermilk that her niece said she was looking for a ghost. That wasn't something intelligent young ladies did. Surely no one would expect him to marry a young lady whose mind wasn't as it should be.

That was a shame, too. She was really very tempting.

He could always say he had to think of the title. Whenever he married it would have to be to a woman of sound mind. His sons would need to strong and intelligent.

Suddenly his stomach twisted. He didn't like using Miss Banning's own words about her pursuit of a ghost to save himself from the gallows called matrimony, but in this instance he might have to.

If her stern-looking aunt didn't already know about her queer searchings for members of the afterlife, she would by the end of tomorrow afternoon.

Five

"From ghoulies and ghosties and long-leggety beasties, and things that go bump in the night, Good Lord deliver us," might be Lord Dugdale's plea after a frightful incident in his home last night, where a family heirloom mysteriously fell from a ledge and nearly landed on his head. But even more intriguing than an unexplained mishap is the tittle-tattle that he was seen in his bedchamber with a young lady new to the *ton*. Is it possible we will see the bans posted for the last of the Terrible Threesome?

Lord Truefitt
Society's Daily Column

OLIVIA TOSSED HER embroidery aside and jumped up from the settee where she'd been sitting for all of three minutes. She wasn't in the mood to take her time with the tedious stitches on the intricate floral pattern. And reading had been impossible for her to concentrate on, too. She didn't know if she had ever felt so restless.

Perhaps it was because she hadn't slept well. Usually she had no trouble finding slumber, but it had eluded her last night.

She'd been up and dressed since dawn, impatiently waiting for her aunt to come belowstairs. When midday had passed and there was still no sign of Agatha, Olivia inquired about her. Their maid Susan replied that her aunt had said she would be down later.

It was fast approaching midafternoon and she still hadn't appeared. A couple of hours before, Olivia had wanted to barge into her aunt's chamber without permission and demand they talk, but after last night, Olivia was reluctant to enter anyone's room without an invitation.

Olivia stood in the middle of the parlor and looked around the room. What else could she do but pace until her aunt chose to join her? Olivia had already lost all patience for trying to read, write poetry, or work with the needle. The constant drizzle of rain had made a walk in the gardens impossible. It wasn't like her to be so twitchy, but then it wasn't like her to let a complete stranger kiss her, either.

What strange phenomena had caused her to behave in such a brazen manner?

She didn't like the unsettled feeling inside her. Her hands dropped to her sides as she strolled around the room taking time to look closely at each object. She didn't particularly want to dwell on the contents of the house, but she was struggling to find something to keep her mind off a certain rogue earl.

The house Agatha had leased for the spring and summer was small but elegantly decorated with exceptional furniture, fine rugs, and expensive paintings. The draperies were rich red velvet trimmed military style with gold fringe and brass rosettes. Even accessories like the candlesticks, lamps, and figurines had the look of excellent quality.

It was clear no expense had been spared with the furnishings or with the kitchen and flower gardens, which were tended every day by the servants who worked for the owners of the house. Olivia knew she and her aunt had only been allowed to lease the town house in the exclusive district of Mayfair because Agatha had known the owners for many years and they were quite fond of her.

Olivia stopped to stare at a painting that hung on the wall by a handsome chair upholstered in a fine Chinese silk. It portrayed a young lady and her beau standing in the middle of a crowded dance floor. The gentleman was bowing as he kissed her hand, but his eyes were looking up at her face. She was smiling back at him.

What surprised Olivia was that she'd been in this room every day for over a month and this was the first time she'd looked at the painting and saw the romance between the two people. The expression on the face of the gentleman spoke of the desire he had for the lovely maiden.

Had Lord Dugdale looked at her like that last night? Had she wanted him to? Had she offered him even a hint of a smile?

All night she'd remembered each touch of the earl's fingertips on her skin. She'd felt the pressure of his lips on hers, the warmth of his arms and the whispered breath of each word he spoke.

Olivia and Agatha had left Lord Dugdale's home immediately after they quit his chamber. Olivia had wanted to stay at the party. She didn't like the feeling that she was running away or hiding from him or anyone else. But Agatha wouldn't hear of remaining. She insisted that leaving was the proper thing to do.

In the carriage on the way home Olivia had expected to get a stern dressing down and to be questioned at length about being caught with Lord Dugdale in his room, but the only thing Agatha had been interested in was whether or not Olivia had seen or sensed any signs that Lord Pinkwater's ghost might be present.

Clearly there were times her aunt wasn't in her right mind, and that worried Olivia.

Agatha told her that everything with Lord Dugdale would be satisfactorily worked out later. She insisted that finding Lord Pinkwater would be the bigger challenge.

The gloomy day had given Olivia too much time on her hands to think about her intimate encounter with Lord Dugdale and his lingering kisses. She'd been kissed once by a young suitor—if their light touching of lips could be called kissing when compared to the way Lord Dugdale had manipulated his lips across hers.

Her stomach quickened deliciously just thinking about the way the earl had made her feel. But when that young man had given her her first kiss, she hadn't felt struck by lightning as she had when the earl's warm mouth covered hers.

She didn't understand it but knew she couldn't imagine not ever feeling that wonderful sensation again.

Suddenly Olivia's breath caught in her throat.

Was it possible that's why her mother had been so attracted to Olivia's rogue father and why her aunt continued to pine after Lord Pinkwater? Had her mother and Agatha felt the same stirrings from those men as she had felt when Lord Dugdale kissed her?

She shook her head to clear away the silly notions and continued her stroll. So much for not wanting to think about the handsome earl. If sewing, reading, and studying lovely objects didn't keep her mind off Lord Dugdale, what would?

She must find something to occupy her thoughts while she waited for her aunt.

"Good afternoon, Livy."

Olivia spun and saw Agatha floating into the parlor looking like a streak of sunshine in a yellow-sprigged dress that flattered her aunt's tall, slender figure.

"Auntie," she said almost breathless, "why have you taken so long coming down? I've been waiting all day to talk to you."

Keeping a smile on her face and the sparkle in her eyes Agatha said, "What kind of morning greeting is that?"

"It's not morning. It's past two in the afternoon. I've been up for hours wanting to talk to you."

Olivia could have added that she hadn't slept more than a wink or two but Agatha looked so cheerful that Olivia didn't have the heart to say anything that might make her feel bad.

"Oh, my dear, I am sorry about that, but I was resting so well I simply lingered over my chocolate and toast and then I had other things to do."

Concern crept inside Olivia. "You aren't feeling ill again, are you?"

"Heaven's angels, no. I'm in the pink. After I rose and dressed I had too many things to do before I could come down. I had invitations to respond to and I had several correspondences to write. Oh, Livy, I feel like I'm home again. I've missed London and I'm enjoying every moment of being here."

Concern turned to confusion. Agatha's behavior had been so irrational of late. Olivia wouldn't have been surprised if her aunt had taken to her sick bed over the incident in Lord Dugdale's chambers last night, but she didn't seem the least upset about it.

That worried Olivia.

"I didn't realize you had missed living in the city so much."

Agatha laughed softly. "Neither did I, but I think I'm coming alive again for the first time in years. I've stepped right back into Society as if I'd just left yesterday. It's a splendid feeling."

A bit of hope sprang up in Olivia. If her aunt felt as if she were coming alive again maybe she'd stop searching for a man who died over thirty years ago. "You are looking wonderful, Auntie. I'm sorry to have kept you away so long from the life you loved."

Agatha's eyes widened then narrowed and softened just as suddenly.

She stepped closer to Olivia. "Never say such nonsense again, Livy. You didn't take me away from anything. I left London because I wanted to take care of you. I was sad for you losing your mother but happy for myself that your father didn't want you. I knew I would never have children of my own, so you were a welcome gift to me."

Olivia's love for her aunt grew. She smiled at Agatha and nodded. "Thank you, Auntie."

"I have loved you as if you were my own daughter and I always will."

Olivia's heart melted. She hugged Agatha's thin frame affectionately.

"I've never regretted a moment I spent in your father's house, but I am pleased to be back in London Society with all its parties, its fame, and its secrets, but that said, I wouldn't be happy if you weren't here with me. The parties have been grand, don't you think? And now there's a little excitement going on, a little taste of scandal in the air. It's just like the old days."

Olivia was incredulous.

"But the scandal is about me, Auntie. How can you be excited about that?"

"Oh, Livy, scandal can be a good thing as long as it is dealt with properly in the end." Agatha smiled triumphantly. "And I assure you this scandal will be."

"How? I'm unsettled about last evening. And I can't understand why you aren't outraged that I wasn't more careful in my chance meeting with Lord Dugdale."

"There's no reason to be. At my age, Livy, few things upset me and even less outrages me. The damage was done once you were seen with him in his room. The only thing left to do is handle it. And I shall."

The way Olivia wanted it dealt with was to return to Kent, find a nice man like Mr. Yost to marry, and live a quiet life. She didn't want to be plagued with remembrances of mint scented soap, whispered words, and stirring kisses.

"But you know I was in there looking for Lord Pinkwater's ghost."

"It doesn't matter if all Society knows. The reason behind the two of you being in there at the same time is not important. How it's settled is. I received a correspondence from Lord Dugdale this morning. He was very prompt. He will be calling on us within minutes."

Olivia's stomach felt as if it rolled over. It was an odd feeling; she wanted to see him and she didn't.

"Why are you forcing him to come over, Auntie? I really wish you wouldn't."

"What an odd thing to say. He's a gentleman. He must."

"But I would very much like to forget that I ever stepped

foot in his bedchamber last night. In fact, I should be happy
never to see him or the inside of his house again."

"You will see him. I immediately sent a note back to
him saying we would be expecting him. I have no doubt
that everything will be worked out perfectly."

"But what is there to work out? I want nothing to do
with the earl."

His kisses made her feel too many things she didn't
want to feel for a titled man with a rogue's reputation.

"That's not a solution. Let me take care of this, Livy. I
have a bit more experience dealing with the rules of Society than you do. I knew I shouldn't have let you search the
house for Lord Pinkwater's ghost. I blame myself for this
and I have every intentions of making things right for you."

"Lady Lynette is such a nice lady, I don't think she
would breathe a word to anyone. Maybe you could persuade the Lord Mayor's wife not to say anything about
what she saw?"

"I'm afraid it's too late for that. The afternoon edition of
the *Daily Reader* was delivered to my room just before I
came down. Lord Truefitt's column has already published
that a young lady was seen in Lord Dugdale's bedchamber."

"What? How did they get the story and print it so
quickly?"

"Gossip has wings like a bird. It flies, my dear."

"Did the column mention my name?"

"No, no names in this issue, but that does not mean
Lord Truefitt doesn't know. And don't even ask how he
finds out about such things. All the writers of scandal
sheets have their little spies at every party. It's simply how
Society works. Something this delicious couldn't possibly
be kept from the eyes and the ears of the *ton*. That would
be unforgivable."

"You think that even if I'm the one being talked about?"

Agatha sounded like she was enjoying this, but that couldn't possibly be true.

"The proper settlement can silence the sharpest of tongues when it comes to scandal."

Olivia cringed. She had allowed the earl to touch her and kiss her. And worst of all, she'd enjoyed it far more than she should have.

"Now, there's no reason to fret, Livy. I've sent a letter to your great uncle, the Duke of Norfolk, seeking his counsel."

"The Duke? He's not really my uncle is he?"

"Of course he is—by way of three or four marriages to be sure, but he's still related to you."

"But why mention last night to him? I don't understand."

Agatha reached down and picked up Olivia's discarded embroidery and looked at it. "For one thing, he's always been a favorite of the king as well as being in excellent standing with the prince. Lord Dugdale would know this. Besides, the duke would want to be consulted in this matter as you are a distant relative and without a close male guardian."

An unusual feeling of unease stole over Olivia. Conferring with the powerful duke seemed over the top for such an innocent—partially innocent—meeting with an earl. Was this really happening? All she had wanted to do was spare her aunt the stigma of being remembered as an old woman who had gone mad and searched houses for ghosts.

"Besides all that, I'm eager to hear what Lord Dugdale has to say for himself," her aunt added.

Olivia was not one to run away from anything, but she didn't want to be pushed into anything, either.

Agatha looked up from the embroidery and said, "I've always said you do lovely work, Livy. You have an eye for color and design."

Olivia wasn't going to be distracted. "Auntie, it's time for us to quit this idea of finding a ghost and go back home."

Agatha laid the sewing aside and looked into Olivia's eyes. "Last night changed everything, Livy. This is home now for both of us."

Her aunt's words were far too final sounding for Olivia. They chilled her.

"Excuse me, Miss Loudermilk," the housekeeper said. "The Earl of Dugdale has arrived."

Olivia's stomach tightened.

"Right on time," Agatha said with a satisfied smile. "Show him in, and then arrange for tea to be served."

Olivia watched the door as her aunt mumbled something more about their distant blood relationship to the Duke of Norfolk.

The earl walked in and Olivia's heart tumbled. His posture was straight but not rigid. His clothing was impeccable yet he appeared comfortable. On him, the tight, intricately tied neckcloth he wore seemed commonly casual. He looked even more impressive today than he had last night. Tall, powerful, commanding.

It was madness the way her breath caught in her throat and her pulse raced at the sight of him.

Their greetings were much more formal than seemed necessary after the events of last night. The earl purposefully looked directly into her eyes. She had the feeling he was trying to intimidate her, but the only thing his magnetic stare managed to do was fascinate her.

She didn't know why, but she found everything about him exciting.

"Is your solicitor joining us later?" Agatha asked.

"No, I'm alone. Had I thought he was needed I would have contacted him. I feel sure that by the end of our meeting this afternoon you will have realized that Miss Banning was not compromised and there is no need to involve anyone else in this matter."

"Perhaps you are right, my lord, and perhaps you are not. We shall see." Agatha looked down at the embroidery hoop. "Both of you please sit down while I put this away."

Her aunt walked to the back of the room and Olivia sat down on the gold-and-green striped settee. Lord Dugdale took a chair opposite her.

As soon as Agatha's back was turned the earl leaned toward her and whispered, "Far more clever ladies than you have tried to tie me by strings of matrimony, Miss Banning."

Olivia drew her brows together in a tight frown. "How presumptuous of you to think I want to marry you," she whispered back to him. "I am only appeasing my aunt by this charade."

"Your innocent act is wearing. Drop it and admit you are trying to trap me into marriage."

"And your arrogance is offensive, sir. I wouldn't marry you if the prince himself demanded it."

"Does your boldness know no bounds?"

"Not when I'm talking to an overly suspicious man who will not listen to the truth."

"I'm sure you are aware that your actions speak louder than your words."

It was proving difficult to best him in a war of words, but Olivia would not give up the fight.

"Why would I want to marry someone who doesn't love me, a man who doesn't even know me?"

"My thoughts exactly. However," he paused as his gaze dropped to her lips and lingered, "I haven't forgotten how well you enjoyed my kisses last night, have you?"

Olivia gasped and glanced back to Agatha. "It's not very gentlemanly of you to even mention such a thing, especially where my aunt might hear you."

"I'm not feeling very gentlemanly right now, Miss Banning."

"I don't think you ever have."

Lord Dugdale chuckled low in his throat. His face was relaxed, handsome in laughter. But his tone was serious when he said, "I don't like the idea of being forced to marry a fortune seeker."

"You go too far, sir. I do not need your financial status, your protection, or your name, nor do I care for your condescending attitude."

"Then why did I find you in my bedchamber, more than willing to accept my kisses?"

Olivia hated having to whisper when what she wanted to do was shout her outrage at this man. She glanced again at her aunt, who seemed to be taking a long time at putting away the sewing basket.

She then leaned even closer to the earl and whispered earnestly, "You are an egotistical beast. I have no desire to force you into anything. There is a *true* gentleman in Kent who has caught my fancy. If I marry anyone it will be him. Not you."

"Excellent. How soon can you leave London and go back to him?"

"Not soon enough, as far as I'm concerned. It is quite clear to me now why you are the only one of the Terrible Threesome who is not wed. No lady in her right mind would marry you."

"Oh, good. Here is the tea," Agatha said, rejoining them and taking a seat by Olivia on the settee. "Let's enjoy a cup while we talk, shall we?"

Olivia was steaming. She couldn't believe her aunt seemed oblivious to the tension between them when she sat down. The earl's dark, honey-colored eyes never left her face while her aunt poured the tea. Lord Dugdale was angry, but so was she. How dare he continue to assert that she designed to marry him?

He took the cup of tea Agatha offered but Olivia was certain his cup would remain as untouched as hers.

Agatha said, "Lord Dugdale, I sent a letter over to Claudette this morning and invited her to join us this afternoon, but I never heard from her. I assume she must have already left her house by the time my note arrived."

"I don't need assistance from my Aunt Claude, Miss Loudermilk."

"An earl need help? Oh, I should think not. However, she and I were friends long before you were born and I felt *I* needed her here. But she and I shall talk another time. Right now, I'd like to hear what you plan to do about the harm you have done to my niece's reputation."

"If I considered that Miss Banning had been violated because of me, I would do whatever was necessary to save her reputation, but that isn't the case."

"Then perhaps you haven't seen this?" Agatha set her teacup aside and pulled a sheet of news print from the pocket of her skirt.

Olivia cringed, knowing that it had to be a copy of Lord Truefitt's column.

Lord Dugdale remained calm as he said, "No, I haven't seen it."

She extended paper to him. "I'll give you time to read it."

The earl put his cup aside and quickly glanced at the paper. Olivia felt as if she were sitting on pins. She hadn't seen the article, either.

"It mentions no names," he said and returned the paper to her before glancing at Olivia again.

"How long do you think it will take before everyone knows her name?"

"Hundreds of scandals have surfaced over the years without names being printed."

"Yes, but I'm sure you are aware that the names are almost always circulated by word of mouth, which is the worst kind of gossip."

"I had hoped not to mention this, but now feel I must. When I happened upon Miss Banning in my rooms she told me she was looking for a ghost. That's not something most intelligent, rational people do. In order to spare her embarrassment, I didn't mention this in front of the other ladies last night. I'm sure you wouldn't want that kind of information about her known."

Olivia pierced him with a hard glare. "Just what are you trying to imply, my lord?"

He sent a cold stare right back at her. "I'm not trying to imply anything. I'm merely making your aunt aware of what you said you were doing in my room."

"I think you are suggesting I'm simple minded or perhaps that I'm insane because I search for someone from the spirit world?"

As soon as she said the words she realized that was her reaction to Agatha when she first mentioned looking for Lord Pinkwater.

"You said it, Miss Banning. Not I."

"Quite frankly, Lord Dugdale," Agatha said, "I would have rather she had been found in that bedchamber with

Lord Pinkwater's ghost than with you. It would have been much easier to explain to the *ton* that she was with a ghost than with you. Obviously, I think that marriage between the two of you as soon as possible should settle this affair quite nicely."

Olivia rose from the settee. "Aunt Agatha, you know I don't want to marry him."

Lord Dugdale rose, too. "Miss Loudermilk, I can't imagine you or anyone insisting I marry a young lady who goes around hunting ghosts in strangers' houses. It goes beyond the pale."

"I am perfectly sane, sir," Olivia shot back at him.

"You won't find it easy to force me to the altar, no matter that your aunt has known mine a long time."

"Olivia, Lord Dugdale, please lower your voices," Agatha said from where she remained seated on the settee, holding her teacup.

When they both looked down at her she continued. "I wouldn't dream of trying to persuade or influence you or Claudette. This sort of thing is best left to a man. That's why I sent a letter to Olivia's uncle, the Duke of Norfolk, this morning asking his counsel in this matter."

"Olivia's uncle?"

"Yes." Agatha paused and smiled charmingly at Lord Dugdale. "You didn't know we were related to him?"

It was quite clear to Olivia that he didn't know she was distantly related to the duke, a crotchety old man who was known for detesting anything that defied convention. In Society's circles he was revered almost as much as the old king and the prince regent, too.

"I suppose I thought Claudette would have mentioned it to you. Naturally, I told him speed was of the essence. No doubt he will be in touch with you within a day or two."

"No doubt, he will."

Olivia looked at the earl, knowing her own expression was filled with outrage that her aunt intended to push them through this forced marriage, but when she saw Lord Dugdale's face, she knew what people meant when they said *if looks could kill.*

Six

When OLIVIA HEARD the front door close behind Lord Dugdale she turned to her aunt, who was pouring herself another cup of tea. Agatha looked far too comfortable and much too pleased with herself to suit Olivia.

And Olivia had a feeling she knew why.

She walked over to her aunt and sat down in the chair that Lord Dugdale had just vacated. "You are serious about this, aren't you?"

Her aunt remained silent, but her expression told volumes.

Olivia was aghast. "You want to force Lord Dugdale to marry me. Why?"

Agatha took a dainty sip of her tea before focusing her attention on her niece. "He's an earl. It's what he must do, considering he compromised you. Society would demand it even if I didn't."

This was incredible.

Olivia saw her dream of a quiet family man for a husband slipping away. "Doesn't it matter to you that I was in that room for you, looking for Lord Pinkwater's ghost? Doesn't it matter that I don't want to marry Lord Dugdale?"

Her aunt looked directly, firmly into Olivia's eyes and said, "No, my dear, it doesn't."

Olivia felt as if she'd been struck across the face. "You don't mean that."

"Of course I do," Agatha said, keeping her matter-of-fact tone.

"You're telling me that what I want doesn't count? You've never done that before."

"I've never had to. If I had been alone when I saw you and Lord Dugdale together in his room, or perhaps even with Claudette there, maybe we could have prevented this and settled it between our two families. As it is, with Dorothy and Lady Lynette knowing and now the scandal sheets no doubt on the verge of telling all, it's impossible for this to go away without your reputation being ruined. The only thing that will save you is marriage to him."

Olivia didn't understand. They had only kissed. True it was more than one chaste little kiss, but their aunts didn't know that.

"What about happiness, Auntie? How can I be happy with a rogue who was forced into wedlock? My mother married a man of Lord Dugdale's reputation and lived a life of loneliness and regret. You were jilted by such a man and never loved again. How can you want me to marry a man like Lord Dugdale?"

"I'm not saying I want you to marry him. I'm saying you must marry him." She placed her delicate cup on the tea tray and turned a serious expression on Olivia. "And as for happiness, Livy, no man can make you happy. That is something that comes from within you. Only you and the way you feel about things inside here." She lightly touched Olivia's chest just above her heart. "Right here in your heart is the only place where you can find true happiness."

Surprising Olivia, Agatha then relaxed her straight shoulders and sat back in the settee and smiled. Her aged gaze affectionately brushed Olivia's face.

"You think that because I've never loved but one man that I haven't been happy all these years?" She laughed gently, briefly. "Nothing could be further from the truth, silly girl. You have brought me more happiness than I could have ever imagined. I have never regretted leaving London to be your guardian."

Her aunt's words touched Olivia's heart warmly. She had always felt Agatha's love and concern for her even though it had seldom been voiced over the years.

Olivia leaned toward Agatha and said, "Then why would you want me to leave you and marry a man I don't know, a man who will never love me?"

"That is life. All species give up their young. I must, too. If I consent to Lord Dugdale's wishes, all your life you will be considered a ruined woman unless you marry someone right away. I couldn't live with myself if I allowed you to carry that shame. Society will never forget, and you would never be welcomed in anyone's home again if you don't marry. On your mother's grave, I won't allow that to happen."

"I would agree to all you said if I had intended to make a match here in London to a titled gentleman such as Lord Dugale. My reputation is ruined beyond repair, but I want to go back to the country and marry a man like Mr. Yost."

"Do you really think that would be possible, Livy?"

"Yes." She smiled, thinking her aunt might be willing to consider seeing this her way.

Agatha settled more comfortably in the settee. She seemed to ponder Olivia's words carefully before saying, "Truly, dear girl? You think Mr. Yost or someone like him will want to marry you after he hears that you were caught with Lord Dugdale in his bedchamber?"

Doubt suddenly clouded Olivia's enthusiasm. It seemed so distasteful when Agatha put it that way. "But Mr. Yost never comes to London. He wouldn't have to know, would he?"

"There's mention of the incident in Lord Truefitt's column. It's only a matter of time before everyone knows the lady in question is you, whether or not it's ever mentioned to your face. And even if someone like Mr. Yost agreed to marry you, do you think he would find himself at times wondering if Lord Dugdale's lips had touched yours with passion, or if his strong hand had caressed your soft cheeks, or if he held you close and whispered lovely words in your ear? Don't you think Mr. Yost would wonder what went on during the time you were alone with the earl in his rooms?"

Olivia's throat grew tighter with every word Agatha spoke. All the things she mentioned had happened. It was as if Agatha had witnessed her moments alone with the earl. How could she have known—but suddenly Olivia had a pretty good idea how her aunt knew.

Agatha had loved a man just like Lord Dugdale. Lord Pinkwater must have been every bit as charming and enchanting to Agatha as Lord Dugdale had been to Olivia. No doubt she and her aunt had had similar experiences with the two men.

Olivia slowly shook her head. Agatha was right. Mr. Yost wouldn't want to marry her. No man would. She wasn't innocent any longer. She had let Lord Dugdale kiss her and touch her and enchant her.

"What will happen to you if I marry? What about my helping you find Lord Pinkwater's ghost?"

Agatha's eyes brightened. The concerned expression faded from her face and she picked up the teapot and poured a splash into her cup. "Oh, I will still need your help with that, my dear. I do believe Lord Pinkwater's ghost is in Lord Dugdale's house. I think he was disturbed that so many people were in the house when he sensed my presence last night and that's why he caused the vase to fall. Don't you think that's why he didn't show himself to either you or me?"

"I don't know," Olivia said, feeling the weight of her intimate interlude with Lord Dugdale on her shoulders.

"It will be different the next time I am in the house. I'm certain Lord Pinkwater will try to contact me again."

A funny feeling stole over Olivia, and she was beginning to have a vague apprehension that somehow her aunt had a grand scheme that Olivia didn't understand.

"Auntie, why do I get the feeling you might be pushing me into this marriage just so I can live in Lord Dugdale's house and help you find that ghost?"

"Heaven's angels, Livy, that's not true," Agatha said adamantly, placing her cup on the table once more. "I've never heard anything so outrageous. I had no way of knowing that you and Lord Dugdale would end up in his chambers at the same time when I agreed you could go in search of Lord Pinkwater's ghost. However, I do feel this was meant to be."

It was true that her aunt couldn't have known that she and the earl would have a chance meeting in his rooms. And they wouldn't have if Olivia hadn't felt that mysterious pull to linger and look over his chamber rather than to leave immediately. If she hadn't been overcome with the desire to touch his things, smell his soap, and feel his presence all around her, this wouldn't have happened.

No, she really couldn't blame anyone but herself for this predicament. She hadn't planned it, but it was her fault.

"I'm insisting on this marriage partly as my duty to your mother and your father. It's what they would have done. I couldn't live with myself if I didn't do this for you. I'll see you wed, and then I'll continue my search for Lord Pinkwater."

Olivia rose from the chair and walked over to the window and looked out. A sudden chill shook her body. She felt trapped.

Was there any way she could avoid this marriage?

A LIGHT RAIN fell on Andrew's hat and his shoulders but he paid it no mind as he stepped down from his curricle in front of his town house. The gray afternoon matched his mood. It had been less than ten minutes since he left Miss Banning and Miss Loudermilk. Their leased abode was decidedly too close to his for comfort.

There was no telling what those country-rustics might come up with next. Who the hell did they think they were to try to force him into marriage?

"Relatives to the Duke of Norfolk," he mumbled begrudgingly to himself as he strode up the walkway.

Just his luck, he thought. They might as well be related to the prince himself. The cranky old duke didn't approve of anything that went against convention. And the duke could make trouble for Andrew if he ever decided to take his place in Parliament or if there were ever any disputes about his lands or holdings.

He was dealing with a beautiful, desirable, but devious young lady who was well-connected. He supposed he should feel privileged she chose him to try to leg-shackle, but her reasoning was too close for comfort for him to be amused or flattered.

Miss Banning was a mixture of self-confidence, innocence, and audacity. And for some reason he was attracted to all three. She was definitely the kind of young lady he would have pursued if he were interested in giving up his bachelor status.

He couldn't help but wonder why she wanted to catch him in the parson's mousetrap if she wanted the attention of another man. Andrew supposed she used the man waiting in Kent as a ruse so he would think she really didn't want to marry him. The clever lady had thought of everything.

Andrew sprinted up the steps and opened the front door of his Mayfair town house and stepped into the foyer. His gaze immediately scanned up to the landing where the heirloom vase used to sit. Thankfully a disaster had been avoided last night when the damned thing crashed. He hoped Whibbs had gotten to the bottom of who left the urn so close to the edge that it fell.

He took off his damp hat, gloves, and cape just as Whibbs came walking into the vestibule. Whibbs had been his manservant, butler, and valet all neatly rolled into one for more than ten years. He was a short, efficient man with thin, graying hair. His round face made him appear heavier than he actually was.

Whibbs was professional to a fault, keeping check on the housekeeper, the cook, the gardener, and the groom. Sometimes Andrew thought Whibbs must stand at the window and watch for his carriage to drive up because whenever Andrew came through the front door, his man was only a step or two away.

"Good afternoon, sir. I trust you had a pleasant afternoon."

"No, Whibbs, I didn't," Andrew said, having always felt comfortable saying whatever he pleased to his servant and having all trust it would never be repeated to anyone.

"Then perhaps I made a mistake."

Whibbs picked up the wet coat and gloves from the foyer table where Andrew had laid them and draped them over his arm.

The last thing Andrew needed was another disaster to deal with.

"About what?"

"A Mr. Howard Thompson is here to see you, sir. I told him you were out and I didn't know when you were expected to return. He insisted he needed to talk and asked if he could wait for you. It appeared urgent so I showed him into the parlor. I'll dismiss him right away."

"No, don't. You did the right thing. I want to see Thompson. Give me a minute to get to my desk and then show him in."

Whibbs nodded once. "Yes, sir."

Andrew walked into his book room and sat down at his desk. He reached into a drawer and pulled out a folder with the name Willard Hawkins marked on it. He hoped the Runner had some good news for him about the man's whereabouts. After last night and his visit with Miss Banning and Miss Loudermilk a few minutes ago, he could use some.

Those two ladies were hell-bent on upsetting his well-planned life. He hadn't come back from a quiet year in the countryside to spend a quiet life in London. He was ready to resume his life as London's premier rake.

A couple of minutes later, Whibbs showed the Runner

into the book room, where Andrew spent the majority of his time in his house when he wasn't sleeping.

Thompson was a tall, broad-shouldered fellow with a full head of dark brown hair and not a wrinkle in his face even though Andrew knew him to be past fifty. Andrew had been most impressed with the Runner's knowledge of how to find a person who didn't want to be found and the fact that he had several men working for him who could search for Hawkins.

Andrew had talked with three different men before settling on Thompson as the person best able to nab the man who had embezzled from the estate for the better part of five years.

"Have a seat," Andrew said, pointing to wide-striped upholstered chair in front of his desk. "Would you care for something to drink?"

"No, thank you, my lord, I'm fine."

Andrew gave the nod to Whibbs that he could leave, then immediately said to Thompson, "Tell me what you have for me."

"Nothing, I'm afraid, sir," Thompson said with all the self-confidence of a man who'd had complete success.

"Then what the hell are you doing here?" Andrew said, a bit more angrily than he intended, but his frustration was running high.

Thompson's wide-set eyes showed no sign of offense at Andrew's irritation as he said, "We've been in Derbyshire over a week. We're watching the house where Mr. Hawkins's mother lives and keeping watch at the taverns and inns, but so far there hasn't been any sight of him."

"That's not what I wanted to hear."

"I know that, my lord. I've stationed men at all three homes where Hawkins has relatives. There have been no reports of anyone coming and going except the people who live at the houses. If he is holed up in any of them, he's not coming out and showing his face."

Andrew made a low sound in his throat that he realized sounded like a growl. Thompson didn't flinch. Andrew liked the fact that he didn't intimidate the Runner. That meant Hawkins wouldn't either.

"Maybe your men are missing him. He could be disguising himself and coming and going at will," Andrew said, knowing that was highly unlikely as soon as the words were out of his mouth.

"I don't think so," Thompson said. "Hawkins is well known in the area. I realize we've only watched the houses for a few days and he could still turn up. If he's in Derbyshire he'll have to show his face sooner or later and we'll get him, but I'm beginning to think he left the area."

"You stand by the trustworthiness of your men on their watch?"

"I do," Thompson said, not backing down an inch. "I hire only the best. You mentioned that Hawkins had been stealing from you for years. Have you given thought to the idea that he might leave the country and make a new life for himself abroad?"

"With the money he stole from me? I suppose that's a possibility. In the months I stayed at my home in Derbyshire I heard talk that he gambled heavily. If that's true, I'm not sure he had enough blunt to get very far."

"I'll see what I can find out about any debts he left owing or if anyone owes him."

Andrew nodded. "That might give you some lead as to his whereabouts."

"I'd also like to have your permission to widen my search and check out other towns, the hells of London and even some of the seaports to see if anyone remembers him boarding a ship."

Andrew hadn't forgotten what it felt like when Hawkins's shot grazed his arm.

"By all means, Thompson, do whatever you must. I don't care if you have to bribe one of the scoundrel's family members to tell you where he is. I want the man found."

"Thank you, sir. I'll get right on it."

"Stay in touch."

Andrew looked up and saw Whibbs waiting in the doorway. He nodded for him to enter and speak.

"The Viscountess Hollingsworth has arrived and would like to speak to you, sir. She's waiting in the parlor."

Andrew let out a heavy sigh and whispered a curse under his breath. He didn't have to wonder what his aunt wanted to talk about. He might as well see her and get it over with.

"After you've shown Thompson out, tell her ladyship I'll be right in."

"Yes, sir."

His aunt couldn't possibly have had time to talk to Miss Loudermilk and then get here, but no doubt she wanted to discuss what happened at the party last night, especially since she had been his hostess for the evening.

Aunt Claude was the matriarch of the family, and she wore her well-earned title with strength. Getting caught with a young lady in his room was not the kind of thing she wanted to happen, but then neither had he.

As much as he hated to do it, he had to face the fact that for the first time in his life a lady had outsmarted him. He didn't know if she was a trickster or a lunatic—neither of which he wanted to marry.

And he had to decide what he was going to do about it.

Seven

❦

ANDREW WALKED INTO the parlor and Claudette rose to greet him. He took her hands in his and kissed the backs of both palms.

"Don't tell me you've come so I can take you on a ride in the park because you've rejected all the handsome suitors who are vying for your hand."

Claudette smiled graciously at him, and then laughed. "If only that were true, but no, I've come on a much more important matter than the possibility of a fourth husband for me."

Andrew folded his arms across his chest and pretended to study what she'd said. His aunt was short and thin, but when she spoke everyone in the family listened. Watching her laughing face, he could see why even at her age men still wanted to pursue her. She had that unique combination of femininity and strength, the same qualities he saw in Miss Banning.

"Let me guess. Does your visit have anything to do with a certain young lady in the care of Miss Loudermilk?"

Claudette took a seat again on the settee. "Of course, why else would I come out on a rainy afternoon? You know how I hate to get my feet wet. I had a note from Agatha today asking me to visit her."

"So you haven't seen Miss Loudermilk?"

"No, I wanted to speak with you first. Pour me a splash of that good port you have, will you, dear?"

Andrew walked over to the rosewood side table that stretched against the back wall. His Aunt Claude usually had a sip or two of the fine, expensive combination of wine and brandy with him every time she visited.

"I can tell you what she wants," Andrew said as he filled two glasses with the port that was more brandy than wine. "She wants me to marry her niece."

"Of course she does. It's inferred because you were alone with her in your chamber. I always knew your recklessness would catch up to you one day. It was only a matter of time."

He handed her a glass and sat down beside her. He sipped from his glass with confidence and then said, "I'm not married yet."

"I'm here to tell you that it has to be."

Anger at being duped welled up in him again. "She designed our meeting in my room."

"Say what you will, but she couldn't have done it without your help. Even so, you must marry the girl."

So much for his aunt's beating around the bush. She came right out with the hatchet.

Andrew drank from his glass again. He held the strong wine in his mouth for a moment before swallowing. "No. There are things you don't know about her."

"She's from an excellent family with ties to the Duke of Norfolk."

"So I've heard," he grumbled.

"So what else is there to know? There's never been a hint of scandal about her. I'm hoping when I go see Agatha I can tell her you will do what's right by her niece and marry her."

"No."

Claudette's voice remained calm even though he sensed she was getting agitated. "It's in the scandal sheets, Andrew. Dorothy must have been the one to have told the gossipmongers. That sweet Lady Lynette wouldn't dare breathe a word of gossip to anyone, but it's only a matter of time before Miss Banning's name is whispered behind fans."

"I gave up long ago trying to find out how they got their gossip or even caring. But you asked what else there is to know about Miss Banning. I'll tell you. I think she's addled or simple-minded or something, because she's obviously not in her right mind."

"What are you talking about? I've talked to her. She's as sane as you or I."

"When I found her in my room she told me she was looking for a ghost."

His aunt's amusement started with a slow smile lifting her lips at the corners, which quickly erupted into soft, comfortable laughter that grated on Andrew's tenuous hold on his anger.

He tried not to show his annoyance. He had no appreciation for being anyone's entertainment, including his favorite aunt.

Grimly he said, "If Miss Banning spoke the truth and she's a ghost hunter, don't you find that peculiar behavior?

How can I marry a young woman who is not right in the mind?"

"We're not talking about you, Andrew. We're talking about her. It's her reputation that's damaged, not yours."

The reminder sobered him and he set his port aside. His aunt would be one hundred percent right had it not been for the fact the young lady had been ruined by her own design. Once they were seen alone in his bedchamber she was accused.

"And if looking for a ghost is all that is stopping you from doing the right thing, forget about it," Claudette said, with a bit of a sly grin on her lips. "Looking for someone from the spirit world does not make her weak in the mind any more than looking for a fourth husband makes me a madwoman, as some of my dear friends accuse me of being."

"I'm serious, Aunt Claude."

"So am I," she said, although the amused smile lingered on her lips. "Half the members of the *ton* have either looked for a ghost or claim to have seen one."

"I have to think about heirs. Miss Banning could truly be mad," he said, not that he really believed that. Her wit had been too sharp and her self-confidence too high for her to be weak in the mind. He didn't believe she was insane any more than his aunt did, but he still didn't want to marry the scheming Miss Banning.

"And so could your friends be mad in the head, but they're not, and neither is she. I can't believe you are even bringing such a thing up. Don't you remember when Lord Dunraven thought a priceless golden raven had been stolen by Lord Pinkwater's ghost?"

"Members of the *ton* thought that, not Chandler."

His aunt gave him a look that let him know she didn't believe him and then continued. "And just last year Lord

Chatwin thought a ghost had spooked his horse and then rode off on it. I believe it was Lady Veronica's ghost. No, my dear, belief in the spirit world does not a simpleton nor a madwoman make."

Andrew laughed, amused that his aunt remembered the rumors and gossip of the past and not the facts. She had made her point well.

His good friend Chandler had never thought a ghost had stolen the raven but somehow the story had gotten started among the *ton* and it made good fodder for the gossip columns. And Andrew knew for a fact that it was no ghost that rode atop John's horse. In fact, the lady who rode his horse that early morn a year ago later became his wife, yet rumors still lingered that a ghost had once ridden John's horse.

"Miss Banning also said something about having her sights set on a man in Kent."

"That could very possibly have been a ruse." Claudette paused. "But if not, you can handle that. She is beautiful and articulate. I'm sure more than one man has been interested in pursuing her."

"You would want me to marry a woman who desires another man?"

Claudette took a sip of port before she looked him squarely in the eyes and said, "As her husband, it would be your responsibility to make her forget any other man she has ever thought about."

"And just how am I supposed to do that?" he said without really thinking about what those words meant.

"In your bed, my dear Andrew. Once you get her there, make her forget any other man exists."

"Aunt Claude, please," Andrew said, not wanting to discuss such matters with his aging aunt.

"Don't act surprised to hear me say that. I've had three marriage beds and I know what a good lover can do. Judging from your reputation you won't fall short in that department."

"You do know how to get to the heart of a matter, don't you?" he grumbled more to himself that to Claudette.

"Miss Banning might have gone into your bedchamber, but you didn't turn her out. You kissed her, we all saw it, and you had her backed up against the dressing table, no less, not the other way around. You might not like the outcome, Andrew, but now you have a moral obligation to make it right."

"I can make it right by finding her a husband who would be pleased to marry such a beautiful and tempting young lady."

"And no doubt he would be much older than you. I know Agatha and she will not allow her niece to be married off to an old lord more than twice her age just to save her reputation. Nor would she allow her to marry a penniless baron who would be supported by her dowry for the rest of his life."

His aunt's words struck him hard just as she'd intended. He had to admit he didn't like the thought of Miss Banning being married off to an old man who couldn't tap into the passion he sensed and felt inside her last night. She had way too much inner anticipation in her to be resigned to that fate.

He didn't like the thought of a young man touching her any better.

Andrew's gaze shifted from his aunt to the Seth Thomas clock on the mantel. It was four thirty.

What was he going to do about Miss Banning?

If she pushed marriage as her aunt indicated by mentioning the powerful Duke of Norfolk, there were several things he could do to counter that. He could simply leave Town under the guise that he was looking for Willard Hawkins. He could even arrange a marriage for her to someone else.

He instantly dismissed those ideas. He might have done something like that a few years ago but not now. Leaving his estates in the hands of others and not taking an interest in his affairs until it was almost too late had cost him dearly. It had also helped him to mature.

If nothing else, his problems with Willard Hawkins had taught him the hard way not to let unpleasant things continue.

It took a while for him to come to this point. He was a year past thirty. He wanted to be active in what went on in his life and not leave what affected him for others to handle.

If something wasn't right, he intended to take the matter fully in hand, which was one of the reasons he wouldn't stop looking until Hawkins was found and thrown in prison.

So what did that understanding tell him about what he should he do about Miss Banning?

He didn't want the entanglements of a wife. He wanted the freedom to flirt with an enchanting miss on a starlit balcony. He wanted to enjoy the pleasures of a mistress in his bed or spend the night gaming and drinking. When he came back to London he had his life all planned out, and it didn't include the responsibilities of a wife.

But Miss Olivia Banning had plans of her own that included him.

Suddenly a picture of her standing in his room framed by golden lamplight filtered through his mind. Her aggressive denial of wanting to trap him whispered past his ear. The scent of fresh washed hair wafted on the air beneath his nose. His tongue tasted the sweetness of her mouth. The pads of his fingers tingled deliciously as he remembered the softness of her skin.

When he'd kissed her, he'd sensed there was deep passion inside her that had not been roused before he touched her. The thought of awaking her womanly desires sent a rush of heat searing through him. He had no doubt Miss Banning was an innocent, but he also had no doubt she would be a bold lover once she learned the intimacies of what could be shared between a man and a woman.

Andrew swallowed to slow his breathing. Just thinking about her excited him.

She might really be a ghost hunter, or she could have been merely curious as she'd said, but he was certain she wasn't a simpleton.

After his aunt finished her port and said her farewells, Andrew dressed for the evening and headed straight for White's. He needed to do something to get his mind off Miss Banning.

It still rankled that he'd been caught with her in his private chamber. He was old enough to know better than to be so irresponsible. And he wouldn't have been had the gel not tempted him beyond his endurance to resist her.

Cards didn't seem to be his game for the evening, so he left the tables and headed to the billiard room and found a challenger. Minutes later Andrew rested the heel of his palm on the billiards table and positioned the cue in the web of his hand and scattered the balls.

Not a one of them went into a pocket.

Half a rueful laugh swept past his lips and he bowed to his opponent.

Not only had fate turned against him, Lady Luck had left him, too.

Andrew barely knew the man he was playing against, but that's the way it had been since he'd returned to London. Before John and Chandler had married he'd always had them to play cards or billiards with so there was no reason to get close with anyone else. He had to get over the fact that neither of his two best friends cared a damn anymore about spending the night at White's gaming and drinking.

"It's your turn," the younger man said.

Andrew looked at his opponent, and then without saying a word tried to put a ball in the side pocket. He missed by several inches. It just wasn't his night. He should have given up long ago and gone home.

He'd lost every card game he'd played, and now he couldn't even win at billiards when he was usually a challenging player. With no current mistress to ease his frustration, the only way to end a night like this was to have another drink and go home.

But that didn't hold any appeal, either. He had to make some inquires and see about arranging for a mistress.

Andrew quickly let the young man beat him at billiards and then replaced the cue on the hanger before settling his bet. He picked up his tankard of ale and turned to head into the club room when he saw Chandler and John walking through the doorway.

His spirits lifted instantly. Damn, there was no way they could know how bad he needed to see them tonight, yet they were here.

"What's this?" he joked, walking toward them as if he didn't have a care in the world. "Are these the two lovesick puppies I saw a month ago? The ones who didn't want to leave their wives for an evening of games at White's or even a horse race in the park?"

"We wouldn't have tonight," John said, "except for the fact that we felt like you needed us."

Andrew's smile faded. That changed everything.

He did need their friendship and companionship, but he didn't want them knowing that. He'd walk through hell unarmed before he'd allow anyone to feel sorry for him, especially these two strong men who had been like his brothers.

Andrew had gotten himself into this trap with Miss Banning and he'd get himself out of it. And looking at the two of them, he knew exactly what he had to do.

Eyeing them warily, Andrew said, "Now why would you two think I needed you? I'm in White's with money in my pockets. I'm gaming," he pointed to the billiard table behind him. "And I'm losing." He pointed to the gentleman who was putting his winnings in his pocket. "And I'm drinking." He held up the tankard of ale he held in his hand. "What more could I need?"

"We're worried about you, and it looks like somebody needs to be, since you aren't," Chandler said with a scowl on his face.

Andrew grinned with ease. "Worried? Since when and over what?" he asked, though he had a pretty good idea why they had come.

"Since last evening when you admitted you were caught with a young lady in your bedchamber. We haven't been able to stop thinking about it."

"Yes," John said. "Obviously you haven't heard, but the incident hit Lord Truefitt's column this afternoon."

"And you know when that bastard gets hold of a piece of gossip he doesn't let it go until he gets to the bottom of every fact and every name," Chandler added with distaste in his tone.

Andrew looked at his two friends. They were worried

about him. They wanted to help him. He saw it in their faces. And that felt damn good, but it also made him even more determined to handle this on his own. And do what he must. Despite the consequences of what he had decided he had to do.

He took a chug of the ale. It was dark, strong, and soothing. Suddenly it was as clear as a cloudless blue sky what he had to do.

"Well, worry no more, my good friends who have come to rescue me. I plan to take care of the problem to the satisfaction of everyone concerned in the matter."

Chandler and John looked at each other with curious expressions on their faces and then they turned their confused expressions on Andrew.

"Wait a minute," John said. "How do you propose to settle this?"

Taking a labored breath, Andrew placed his empty tankard on a nearby table and clapped both men on the back as he said, "The old-fashioned way. I'm going to marry her."

Eight

THE BALLROOM OF the Great Hall glittered with lights
from hundreds of candles. Stately columns had been draped
with ivory tulle, wrapped in green vines and scattered with
sweet-smelling blossoms. Large doors were swung wide so
the night's gentle breeze could flow through the room and
keep the guests cool as the dancing, laughter, and chatter
heated up the rooms.

Olivia twirled, side-stepped, and curtsied as she covered the dance floor with a man who looked to be twice her
age. Agatha had told her the Marquis's second wife had
died in childbirth and he was looking to find his third bride
to take care of his four children before the Season was out.

She was certain her aunt wanted her to realize there
were worse things than being forced to marry a handsome
earl. And this titled gentleman who kept smiling at her
made a believer out of Olivia.

Facing him in the quadrille was as close as she wanted

to get to him. He wasn't unattractive. In fact he seemed very fit and quite intelligent, but Olivia felt no spark of interest when she looked at him. She had no intentions of becoming his next wife. As soon as this dance was over she was heading to the ladies' retiring room to spend a few quiet moments alone.

Aunt Agatha considered herself a master in knowing how to handle all issues concerning the dos and don'ts of Society affairs. As a well-respected spinster among the *ton* for many years she'd had countless opportunities not only to see but also to help direct how delicate matters such as compromising situations were maneuvered to create the least amount of scandal.

Olivia had assumed they would not attend any more parties in London after Agatha had insisted they quit Lord Dugdale's party last night immediately after they'd left his bedchamber.

But Olivia was wrong.

Her aunt had said they must be at the biggest party of the evening tonight. Agatha wanted Olivia seen dancing with handsome gentlemen, laughing with young ladies, and charming aging dowagers, and that was exactly what she'd been doing.

Olivia had dined, danced, and chatted for what seemed like hours. She felt confident that no one, other than the intimate group last night, knew she was the young lady written about in Lord Truefitt's column. Surely someone would have mentioned it to her or at least shied away from her if they knew.

Agatha had assured her, however, that it was only a matter of time before her name trickled out into the open and then it would be on everyone's lips.

Only once had she felt even slightly uncomfortable, and

that was when Lady Lynette joined a group of ladies with whom Olivia was conversing. Thankfully the duke's daughter had made no reference to what she'd witnessed the night before. Her silence had made Olivia like her even more.

At last the lively dance came to an end and Olivia allowed the bride-hunting Marquis to lead her back to her aunt.

"Do you like children?" the Marquis asked as they walked across the dance floor.

"I suppose so," she answered truthfully. "I was an only child so I've never had the opportunity to be around children."

"There's not much to do. The governess takes care of them during the day and a nurse cares for them at night."

"Oh, how nice. Aunt Agatha is over there," she said, changing the subject and picking up her pace.

The truth was that Olivia had never given the idea of children much thought. Having children was just something she knew would happen after she got married. She didn't want to think about the possibility of marrying a man who already had four.

The dapper Marquis led Olivia over to Agatha, who was standing with Lady Lynette, Mrs. Farebrother, and several other women. The Marquis spoke to the ladies and soon had all of them except Olivia listening to his story.

Olivia had caught a glimpse of Lady Lynette looking at the Marquis of Musgrove Glenn. Lynette's lovely green eyes were transfixed on the man and she had an adoring expression on her face. She was taking in every word he said as if she were trying to memorize them.

At one point the Marquis's gaze met Lynette's for a moment and he smiled at her. Olivia saw the older woman blush as easily as an innocent schoolgirl with her first thought of love. Olivia couldn't help but think that Lady Lynette had designs on the Marquis.

When he finished his story, Mrs. Farebrother started talking to Agatha, but Olivia kept her attention on Lynette and the Marquis.

Lynette asked him about his four children, calling each of them by name. She asked about his ailing, elderly mother. Olivia could see the Marquis was pleased that she showed concern for his family, and then he in turn asked about her father.

When the Marquis bid his farewell and left, Lady Lynette watched him walk away. The adoring expression stayed on her face until he walked up to another lady and headed to the dance floor with her. Only then did Lady Lynette look away. The glimmer of happiness had left her eyes and in its place was sadness.

It occurred to Olivia as she continued to study Lady Lynette that she had that same faraway look that came over her aunt when she was thinking about Lord Pinkwater.

Lady Lynette was in love with the Marquis and Olivia wondered if the man had any idea. And if he didn't, what could she do to help him realize it?

Olivia cleared her throat and spoke softly so her aunt and the other ladies standing near them couldn't hear her say, "Thank you, Lady Lynette, for not mentioning what happened last evening when we were talking with the group of ladies a short while ago."

"Oh, I wouldn't have brought that up in front of anyone, Miss Banning." She leaned in closer to Olivia and added, "But now that we're alone, I would like to say that I hope everything is being handled appropriately and to your satisfaction."

"Yes, thank you. Aunt Agatha and Lord Dugdale talked today."

"Good."

Olivia knew that perhaps she should leave well-enough alone, but she wanted someone other than her aunt to know and believe that she hadn't planned a rendezvous with Lord Dugdale.

"I feel like I owe you an explanation about last night."

Lady Lynette's green eyes widened a little and she moved a little closer to Olivia, turning so that she blocked Olivia from the other two ladies.

"Oh, no, don't think you have to explain anything, but if you would like to, I shall be happy to listen to anything you have to say."

"It truly started very innocently. I did not arrange to meet Lord Dugdale in his rooms. It's true we'd never even met. I was only peeking inside his room when curiosity got the better of me and I wandered inside to look around. I've never been in a man's chamber and I wanted to see what it was like. I had no idea he would come in while I was there."

Lynette smiled. "I probably would have done the same thing. I've never been in a man's room before either and I'm a few years older than you. What was it like? Did you feel absolutely sinful for being in there?"

"No, I felt—" She paused. *Safe. Comfortable. Welcomed.* "All right, yes, I felt a little naughty," she answered with a sheepish smile, knowing that's what the duke's daughter wanted to hear.

"I'm certain that every young lady who's ready to wed wishes she was the girl who'd been caught in his room."

"Do you really think so?"

"Of course. He's handsome, titled, and considered unattainable. He's the last bachelor of the Terrible Three-some. What more could a young lady want?"

"Love?"

Lynette sighed quietly. "Of course. How could I have for-gotten? It's such an elusive thing, is it not, except, maybe for Lord Byron? He seems to know just how to explain what it feels like to be in love, doesn't he?"

"He has a way with words like none other, Lady Lynette."

"Oh, please, you must call me Lynette. We certainly don't need to be formal, do we?"

Olivia smiled, remembering how Lynette looked at the Marquis. "No, not at all, and please call me Olivia."

As they continued to chat Olivia's attention was drawn to the red birthmark on Lynette's cheek. Olivia recalled what Viscountess Collingsworth had said about trying many different kinds of creams from the apothecary on her face. Olivia couldn't help but wonder if Lynette had ever tried a concoction to either fade or cover her birthmark.

They talked for a few more minutes before Olivia ex-cused herself and headed for the retiring room. Halfway across the floor she stopped. It appeared as if the crowd was separating down the middle and standing to one side. She started to step aside, too, until she saw Lord Dugdale walking straight toward her in that tall, powerful, and com-manding way.

Her breath caught in her chest. He wore a superbly cut black evening coat and trousers. His crisply pressed collar, narrow neckcloth, and fancy brocade waistcoat were all in shades of white. He had such unassailable poise that her heart tripped.

Stopping in front of her he bowed and then said, "Good evening, Miss Banning. You're looking lovely tonight."

His voice was soft and caressing. He had such a confident smile on his face that if she hadn't known better she'd have thought he was happy to see her.

His gaze didn't leave her face, but now that he was closer she could tell that the smile was forced. There was tightness around his lips and his eyes. He wasn't happy to see her. A pang of foolish disappointment seeped inside her.

He was playing for the crowd.

She curtsied stiffly but couldn't manage a fake smile nearly as well as he had. "Lord Dugdale."

"I trust the rest of your day went well after I left you this afternoon."

She didn't look around but she sensed that every pair of eyes in the room was on the two of them. No doubt this grand display of their meeting in front of this crowd was planned by him.

But why?

"I don't believe anything has gone well for me since I met you," she said honestly.

He chuckled softly so the onlookers could see him laugh but only she could hear the low ruefulness of his tone and see the unrelenting firmness to his lips as he smiled.

"I echo your sentiment exactly. You have effectively turned my life upside down with one simple ploy."

"Although you've made it clear you don't believe me, my lord, my life is not on the course I desired, either. However, I refuse to explain last night again."

"There's no need. I understand perfectly."

"No. You believe only what you want to and that is what suits you."

His eyebrows raised a fraction. "And you think I should believe only what you think is truth and what I believe doesn't matter."

"The certainty is that if you had allowed me to leave your room when I wanted to no one would have seen us together."

An incredulous gleam shone brightly in his eyes and the corners of his mouth tightened again. "From the beginning you have said that this entire debacle which you created is my fault."

"Very much so."

"You have some nerve, Miss Banning. If you had not tempted me to kiss you no one would have seen us together."

She knew her hands had made fists at her sides but she was powerless to stop them. He could light her temper faster than anyone ever had, yet she was immensely attracted to him.

"How did I tempt you, my lord?"

"When you asked me to search you."

Forgetting where they were, she took a menacing step toward him.

Lord Dugdale didn't flinch, but quietly said, "Careful, Miss Banning, you don't want the eyes watching us to think we are having a spat, do you?"

She relaxed and glanced around the room. A few people were looking at them, including her aunt and his.

"If not for my aunt, I wouldn't care who watched. I am a properly educated lady. I never thought a gentleman would actually touch me."

His eyes narrowed, his voice lowered as he said, "I am a man and you are a beautiful woman. Of course I wanted to accept your invitation and touch you, embrace you, and kiss you."

"You shouldn't say things like that to me," she said, but all she could think was how wonderful it would be to experience his touch, his taste, his scent once again.

"I'm speaking the truth." His features relaxed and so did his stance. He folded his arms comfortably across his chest. "Even now, knowing how scheming you are, knowing what you planned, I find you extremely exciting, and take my word for it, Miss Banning; I would very much enjoy kissing you again."

Olivia huffed at his audacity. "Sir, you are positively wicked."

He smiled at her and this time it wasn't forced. It was more of that charming smile she'd seen a hint of when she told him she was looking for a ghost. The tightness that was in his features had evaporated, too, and she saw nothing but a very handsome man who set her pulse to racing standing in front of her.

"You have no idea, Miss Banning, how wicked I can be, but the time is coming when I will show you."

"Is that a threat?"

"Yes."

"After the mauling you gave me last night, I think I have a fairly good idea of what you could show me," she challenged him.

"Mauling?" Lord Dugdale chuckled again.

She loved looking at his face in laughter. There was a quality about his face that set her heart to fluttering.

His eyes swept up and down her face so intimately that her stomach quivered with anticipation.

"Don't tempt me to prove to you just how much you enjoyed being in my arms."

"I have no desire to tempt you concerning anything, my lord."

"We're attracting more attention than I anticipated. Come walk with me to the buffet room and I'll get you a glass of punch, or would you prefer champagne?"

"If I'm going to be talking to you I think I need something stronger than punch or champagne."

Lord Dugdale chuckled again and for some strange reason the sound peppered her with shivers of anticipation. He wasn't even trying to be nice to her, so why did she find him so enthralling?

She fell into step beside him, the top of her head reaching just above his shoulder. She realized she felt quite comfortable walking beside this dashingly handsome man, and she couldn't help but notice that some people they passed openly watched them while others whispered behind fans and hands.

"I don't know how you can laugh about this, my lord. It's really quite distressing."

"It's preferable to the alternative."

"I think that is the first thing we've agreed on."

"Perhaps we're making progress."

"We need to. We have a disaster on our hands. My aunt has decided to take her job as my guardian very seriously."

"I know. I've come to the conclusion that I must make the best of a disagreeable situation. No matter the circumstances that brought us together, I have only one honorable choice open to me. I must marry you."

Olivia gasped and stopped so quickly a man who was following them ran into her from behind. Lord Dugdale quickly slid an arm around her waist and pulled her against his chest.

She felt his heat, the strength in his large, steadying hands as they held her. She smelled the scent of his soap and she heard his growled oath to the man who immediately apologized and hurried away.

Lord Dugdale slowly let go of her and stepped away. "Are you all right?"

"Yes, of course," she mumbled and continued walking. Her thoughts were reeling. His words echoed in her mind as he led her into the buffet room and picked up a glass of champagne for both of them.

"Let's move over here," he said and ushered her to an area that wasn't crowded with people.

Olivia took the glass straight away and sipped from it. The champagne was so soothing to her tattered sensibilities that she quickly took another sip. She had to calm herself and think about the consequences of what he'd just said. It was one thing for her aunt to insist on marriage, quite another for Lord Dugdale to fancy the idea of it.

She looked up at the earl and said, "I thought you were going to fight this crazy notion my aunt has of us marrying."

"That was my first plan, as you well know. However, after much thought, I must do the honorable thing. Under the circumstances the only thing I can do is make you my wife."

His words chilled her, and for a fleeting moment she thought they thrilled her as well. She looked into his eyes. They were as serious as his tone and that told her he felt he had to marry her, but he didn't have to like it.

She wasn't sure how that made her feel.

"I don't understand. Just this afternoon you accused me of being simple-minded or insane because I searched for Lord Pinkwater's ghost."

He lowered his lashes for a moment before looking at her again. "That was a bit harsh. Anyone can see that you are extremely intelligent, including me."

That wasn't exactly an apology, but it was a concession she appreciated.

"Thank you."

"The man in Kent who waits for you, are you wiling to give him up?"

Mr. Yost. He hadn't crossed her mind all evening, but she didn't want Lord Dugdale to know that. "I fear that circumstances give me no choice."

His eyes narrowed, telling her he wasn't exactly pleased with her answer. She didn't know that she was, either. She would be giving up her dream to be the wife of a country squire to marry a handsome, titled lord whom she was certain would make her unhappy.

"I'll apply for a special license tomorrow, and we'll plan a small ceremony for one day next week. That should fulfill my duty and satisfy your aunt."

She had always wanted to marry a man who wasn't connected to the *ton* or titled and a man who loved her. Was she willing to give that up? Should she continue to fight this or, as Lord Dugdale had said, should she forget her dream and make the best of a disagreeable situation?

She was definitely attracted to the earl, much more than she should be considering his insufferable behavior. She couldn't imagine that any other man's kisses would make her feel the way Lord Dugdale's had.

"I'm waiting for an answer," he reminded her.

"It's difficult, my lord."

"It's the only option, Miss Banning."

"Next week," she whispered. "It all seems so cold. I in

no way envisioned my wedding to be a hurried, forced affair. I never dreamed I'd feel so melancholic when discussing my wedding."

"A hasty marriage wasn't on my list of things to do when I returned to London either. I'll ask Aunt Claude to make all the necessary arrangements with your aunt. I'm afraid I have pressing business in London and I can't get away for a honeymoon."

"Thank God," she whispered.

"Don't sound so pleased, Miss Banning. We'll have plenty of time alone together."

She glanced up at him. "No offence intended, Lord Dugdale. I simply don't relish the idea of leaving my aunt for a grand tour right now. She's been very ill until recently, and she still has some problems and might need me."

"Really? She looks to me like she's never been sick a day in her life."

Olivia was thinking more of her aunt's mental state than her physical condition, but she couldn't tell Lord Dugdale that.

"You would think that by looking at her, but believe me she's not completely well, my lord."

"Since we're to be married next week, there's no need for us to be formal. My name is Andrew."

"All right."

"Say it, Olivia. Say my name."

Her skin prickled deliciously at his insistence. "Andrew. Andrew," she said a second time just to let him know she had no fear of using his name.

"That's better, Olivia."

Olivia looked around to see if anyone might be close enough to hear her before she softly asked, "Will you—I mean, do you plan to—" She stopped, not sure how to phrase what she wanted to say.

"Do I plan to what?"

Something in the way he looked at her let her know that he knew what she was trying to ask but he wasn't going to help her. That gave her the courage to say what she wanted.

She lifted her shoulders and her chin and asked, "Do you plan to make this a real marriage?"

"In every sense of the word."

Olivia swallowed hard at his suggestive words.

"As far as I know there is no other kind of marriage. I intend to take you to my bed. I will need a legitimate heir. But don't worry overly much. I'll have my mistress discreetly on the side, and I'll not to come to your bed often."

Another unfamiliar feeling struck her chest. Was that jealousy? No, it couldn't be. She didn't even like this man, did she? But she liked even less the thought of him taking another woman to his bed, though she wouldn't let him know that.

She lifted her chin defiantly and asked, "Should I thank you for that, Andrew?"

He leaned in close to her. A hint of a smile played on his lips. "You decide if you will thank me or curse me, after you've spent a night in my arms."

His words caressed her as easily as a fine piece of silk. She wished she didn't find everything about him so intriguing, attractive, and appealing.

"You are an arrogant beast."

"Remember that and don't try to change me once we've wed. Finish your champagne, Olivia. We must dance at least once tonight, and twice would be better."

Olivia put the glass to her lips and polished off the contents in a most unladylike fashion and then wiped the last traces of the champagne off her lips with her tongue.

She looked directly into Andrew's eyes and said, "People marry for many reasons, my lord. Unfortunately we are marrying because we had the poor judgment to exchange a few dull kisses."

"Dull kisses? You do like to issue challenges, don't you, Olivia?"

"I stated a fact." *Just not a true fact,* she admitted to herself. She was immensely attracted to him.

"Then I'll just have to prove you wrong, again, but maybe that's what you want. For now you might as well put a smile on your face and act like you are enjoying my company. As of this moment, you and I are betrothed."

"Some things are not possible, sir, but perhaps I could force myself to look happy if I imagine you on a stubborn ass somewhere in the Northern Country on a dark, cold, and stormy night, dripping wet."

A hint of a smile touched his eyes before they turned serious once more. "What you don't know, Olivia, is that I love cold, dark, and stormy nights."

Nine

$\mathscr{E}$VERYONE IN THE church knew it wasn't a love match and no one was surprised when the wedding ceremony ended without a kiss. But that didn't keep Olivia from feeling a little bereft that she hadn't even received a chaste touching of Andrew's lips against her cheek when they were pronounced man and wife.

She hadn't come anywhere close to forgetting how the earl's kisses had made her feel the night she was alone with him in his room despite her many attempts to do so. And she couldn't stop the growing feeling that she wanted to experience those lovely sensations again. She was made even more aware of them as they silently rode in the carriage back to his house where the breakfast was to be held.

Olivia's pearl-colored gown had been designed by her aunt. The neckline was low and the waist high, fitting tight underneath her breasts and banded by a thin satin ribbon. The skimpy bodice was held together by straps that pulled up from the front and back and were tied into a simple bow on the top of each shoulder. The skirt was three slender cut pieces of tulle with a satin underskirt.

Olivia's hair had been pulled loosely from her face and twisted into a neat chignon low on her nape. A small satin ribbon circled the bun and a simple sheet of netting fell from the ribbon down her back. Around her neck she wore her mother's pearls, three short strings that were held together at the throat by a large sapphire broach. Her earrings were pearl teardrops.

A long table covered in a snow white cloth had been set up in the dining room at Lord Dugdale's home for the buffet. Lighted silver candlesticks graced each end of the table and a small arrangement of fresh flowers had been placed in the middle.

The table was laden with silver trays holding thin slices of salty ham, racks of tender lamb chops, and thick cuts of roast beef. There was a variety of steaming green and yellow vegetables in hand-painted bowls, a tureen of turtle soup, as well as cooked figs, honeyed pears, and plums in champagne sauce. A separate smaller table was filled with an array of apricot tarts, scones, and sweet cakes.

Immediately upon arriving at the earl's house a receiving line was formed and Olivia stood beside her new husband and greeted all the well-wishers who filed by, but her mind was distracted by other thoughts.

In the week following Andrew's assertion that they would marry, Olivia had hardly had time to breathe. From the time she rose in the morning until she fell into bed at night she was being fitted for gowns, approving menus, choosing flowers, and going to teas.

In the evenings she attended two and three parties before returning home. She didn't know how, but Lord Dugdale managed to join her at almost every party and dance with her at least once. They were polite but distant with each other at each meeting. It amazed her how detached she and Andrew were about something that would alter their lives forever.

But what astonished her most of all was how quickly she'd put Mr. Yost out of her mind once she had accepted Andrew's proposal. She had wanted to feel some great loss or at least disappointment knowing she would never see him again, but she didn't.

Olivia had been hesitant that morning when her belongings had been picked up. She was leaving her aunt's rented home and moving to Lord Dugdale's. She had lived with her aunt for so long, but Olivia wasn't one to dwell on the things that couldn't be changed. She had shored up her courage and decided to make the best of her new life as this man's wife.

The gathering was small. Not so much because the wedding was hasty, but because Olivia had not wanted dozens of people she didn't know attending what she considered a very private affair. Aunt Agatha and Aunt Claudette had reluctantly whittled the guest list to under fifty. They both had smiled at her when she insisted that Mrs. Farebrother's name be stricken from their list.

The only person Olivia had personally added to the guests was Lady Lynette Knightington. The duke's daughter had been a welcome friend to her since their first meeting. It also seemed to Olivia that Lynette was the only young lady who wasn't unhappy with her for taking the last of the Terrible Threesome earls off the marriage mart and in such an egregious way.

She tried not to let it bother her that young ladies who'd been so pleasant before the announcement of her marriage to Lord Dugdale were suddenly treating her as an interloper. Her aunt insisted that was all part of Society's game and that it would change once the nuptials had been completed. What the ladies didn't know was that Olivia would gladly give him back to them if she could.

As soon as the receiving line ended, the musicians started playing a slow waltz. Andrew took her hand and led her to the center of the parlor and then into the first steps of the dance. She and her new husband danced just as quietly and skillfully as they had all week.

After the dance, Olivia met Andrew's two best friends and their wives. Lord Chatwin, who insisted she call him John, and his wife, Catherine, and Lord Dunraven, better known as Chandler, and his wife Millicent. Both ladies were lovely and polite. At different times they each said they would have her over for tea soon.

Although nothing improper had been said by either lady, Olivia was sure they knew that this marriage was taking place solely to save her reputation. Surely Andrew's friends had expected him to select his own bride and not be trapped into a forced marriage.

After several more tedious introductions to members of the *ton*, Olivia excused herself and went in search of the friendlier Lady Lynette.

She found the tall, buxom young lady in the dining room filling a plate with food. Olivia just watched Lynette for a few moments. She hadn't forgotten how Lynette had looked when she was with the Marquis of Musgrove Glenn. It was clear to Olivia that Lynette had deep unrequited feelings for the man. Aunt Agatha had said the Marquis was looking for a wife who would take on the responsibility of caring for his children.

Lynette would be the perfect lady for him.

Olivia walked up to Lynette and said, "Thank you for coming today. It meant a lot to me to see a friendly face in this crowd."

"Oh, Olivia, I wouldn't have missed it. I canceled my other plans. I was delighted to be included in this happy occasion. You make a lovely bride. Perfectly lovely."

Olivia gave her a resigned smile. "I wish it were a happy occasion. You of all people know this is not a love match."

"That doesn't mean that it won't be some day." Lynette smiled and added an apricot tart to her plate and then said, "Are you ready to dine?"

Just looking at the food made Olivia's stomach quake.

"No, not yet."

"Do you mind sitting with me while I eat?"

"Of course not. That's why I came in search of you." The last thing she wanted to do was make conversation with people she didn't know, and her aunt was busy talking to the minister.

They walked over to a small table in a corner of the room and took their seats.

Lynette cut into the slice of ham and said, "This may not be a love match, but that is no reason to be unhappy. You just married the most eligible man in all of London. Women of all ages have tried to catch him for years."

"Its too bad one of them didn't catch him before I ended up in his bedchamber."

"Don't sound so serious. I have a feeling you two will suit in a matter of time. He's handsome and you are beautiful. Neither of you have wed before. You both are from excellent families. You're both strong-minded. I don't see how you can keep from being happy."

Olivia laughed lightly as she looked into Lynette's beautiful green eyes. She realized now that she was getting to know the duke's daughter that she didn't even notice the red birthmark on her cheek and others must feel the same way. Still she wondered if Lynette had ever tried to fade it or hide it.

"I wish everyone felt the way you do. I fear I won't be as welcomed with Andrew's friends Lady Dunraven and Lady Chatwin as if he'd chosen his own bride."

Lynette's forkful of ham stopped halfway to her mouth. "You think that only because you don't know the history. There was a long time that Lord Dugdale did not like Catherine, Lady Chatwin. I believe they had words more than once."

"Really?" That seemed unbelievable. "Is this true?"

"Yes. But Catherine recently told me they settled their differences. And I'm glad they did. I know Millicent and Catherine very well. They are lovely ladies with their own stories to tell about how they each captured their Terrible Threesome husband. You ladies will have much to talk about when you get together."

"I don't doubt they are lovely. Perhaps it's just me, but I get the feeling that everyone is looking at me as if I stole something."

Lynette laughed softly. "You did, Olivia, but someone was bound to trap Lord Dugdale—I mean, take him off the market—sooner or later. But now that I think about it, I'm not sure Lord Dugdale ever would have willingly given up his freedom. There was a time he needed to make a financial match in the worst way, yet he didn't. Of course that issue has been settled now. He's quite prosperous once again."

"What happened?"

"I don't know much about it except he discovered his estate manger was stealing from him."

"How horrible."

Olivia had remembered reading something about his light pockets from old issues of Lord Truefitt's column.

Lynette laid down her fork as excitement flared in her eyes. "I have an absolutely perfect idea."

"What?"

"There is another lady I would like you to meet, Lady Colebrooke. She has a reading group that meets every Tuesday afternoon. Would you like to join me next week?"

"Do you think she would mind?"

"I'm certain she won't, but I will send her a note and ask if I may bring a guest."

Olivia's heart seemed to swell with affection for this gracious lady in front of her. "Thank you, Lynette. It's kind of you to want to include me. I think that would be lovely."

"I'll be back in touch with you after I've arranged everything."

"Tell me," Olivia said, completely changing the subject, "how long have you known the Marquis of Musgrove Glenn?"

Lynette's eyes softened and that thoughtful look settled in her eyes. She laid down her fork. "Since I attended my first coming-out party, and that would have been about twelve years ago."

"Was he married then?"

"No. He was so handsome and dashing." She stopped and smiled wistfully. "I thought of him as my Prince Charming." Lynette seemed to catch herself reminiscing and cleared her throat. "He married his first wife later that same year."

"And his first wife died."

"Sadly, yes. Consumption. And his second wife passed on just over a year ago, leaving him with all those children to care for. It must be difficult for him. Most men just don't know how to care for children even if they have the help of a governess and a nurse."

Olivia could see genuine pain in Lynette's eyes for the Marquis's losses, for his children. Lynette had obviously loved him for a long time. How difficult it must be for her to witness him looking for yet another wife.

"I believe that," Olivia said, knowing her own father had no desire to have her in his life. "My own father certainly didn't know how to deal with me. He asked Aunt Agatha to take care of me after my mother died."

"And where is your father now?"

"Dead many years. My mother died before him. Aunt Agatha and I have managed quite well."

Lynette smiled. "I can see that."

"May I ask you a personal question?"

"Of course."

"Have you ever tried to capture the attention of the Marquis of Musgrove Glenn?"

Lynette's green eyes rounded in surprise. "Me? No, of course not."

"Why not? You are a lovely woman and you'd make him the perfect wife."

There was sadness in Lynette eyes as she said, "He wouldn't consider me. Both his wives were beautiful ladies. You are kind to say I'm lovely, but I knew after my first party that my birthmark made men shy away from me. Lord knows I would have had it removed if the many physicians I consulted would have attempted it."

Olivia remembered Lady Collingsworth mentioned a new apothecary who worked miracles. A thought crossed Olivia's mind. She realized she was stepping over polite boundaries to bring it up, but she wanted to help Lynette.

"I heard there is a new apothecary in town and that he does wonderful things to ladies' faces with creams. Have you heard of him?"

"No. Someone new? Years ago I exhausted the list of potions both trustworthy and bogus that promised to fade birthmarks. I finally gave up all hope and stopped torturing myself, but if there's someone new . . . perhaps I should look into it."

"Would you like for me to go with you to see him?"

Lynette put her hand up to her cheek and touched her birthmark. "Do you think he can do anything?"

"I don't know. The question is do you think it's worth a try?"

"Maybe I will. Just maybe I will."

Olivia watched Lynette closely. Another thought struck Olivia. She wondered if there was some way she could help the Marquis see that Lynette would make him the perfect wife and mother for his children. Olivia had only danced with him one time, but perhaps there was something she could do. It would certainly give her more to think about other than herself and her new husband.

As the afternoon faded to evening the wedding guests started departing until only a handful of people remained. Olivia hadn't noticed that her aunt had slipped off to a far corner of the parlor and had become very quiet. Agatha had that dreamy look in her eyes that she got when she was thinking about Lord Pinkwater.

Olivia walked over to her and took a seat in a chair beside her aunt.

"Are you all right, Auntie?"

Agatha looked into Olivia's eyes. She patted Olivia's hand and said, "Of course. I was just thinking that this house is now your home. I think you're going to like it here."

Olivia looked around the expensively appointed room. "Yes," she said with a sigh, not wanting to show her true feelings and upset her aunt. "Right now it feels a bit strange. I shall have to get used to it."

"It won't take long. You know, Livy, now that most of the people have left and it's a bit quieter, I feel his presence."

An uneasy feeling stole over Olivia. "Who, Auntie?" she asked, though she knew.

"Lord Pinkwater." Agatha's eyes glowed peacefully. "He's here. I know it, but he won't make himself known to me because there are still too many people around."

Her aunt looked as sane as every one else in the room but Olivia knew Agatha's mind was troubled. She wanted to get her aunt off the subject of Lord Pinkwater as quickly as possible before someone overheard them.

"Perhaps you are right, Auntie," Olivia said. "Why don't you come over tomorrow? You can feel free to roam about the house until he contacts you."

Agatha's eyes widened and she sat back in her chair. "Oh, I couldn't do that."

That was not what Olivia had expected her to say. "Why not? You just said this is my home now. You can come and search every corner in every room until your heart is content."

"Yes, I understand that, my dear, but I couldn't possibly do it tomorrow. It's bad enough that you aren't going away on a proper wedding journey. No, you must have at least a week, maybe two, alone with your husband before I make a visit."

"That's ridiculous, Auntie."

"Not as far as I'm concerned. I won't allow myself to interfere into your lives so soon."

"Auntie, you could never get in the way. I love you. I'll miss you. I want you to visit often."

"And so I shall, but until then you must promise you will let me know if Lord Pinkwater makes himself known to you."

Her aged eyes still held that wistful, faraway look in them. How sad that Agatha had spent her whole life pining for a man who never loved her. And now Olivia was facing the same fate except for the fact that she was married where her aunt had remained a spinster.

It was Olivia's turn to pat her aunt's hand. Given her aunt's current state of mind, Olivia wanted to make sure she saw her every day.

"Of course I will let you know if Lord Pinkwater appears."

"Good. You know I'm only ten minutes away. You'll see me often. And don't fret. You will adjust and adapt to married life. Young ladies always do."

"I will do my best to be a loving wife to Lord Dugdale."

"I'm not worried about either of you where this marriage is concerned. Say what you will, but you two are not indifferent to each other. I saw the looks on both your faces that night we were standing in the receiving line outside his house. There was a fascination between the two of you and it will only get stronger. Now walk with me to get my cloak. I'm ready to go home."

A few minutes later Olivia and Andrew stood at the front door and waved good-bye to his aunt, the last of the wedding guests to leave. When he shut the door, he turned to Olivia and just looked at her for a moment. She watched his gaze linger on her face, slide down the column of her neck, graze over her breasts, and drift back up to her eyes.

"Let's go upstairs," he said.

Just like that? *Let's go upstairs?* Where were the wedding night things she'd dreamed of—sweet words, touching, kissing? Where was the romance? Was getting her upstairs in bed the only thing he had on his mind?

Of course.

He had no soft, loving feelings for her. She was not the bride of his choosing. But still . . . she had expected a little more consideration from him than the command to go upstairs.

But if that wasn't to be, she'd manage. She had married him because her aunt insisted she must. She had already vowed to make the best of this marriage.

She tried to slow her breathing. It was fine to let her aunt see her weakness, but she'd never let Andrew see that she was a wee bit frightened. She was a grown, married woman, and wives slept with their husbands. There was nothing to be alarmed about.

She inhaled softly and said, "All right," and then she started up the stairs.

Olivia heard his footfalls on the treads behind her, and her breaths grew shorter, deeper, and more ragged with each step. She wasn't as brave as she wanted to be. She'd do her best not to let Lord Dugdale know her insides were trembling like an autumn leaf in an early snow storm.

When she made it to the top of the stairs the corridor seemed too long and too dimly lit and her legs too weak to carry her to the end. Putting one foot in front of the other, she managed to walk all the way down and stop in front of Andrew's chamber, the now infamous room she had foolishly entered just over a week ago.

Olivia stood there, trying to calm her racing heartbeat, and waited for him to say something, to open the door, to do whatever husbands do. He remained quietly behind her for a moment. She felt his heat, heard his light breathing, and smelled the musky mint of his shaving soap as it wafted past her.

Suddenly, for reasons she didn't understand, her skin tingled with anticipation. She didn't understand how she could be frightened and excited at the same time.

His hand slid around from behind her and he opened the bedroom door. Light spilled into the room.

Olivia took a deep, silent breath and stepped inside his chamber. It was just as she remembered: expensive, dark red fabrics, large masculine furniture, and dreamy lighting from the lamp on his dressing table casting shadows across the walls.

She walked immediately to the far end of the bed and turned to face him.

Andrew shut the door behind them and stopped a few feet away from her. He stared at her rather oddly as if he were surprised or maybe confused. She wondered what he saw when he looked at her; a frightened young lady, an annoyed miss, or a woman waiting to be shown the secrets of the marriage bed.

She put her hands behind her back to help steady her and leaned against the drapery-covered bedpost. She was grateful for something to support her weight other than her wobbly legs and wooden feet.

Without saying anything he took off his black evening coat and threw it across the bed. With one pull of the bow his neckcloth came unraveled. He wound it from around his neck and tossed it and his collar on top of the coat. Next he unbuttoned his brocade waistcoat and shrugged out of it and then sent it the way of his other clothing.

Olivia felt her eyes getting bigger with each article of

clothing he tossed aside; still he said nothing as he undressed and stared at her.

In one fluid motion he ripped the tail of his white shirt
out of his black trousers and pulled it over his head and
threw it onto the bed. Olivia didn't want to look at him but
she couldn't force her eyes away.

The soft, amber lamplight made his skin appear a rich
golden color. His chest was wide, his shoulders broad and
thick with muscles rippling beneath firm skin. His trousers
rode low on his narrow waist, fitted his slim hips, and
showed the flat firm muscles of his stomach.

Her mouth suddenly went dry.

Olivia had never seen a man without his shirt and she had
no idea a man's body would be so beautiful. She had a
strong urge to reach out and glide her palm across his naked
chest to see if it was as firm as it appeared, as warm as it appeared, as tempting as it appeared.

"Are you enjoying looking at me, Olivia?" he asked in a
low, seductive voice.

"Yes," she whispered unconsciously and immediately
realized what she had said. Heat flushed up her neck to her
cheeks. Her gaze flew up to his eyes and she quickly added,
"I mean, I've never seen a man's chest before. That is, except in works of art."

"But obviously you like what you see in the flesh."

She decided it was best to ignore further discussion of
his Adonis body so she said, "I didn't expect you to get undressed quite so quickly."

"Why not?"

"I thought you'd give me more time to get to know you
before you—"

"What?"

"Before you undressed in front of me."

"You are in my room, Olivia. This is where I usually undress."

"Of course," she said wishing she knew more about what was going to happen.

"You've had a week to get to know me." He stretched his arms out wide from his chest. "Look at me all you want."

And she did. He was magnificent.

But what was she to do? She'd wanted a loving husband, not necessarily a handsome one. Days ago she had made up her mind that if she had to marry him she would be a dutiful wife and not end up a lonely, discarded woman like her mother.

If he could undress without embarrassment in front of her, she could disrobe for him.

Olivia moved away from the bed. She no longer needed its support. She reached up with both hands and simultaneously untied each bow at the top of her shoulders. The bodice fell away from her breasts, exposing her low-cut off-white corset with its tiny trim of lace.

For a flashing moment she was sure Andrew looked as startled by her action as she was. Slowly he walked toward her and when he was close enough he reached out, circled her with his arms and pulled her to him. Without saying a word he dipped his head low and kissed her.

His lips were warm, soft, inviting as they pressed against hers in a slow, lingering kiss. He tasted of red wine and smelled of clean, fresh mint. His kiss was confident and commanding. She responded by instinct and parted her lips. His tongue darted into her mouth and explored the inside with slow, sensual movements.

Olivia's stomach, abdomen, and between her legs tightened at the thrill that spiraled through her body as his kiss became more passionate with each second that passed.

She reached up and wrapped her arms around his strong, muscled back and seemed to melt into the warmth of his body. He was broad, powerful, and she stretched her arms wide. She felt small, comfortable, and safe in his big, protective embrace.

Nothing she had ever experienced in her life had prepared her for how wonderful Andrew's naked chest felt next to hers. She couldn't keep her hands still on his muscled back.

"Do you still want the attention of the man from Kent?" Andrew asked, his lips against hers.

"Who?" she whispered before she realized what he'd asked.

She heard Andrew chuckle, and then he deepened their kiss and Mr. Yost was forgotten.

Olivia heard a whispered sigh but didn't know if it came from her husband or herself.

Suddenly his lips left hers and kissed their way down her cheek, over her jawline to her neck, sending little shivers of exhilaration popping out all over her skin. At the touch of his moist lips upon the fullness of her breasts, her breaths jumped erratically.

With his teeth he grabbed hold of the bit of lace on her corset and pulled the garment away from her breast. His mouth covered her nipple so quickly and sucked it inside his mouth that all Olivia could do was gasp.

The sudden pleasure caused a tightness low in the center of her womanhood. Her stomach quickened with surprise at the sensation as gasps of pleasure continued to escape past her lips. It seemed natural for her to lean her head back and thrust her chest forward to give him better access.

"Yes, Olivia, free your other breast for me," he whispered against her skin. "You are so soft and so lovely."

Without hesitation she reached up and yanked the fabric from her body, freeing her breast so his tongue could do those delicious things that made her want to groan with pleasure.

Something she didn't understand made her lift her hips up to his.

Andrew moaned his approval as his large hands slipped down her back and cupped her buttocks, firmly pressing her against the hardness beneath his trousers.

Olivia had no idea what she was feeling or why she was feeling this way. She only knew that it felt right, natural, and she didn't want it to go away.

A tremor shook his body and she realized he was as affected by these strange new sensations as she was, and that thrilled her.

Olivia had little knowledge of what was to come, but there was no doubt she was eager to continue with this wedding night.

Slowly his lips left her breasts and traveled back up to her lips for several quick kisses. The pressure on her buttocks eased and she had to fight the temptation to press harder against him again.

Andrew raised his head. His gaze swept down her face to her chest.

His voice sounded husky and raw as he said, "You are so tempting and so beautiful, Olivia."

"Thank you," she answered just as huskily as their eyes met and held. It pleased her that he thought her body beautiful.

Andrew's expression relaxed and he slowly moved

away from her. He took hold of her arms and gently pulled them from around his neck. She let them fall to her side.

Calmly he said, "You are inquisitive and eager for my touch and all that I can teach you."

"Yes," she whispered.

"I like that." He pulled up the straps to one side of her bodice and tied it in a bow as he said, "And I shall make you mine, Olivia. Make no mistake about that, but it won't be tonight."

Olivia blinked rapidly, not sure she comprehended what he was saying. "I don't understand."

"I have other plans," he said and pulled up the other side of her bodice and tied it onto her shoulder. "I'm going out for the rest of the evening, and when I return I'll spend what's left of the night alone in my bed and you will be in yours."

"Oh," Olivia said, not knowing what to think, not knowing what to say, not knowing if she understood. "You mean you're not going to stay here with me on our wedding night?"

"That's right."

Suddenly she felt rigid and empty. "Did I do something wrong?" she asked, confused by the quick change in him.

"No, you did everything right. We might be married, Olivia, but I don't intend to change my lifestyle. I go out most evenings and I usually stay out late."

She gasped. She was horrified. Humiliated. How should she react to him?

Did he expect her to say, "All right, please go ahead? Don't wake me when you return"? She couldn't say any of those things because all she could think was that he didn't want her.

But she'd known that before she married him.

"You mean you're not going to—to . . ." She stopped, unable to say the words.

"Take you to my bed and make love to you? Eventually, yes. But there will be plenty of time for that in the future. We have our whole lives ahead of us, do we not?"

She was still breathless, but for a very different reason. "Then why bring me up to your room? Why undress in front of me?"

"You led the way. I was following you. I expected you to stop at your door and tell me good-night."

How could she have been so naïve? "So you never meant for me to come into your room?"

"No, but I'm not unhappy you did. I enjoyed kissing you and touching you."

And making me want you.

She lifted her chin and said, "Very well. I'm sorry I misunderstood."

"I don't mind you seeking me out anytime you want to, Olivia, but your room with your things in it is right down the hall."

She was stunned. She was being shown out of her husband's bed before she even got in it.

Her heart felt heavy and the pounding in her chest slowed to a strong, steady beat. She had a husband just like her father.

"Of course. I don't know how I could have mistaken your intentions."

He walked over to the door, opened it and said, "Sleep well, Olivia."

Ten

"How could you?" Olivia whispered into the emptiness of the dimly lit corridor as soon as Andrew shut the door behind her.

How dare he kiss her and leave her feeling so, so, what? So wanting of more of his kisses, his caresses, and so wishing she'd never married him.

Yes!

This was their wedding night and he was throwing her out of his bedroom. Not only that, he was leaving her alone in his house and going out.

But where? To his club? To his mistress?

What kind of man did that? What kind of husband did it?

The kind her mother had.

She squeezed her eyes shut for a moment as she stood outside his door. That was the last thing Olivia wanted to happen. She wanted to be a loving wife. She wanted a husband who loved her.

A sudden fear gripped her. Would her life be just like that of her aunt and her mother, always wanting the love of a man who would never give it?

Andrew Terwillger, Earl of Dugdale, was a scoundrel of the highest order.

She would not put up with this kind of treatment. She'd show him. She would go back to her aunt's house first thing in the morning and never come back.

Olivia's shoulders dropped. Her hands made fists at her sides.

But only two seconds later she lifted her head and her shoulders and whispered earnestly, "No. I will not run away. He will not do this to me."

But what could she do? She had to think rationally. How could she force him to treat her differently? She didn't know, but she wasn't going to give up without a fight. She had to remember that he wanted her. She felt it inside him, but for reasons she didn't understand he chose not to make her is wife tonight.

Olivia made her way down to her bedroom door and opened it. When she stepped inside she saw a young woman standing by a large, framed looking glass that hung on the wall near her bed.

Startled, the woman jumped and moved away from the mirror. It was clear from the way she was dressed that she was a maid, but Olivia hadn't seen her earlier in the evening.

"Who are you?" Olivia asked, walking farther into the room.

The maid curtsied nervously. "I'm Ellie, Countess. I'm to be—that is, I want to be your lady's maid. I heard you were inquiring about one. I'm at your service. Just tell me what you want me to do."

Olivia had always shared her aunt's maid. She knew

that now she had to have her own personal maid and she planned to interview for one later in the week. As long as Lord Dugdale had household maids and kitchen staff she would have all the help she needed until she found a suitable person.

"I've planned to interview others for the job as my personal maid. I'm quite capable of taking care of myself until I hire someone."

"Oh, please don't dismiss me without giving me a chance, Countess." The young lady clasped her hands together and held them under her chin. "I need this job to help care for my ailing mum and the younger ones at home. I can suit you if you'll give me a chance. I know it. Mr. Whibbs has already said he would have to dismiss me if I did one more thing wrong. You're my only chance to keep my job. I don't know what I'll do if I don't please you."

The pleading maid was short and slight of frame. Her complexion was unusually white. A mop cap completely covered her hair and her pale blue eyes looked almost too big for her thin, long face. She had a desperate look in her expression that Olivia couldn't ignore.

Somehow she identified with the young woman's feeling of rejection, but Olivia didn't know if the maid was capable of moving from household duties to being a lady's maid. That would be a grand promotion for her.

"Surely there is something else in the house you can do. I'll speak to Whibbs for you."

"No, Countess. If you don't have use for me I'm fearful Mr. Whibbs will turn me off tomorrow."

Olivia sighed. She suddenly felt very weary. She didn't want to have to handle anything like this after her debacle with Andrew. She just wanted to be alone in her room.

Suddenly Ellie's eyes brightened and she smiled. "I'm

not too good with household chores, but look at all I've done for you. I turned back the covers."

She rushed over to the bed and pressed an imaginary wrinkle out of the sheet with a frail, trembling hand that looked much too old for her young age.

"And I've laid out your nightrail real pretty for you." She straightened the bow at the neckline of the garment that had been neatly folded and laid on the bed. She then hurried over to the dressing table. "And look, I brought you up some milk and a plate of apricot tarts just in case you didn't get to eat much tonight with it being your wedding and all. I can go down to the kitchen and get you something else if you don't like apricots."

"No, no that's fine. Thank you, Ellie, all you have done is very nice."

Ellie's smile broadened and she said, "Thank you, Countess. I just poured hot water in the basin for you in case you want to wash."

Olivia could see hope struggling with fear in Ellie's face. She felt she had to smile at her and say, "That was thoughtful of you."

"Shall I help you undress? I can take down your hair and comb it out for you without pulling it once? I'm real gentle."

"No, no, Ellie. I can manage everything for myself tonight. You go on to bed and we'll discuss this further in the morning."

"You mean you'll keep me?" she asked with a hopeful look in her eyes.

Olivia relented. "Yes. I'll speak to Whibbs and tell him you will be my maid."

Relief washed down her face like sunshine chasing away gray clouds. "Thank you, Countess." She curtsied and smiled again. "What time should I wake you, and would you prefer tea, chocolate, or something else?"

"I've always preferred to be up and dressed before having tea. And I don't know how long I shall sleep tomorrow, so don't disturb me. I'll tell Whibbs and we'll discuss everything at that time. Right now I'd really like to be alone and go to bed."

"Certainly, Countess, I understand. Thank you," she said with a grateful look and softly closed the door on her way out.

By the time Olivia had dressed for bed and splashed the warm water on her face she felt drained from the day's events. She sat down in front of the looking glass on her dressing table to take down her hair and noticed the milk and three small tarts on a plate.

Her stomach rumbled. She hadn't eaten anything since morning, and the golden-colored treats looked delicious. She quickly consumed all of them and realized she actually felt better, stronger after eating.

Somehow this servant Olivia had never seen before knew exactly what she'd needed tonight: food, warm water for washing, and a freshly laundered nightrail. All these things had helped soothe her.

Olivia took down her hair and brushed it. Andrew truly felt she had tricked him into marriage. She could understand how that could make him so angry with her he wouldn't take her to his bed even though he wanted to. Maybe that was why she couldn't find it inside herself to stay upset with him.

But Olivia wasn't one to give up without a fight. She was Andrew's wife and she would find a way to be a part of her husband's life.

*A*NDREW HAD EVERY intention of spending the night at White's when he climbed into his carriage a few minutes after dismissing his wife from his bedroom. But when his driver had stopped the phaeton in front of the nondescript building on St. James Street, Andrew couldn't bring himself to get out.

Instead he gave the man another address to take him to.

The carriage clipped along the road at a brisk pace and Andrew brooded, something he wasn't used to doing. But then he wasn't used to getting married, either.

He was restless and wondering why in bloody hell he hadn't stayed home and taken from his wife what she was more than willing to give. She was eager to learn and explore the pleasures between a man and a woman, and Lord knows he was willing to teach her. She had him trembling with wanting her.

Damn, she had been tempting.

He'd been so hard for her that it had been physically painful to set her away from him. But suddenly he'd remembered how she'd manipulated him from the moment he saw her, and he had to stop himself. It hadn't been a show of strength as much as it was a challenge to himself to make sure he could deny her.

She had forced him into the marriage.

She'd responded to his touch with an eager innocence that had him hurting for release. The only thing that had given him the willpower to do it was knowing that she wanted him to take her to his bed. It was all part of her plan from the beginning. She'd marched up to his room with all ease and calm and had watched him undress.

What man wouldn't get hard over that?

It was her way of trying to continue to manipulate him to get what she wanted. Something inside him said he couldn't let her win again. If he'd taken her and given her the loving their bodies had yearned for she would have gotten everything she wanted from him.

It wasn't easy, but not taking her to his bed gave him control over her.

She'd gotten the marriage and that was all he was willing to give.

For now.

He could change his mind any time he wanted and he planned to. His body was telling him to stop being a scoundrel and do it tonight.

And what of this man in Kent that she purported to fancy? Had she really forgotten him? Perhaps he had been just part of her ruse to make Andrew think she hadn't planned this whole thing? There was little or no reserve in her kisses and he felt sure there would have been if she was attracted to another man.

Andrew decided he must be restless because he didn't have a mistress to help get him through the long nights, and he didn't have a mistress because he hadn't put any effort into finding one since he'd been in Town.

He was eliminating that oversight tonight.

The carriage stopped in an area far removed from the elite section of Mayfair where Andrew lived. He opened the door and stepped down. It was still early in the evening, so there was a chance that Haversham was still at home. The tradesman had sent him a note saying he'd heard that Andrew was seeking a mistress. That could only mean one thing. Haversham knew of a woman who was looking for a lover.

The night was dark, damp, and foggy, matching his mood. He strode up to the door where a single hazy light shone through the dense fog, lifted the knocker, and let it fall. The sound echoed inside the house. Outside, a chilling breeze reminded Andrew of how warm and comfortable Olivia's body had been, nestled so close to his. The moist air had him thinking about her malleable lips that fit perfectly, eagerly against his, how soft her woman's body was against his hardness.

He wanted her.

He was being foolish in denying himself his wife, but he couldn't seem to stop himself.

She had left him with no doubt that she would be an amazing woman to have in his bed, and the thought ran through his mind that he was the worst kind of fool to be looking for a mistress when he had Olivia.

A well-dressed butler answered the door.

"I'd like a word with Haversham if he's home and receiving guests," Andrew said.

"Who shall I say is calling, sir?"

"Lord Dugdale."

The butler stood aside and allowed Andrew to enter. "Wait here in the foyer, my lord; I'll see if Mr. Haversham is in."

"Thank you." Andrew handed him his hat, coat, and gloves.

Andrew looked around the wide foyer. The furnishings were of fine wood and the draperies of fine fabric. He stood on an expensive wool rug. Obviously Haversham's business was doing well.

The butler came back a couple of minutes later and showed Andrew into the parlor. The warmth of a low burning fire was the first thing Andrew noticed. The room smelled of tobacco, burned wood, and beeswax. The room was big and filled with elaborate furniture, further evidence of Haversham's wealth.

"Come in, Lord Dugdale," Haversham said from the back of the room, where he was pouring what looked like brandy into two crystal glasses.

He was a tall, portly gentleman, but the expert cut of his clothing hid his rounded middle. The man's gray hair was thick and trimmed closely to his head. His mustache had been shaved to a thin line on his upper lip and it came around and met his goatee.

"I'd heard you were back in town, my lord, and getting married I believe. When is the happy occasion?"

"I was married today," Andrew said and instantly didn't like the way the admission made him feel, considering what he was doing at Haversham's house.

Haversham never blinked an eye, never raised a brow, never showed a hint of surprise in his features. There probably wasn't much this man hadn't heard.

Andrew swallowed his moment of guilt.

"Congratulations."

"Thank you."

He handed Andrew the drink and said, "Have a seat and make yourself comfortable."

Andrew didn't want to get drawn into a friendly conversation with this man and he didn't want his liquor. A business deal was the only thing he was looking for from him.

"I can't stay."

"I understand."

"Your note indicated you have a name I might be interested in."

Damnation!

What was wrong with him? He couldn't say the word *mistress*. It was a wonder that Haversham wasn't laughing at him.

The portly man tapped his lips with his forefinger and

seemed to study the request for a moment. "Yes, I do. Three, presently, that you might be interested in becoming acquainted with."

Andrew liked the fact he didn't question him about anything.

"Good. Could you arrange for me to meet one of them?"

"Absolutely. In fact I have one that I can say with all faith that would be available tomorrow if you're interested. I believe you know her. Arabelle Woodward has just become unattached."

Andrew felt a jump in his loins. Arabelle had been his mistress five or six years ago. She was a bit older than him as he remembered, but well versed in knowing how to please a man and knowing how to enjoy a man's touch. If she was available, she was more than acceptable.

"Yes. I know her and I wouldn't mind seeing her again."

"I'll send you a time that is convenient for her first thing tomorrow morning."

"Good."

Andrew set down the untouched drink and turned and walked out.

He stepped out into the damp fog again and realized he felt as black as the night. He didn't feel good about what he was doing and he didn't exactly know why.

Bloody hell.

What was bothering him? A man had every right to have a mistress if he so chose. Maybe what plagued him was that most gentlemen didn't go looking for mistresses on their wedding night.

*S*OMETHING DISTURBED OLIVIA'S slumber.

Her lashes fluttered upward and her eyes popped open to complete darkness. She lay on her side with her cheek flat against the pillow. Not sure what had awakened her, she didn't move.

Was that breathing she heard? Was it her own?

She looked around without lifting her head but saw nothing. She heard the soft sound of rustling movement. Someone was in the room with her.

Had Ellie returned after she told her not to disturb her? No, the maid was too frightened of losing her job to disobey Olivia.

Had Andrew changed his mind when he returned and come into her bedroom? Her heart beat faster. Did this mean he wasn't immune to her after all?

But how would he have gotten in? She'd locked the door before lying down.

It's his house, he would have a key.

Should she pretend to be asleep? It would serve him right, but did she want to do that?

As she contemplated what to do she heard the squeak of the door opening. Quickly she rose in the bed and turned toward the door. In the darkness she saw what looked like a man disappearing through the door as it closed. For a moment she thought perhaps Whibbs had come in, but as her mind cleared she knew he would not invade her bedroom, and the man she saw was much too tall to be the butler.

She started to call out to Andrew but something stopped her. He obviously hadn't wanted her to know he was there.

After a few moments, she lay back down, trying to decide if she were hopeful or angry that Andrew had slipped into her room after throwing her out of his.

Eleven

❧

$O_{LIVIA \; SLEPT \; SOUNDLY}$ after her midnight visitor left her
room and she awakened with a sound purpose in her mind.
She had decided she was going to win her husband's respect,
if not his love, with kindness and duty. She would not feel as
if she were an interloper in a house that was now her home,
nor would she be sent to the countryside to live out the rest
of her days in seclusion as her mother had been.

She was certain Andrew was drawn to her just as she
was drawn to him by some emotional force she'd never en-
countered before. She had seen it in his eyes, felt it inside

him that he wanted her. She'd sensed it in the tremor that shook his body when he'd held her in his arms last night. She could only assume that because he believed she had trapped him into marriage he'd pushed her away. Her instinct told her that in time he would come to know her and realize that she wasn't capable of such a devious act.

Olivia looked at every dress in her wardrobe before selecting a pale lilac-colored morning dress that flattered her coloring and her hair. The current style of dresses for day or evening wear was an embarrassingly low-cut neckline and high waist that amplified a woman's breasts. None of Olivia's dresses were an exception to that rule, so for modesty's sake she added a lace fichu.

After donning the dress she arranged her hair on top of her head, added a light dusting of powder to her face, and fastened a gold chain with a large, oval amethyst around her neck before heading downstairs.

A quick peek into each room she passed showed that every cup, glass, and plate from the wedding party had been cleaned up, and the house seemed in perfect order.

Lord Dugdale obviously had an excellent staff. It didn't look as if there was much for her to do, but surely she could make an improvement somewhere and prove her ability to manage a household.

That should please her new husband.

When she walked into the dining room she saw the butler talking to a maid who was adding hot water to a silver teapot.

"Good morning, Whibbs," she said in a cheerful tone and with a bright smile.

"Good morning, Countess," he said, clearly surprised to see her. "I'm sorry, we didn't expect you down so early. The buffet isn't quite ready. I'll let cook know you're here."

"No, please don't on my account. I'm in no hurry. Tell me, what time does Lord Dugdale come down for his breakfast?"

"He has no set time, but he usually has coffee and reads the *Times* while his food is prepared."

Although Olivia didn't grow up with a man in the house, perusing the paper sounded like a reasonable thing for a gentleman to do.

"I see. In that case, I think I will wait and eat with Lord Dugdale."

"As you wish, Madame."

Olivia looked over at the table. It was covered in a white cloth, but only one place setting had been laid and it was at the head of the table. A copy of the *London Times* was beside the plate.

Obviously Whibbs knew where her mind was going because he suddenly offered, "I assumed you would take your breakfast in bed. I was going to send one of the maids up with chocolate a little later in the morning."

She smiled at him to let him know she was not offended. "Thank you, Whibbs, that would have been nice, but I prefer tea to chocolate in the mornings, and I never have it in bed. I'm always an early riser even when I've been out late the night before."

"Yes, Madame, I'll remember that."

"I think I should like to have a cup of tea and walk through the garden while I wait for Lord Dugdale to come belowstairs."

"I'll get it right away."

"There's one other thing, Whibbs."

"Yes." He stopped.

"You and your staff take excellent care of Lord Dugdale's home."

"Thank you, Madame."

"I should like to meet with all of the staff at two this afternoon. Do you think you could arrange that for me, please?"

"Of course."

"Good. And after I meet everyone, I'd like a few minutes of your time to discuss the managing of the servants and to go over the household account. If that meets with your schedule?"

"Whenever you say, Madame, will suit me. I have everything in order for you."

"I have no doubts on that. Our meeting should go smoothly. And one last thing. I'd like for Ellie to be kept on as my personal maid."

His brows shot up again in surprise, though he only said, "If that is your wish, Madame."

Ellie had already admitted to Olivia that she couldn't please Whibbs in her household duties, and by the cleanliness of the house it appeared Whibbs's standard was high. But Ellie had seemed to know exactly what Olivia needed last night. For that reason alone she wanted to give the maid a chance.

"It is," Olivia said without further explanation. "Make any arrangements that are necessary for her to remain with us."

"Yes, Madame, I'll take care of it," he said a bit stiffly, but he didn't question her further.

Olivia gave Whibbs a genuine smile. "Thank you. I'll take that tea now."

After receiving her cup, Olivia stepped out the back door to the garden feeling good that her first task as lady of the house had been handled and had gone quite well. She hadn't expected any trouble with Whibbs and there hadn't been any.

So far everything was going along nicely. She supposed it was only natural for Whibbs to be a bit surprised that she wanted to keep a servant whom he had considered dismissing.

Olivia inhaled deeply and took in the fresh morning air. It was a gloriously beautiful day. Cool but not chilling. The sky was a bright blue, scattered with patches of wispy white clouds that appeared as thin as gossamer. Warm sunshine had already dried the dew off the grass, shrubs, and flowers, leaving them washed clean to show their vibrant spring colors.

Back in Kent, their garden had been large and lush with greenery, fountains, and vistas. Tall yews had been trimmed close to form a maze of arches, nooks, and pathways that led the wanderer on a merry chase through the grounds.

The garden at her new home, though small, was as exceptionally tended as the house. Not much needed her attention. Whibbs was a master at taking care of Lord Dugdale's house. It would be hard for her to impress Andrew with her skills at managing his household and staff when it was already being run proficiently. But there had to be a way to gain favor with her husband, and she was determined to find it.

A few minutes later when she walked back into the dining room, she saw Andrew sitting at the table with the *Times* in front of his face. He lowered the news print and rose when he heard her walk in. His gaze swept up and down her. It was clear he appreciated the time she'd taken with her appearance.

Olivia looked him over, too. He was completely dressed for the day, down to his waistcoat and perfectly tied neckcloth. He looked so handsome standing there watching her that her stomach felt as if it rolled over. And she couldn't help remembering how he looked last night without his shirt. Just the thought made her tremble with expectancy.

It was almost laughable. She had taken such care with her toilet trying to impress him and gain his attention, yet just being in the same room with him filled her with pleasure.

When their gazes met, they held much longer than was necessary.

He said, "Good morning, Olivia."

She smiled at him and said, "Good morning, Andrew. I trust you slept well after you came in last night."

"Very well indeed."

"Good."

Andrew continued to stand so she said, "Please don't let me disturb you. Sit back down and finish your reading. I'll join you as soon as I refresh my tea."

She walked over to the buffet and placed her empty cup on top of it. She had to get control of herself. She couldn't allow her legs to turn buttery every time she looked at him.

He sat back down and quickly gave his attention to the *Times*. Olivia took her time pouring tea into her cup, adding sugar and cream and stirring it much longer than was necessary before walking over to the table to take her seat. Andrew quickly laid the paper back down, rose, and pulled out her chair for her.

"Thank you," she said.

He then seated himself once again and picked up the news paper.

Olivia sat quietly for a few moments sipping her tea. She had grown up having her morning meal alone in the dining room. Agatha wouldn't think of rising from bed before finishing her chocolate and toast. Olivia's mother had been the same way. Spending the morning in bed was not for Olivia. She had always been too eager for the day to begin to waste a moment more than necessary lying down.

She'd never minded dining alone, either, but it hadn't

taken more than a few minutes to realize she didn't like to be ignored across the breakfast table. Suddenly she was tapping her fingers softly on her saucer just to have something to do.

Softly clearing her throat, she looked around the formal room. A gold-leaf girandole looking glass hung over the fireplace with two brass sconces on either side of it. In the corner behind the head of the table stood a larger-than-life-size suit of armor complete with shield and pike, and against the far wall was a lovely Chippendale side board with two tall French gilt porcelain urns on it.

The only window in the room was framed with dark green velvet draperies which were pulled back on each side showing lace sheers. Bright sunshine streamed through small panes, throwing prisms of blue, yellow, and red across the white walls.

She didn't know why Andrew's reading the paper bothered her. But somehow being disregarded by someone present had a different feel from just being alone. It was a feeling she didn't like.

"Andrew," she said when she couldn't stand the quietness any longer. "I'm sorry to disturb you again."

He lowered the paper and looked at her with a distracted expression. "Yes?"

"Perhaps you can tell me what parties you planned to attend tonight and for the rest of the Season so I can be prepared."

"It makes no difference to me. Have Whibbs give you the invitations I've received and select the ones you want to grace with your presence." And with that he went back to reading.

The way he said that raised another question. "By that statement do you mean that I should go alone?"

Without looking up he said, "No, Olivia. I'll play the dutiful husband and escort you wherever you want to go."

At least that was a start. He didn't plan to completely ignore her and force her to stay at home alone every evening.

But was a reluctant husband any better than an absent one?

She managed to stay quiet a couple more minutes until she couldn't bear to hear the rustling of the paper one more time.

She asked, "Why did you come into my room when you returned last night after making it quite clear you didn't want me in your chambers?"

Again he didn't bother to lower the paper, but in an uninterested tone he said, "I have no idea what you're talking about. I didn't enter your room last night."

It surprised her that he denied it. "I beg your pardon, my lord. Although I didn't rise and speak to you I was awake and knew you were there. You don't need to pretend you were not."

"I'm not pretending anything, Olivia, I'm trying to read the *Times*," he said in an exasperated tone.

"And it's very difficult for me to talk to you with it in front of your face."

Andrew slowly lowered the sheets of paper to the table and stared rather oddly at her. "I've read my paper while having my coffee every morning for the past twelve years. I don't intend to stop now."

That was as good as telling her she was intruding on his time.

She should have accepted that so she could be the kind wife she wanted to be for him; kind, dutiful, seen but not heard. She wanted to be all those things for him.

But Olivia couldn't keep quiet.

She felt compelled to say, "Perhaps now that you are married and have someone to talk to you could take a few moments for conversation."

"All right, talk."

His annoyed expression told her she should have stayed quiet and she certainly shouldn't say another word, but Olivia realized she was too accustomed to speaking her mind to slip easily into the role of a dutiful wife.

"Very well. Let's go back to the exchange we started earlier. It was completely dark in my room last night, but I saw the back of your white shirt as you went out the door. Why do you deny your entrance?" Her words were more defiant sounding than she had intended.

So much for thinking she would win her husband's favor with kindness. She was acting like a shrew, but couldn't seem to stop herself. If he would simply admit he'd been there she would let it go.

"You say it was dark in your room when you thought you saw me? That proves you could not have seen me, Olivia. Shortly after you left my chamber, I left this house and it was daylight before I returned."

Something close to a chill shook Olivia, but there was more to it than just the intruder in her room. It was because he hadn't come home on their wedding night.

Denying the hurt that gripped her she said, "Who could have been in my room?"

"No one, I'm sure. Perhaps you were dreaming."

"I was not dreaming, my lord. I felt a presence in the room and when I heard the door open I rose up and I saw a man leaving. I assumed it was you."

"It wasn't me."

He was serious. She could see it in his eyes. "If not you, who would dare enter my room?"

A half smile lifted one corner of his mouth, making him devastatingly handsome. "Perhaps you saw that ghost you are so famously looking for. Who is he? Lord Pinkwater, I believe?"

Andrew was mocking her but he didn't know how right he could be. What if her aunt was right and the ghost of Lord Pinkwater was in this house? What if he'd known Agatha was in the house yesterday and he'd come looking for her last night?

Could that possibly be? Was a ghost really in her bedroom last night looking for her aunt?

"No. It had to be you," she whispered more to convince herself than to argue the point.

"Believe me, Olivia, if I had wanted to enter your bedroom last evening I never would have dismissed you from mine. I thought I made it clear last night that I don't intend to change my life simply because I now have a wife."

Olivia suddenly pushed back her chair and rose so quickly that the chair tumbled backward to the floor. Andrew stood up at the same time and just at that moment the iron pike from the suit of armor that stood in the corner behind Andrew's chair fell hard across his shoulder. It bounced off him and onto the table, breaking his plate.

"Heaven's angels," Olivia whispered.

"Damnation." Andrew looked down at the dangerous-looking pike as he grabbed his shoulder.

Olivia rushed to his side. Taking hold of his forearm, she asked, "Andrew, are you hurt?"

"No," he said with a grimace. "I'm fine. I'm just wondering how in the hell that damned thing fell."

Olivia didn't believe he was all right. "It must have injured you. Take off your coat and let me have a look."

She put her arms up to grab the lapels of his coat and

started to help him take it off, but he gently took hold of her wrists and stopped her motion.

He calmly looked down into her eyes and said, "I'm not hurt. If it had been my head instead of my shoulder I might not be saying that, but as it is there was no harm done to me."

In that moment Olivia wanted to throw her arms around him and hold him tight and she sensed he felt the same way. The thought of him being injured tore at her heart. She knew he could see the fear for him in her eyes but she didn't care. From the evening she'd watched him standing in the vestibule of his house she knew she felt differently about him than any other man.

His gaze swept down her face to her breasts. Her breathing became shallow as she watched him staring at her with something in his eyes that looked like wanting or hunger.

"My lord, I heard a crash, are you and Lady Dugdale all right?" Whibbs asked as he came rushing into the dining room.

Andrew let go of Olivia and she stepped aside. "Yes, we're fine," Andrew said. "But for some reason that damned thing fell." He pointed to the pike that lay on the edge of the table.

Whibbs picked it up and looked at it closely before leaning it in the crook of the suit of armor's arm.

"I don't know how this could have happened, sir. Perhaps the same maid who dusted the vase in the foyer and didn't put it back in its proper place also dusted the pike and failed to secure it when she was finished."

The butler didn't look at Olivia, but she had little doubt Ellie must have been that maid.

"May I suggest we have the armor taken out of the dining

room and put in the attic until we decide what to do with it?" Olivia asked.

"Yes, Madame. I'll have someone take it away immediately," he said and walked out of the room.

Olivia swallowed with difficulty. Softly she asked, "Are you sure your shoulder is all right?"

"Positive."

"I'm glad you weren't seriously hurt. I shudder to think what would have happened if you hadn't moved when you did. That pike could easily have hit the back of your head."

"But it didn't." He looked into her eyes as if he were searching for something from her, but said, "I'm going out for the day. I'll be back in time to take you to the first party tonight."

He walked past her and out of the room.

Olivia was left staring at the unfinished *Times* lying on the table and the suit of armor.

If it was indeed a ghost who'd entered her room last night, could a ghost have caused that pike to fall? And if so, what would be the purpose of the spirit wanting to hurt Andrew?

She had never believed in ghosts, and certainly not ghosts that created mischief.

But she was positive that someone was in her room last night. Maybe she was just dreaming after all, but if so, it didn't feel like any dream she'd ever had before. She walked to the window and looked out over the back lawn. In her mind she went over everything she'd felt last night when she been awakened.

No. It was no dream. Someone or something had been in her room last night. She was sure of that.

If it wasn't Lord Dugdale, could it have been Lord Pinkwater's ghost?

Twelve

❧

*A*RABELLE *W*OODWARD *WATCHED* Andrew with dark, beautiful eyes that told him she'd welcome his advances if he were so inclined.

When he'd first arrived at her modest home it had been easy to spend time with her because they were very familiar with each other. They talked of old times together and various people they both knew. But after she'd poured the second glass of wine their conversation lagged.

He kept trying not to compare her to Olivia but hadn't met with much success. Not only did Arabelle have dark hair, eyes, and skin while Olivia was blue-eyed, fair, and blonde, his former mistress was at least twenty years older than Olivia, though she wore her age well.

But there was another more important difference between the two. Arabelle didn't challenge him. She said all the right things, agreed with him on everything, and smiled at him with every word she spoke.

Not so for Olivia.

Andrew didn't think Olivia had ever agreed with him on anything, and he was certain she'd never smiled at him. Yet, he wasn't put off by her lack of coquettishness. He was intrigued by her boldness and the way she took him to task about everything. He found Olivia infinitely more interesting than this woman he'd known intimately.

He had thought coming to see Arabelle would satisfy his need for a woman in his bed. And get his mind off Olivia. When he'd held Olivia in his arms and tasted her sweet breasts it had almost sent him over the edge. It had taken all the willpower he could muster to push her away.

And he'd damned himself for it.

He had been hard for her ever since. That was why he was sitting with his former mistress, trying to make himself want her.

But being with Arabelle had only made him aware that he didn't want her and that there were more differences between her and Olivia than the one being a lady and the other a mistress.

While Arabelle talked about her recent trip to Bath, Andrew's thoughts drifted to his conversation with Olivia that morning.

He should be angry as hell with her that she wouldn't let him read the news in peace. But he wasn't. For some reason he actually approved of Olivia taking him to task about it. It was rude of him to keep the paper in front of his face and ignore her on the first day of their marriage. And he'd been a damned fool spending the night at his club gambling with men he hardly knew rather than under the sheets with her.

The real reason for his bad behavior was that he didn't want Olivia putting any restrictions on him. No one had set boundaries or limitations on his actions since he was fifteen and his father died. He had no intention of letting his new bride change his lifestyle just because she'd changed his status from bachelor to husband.

Olivia had looked like an angel when he glanced up from the paper and saw her walking into the dining room. The thin material of the dress she wore clung to her body and legs as she walked, outlining her shapely form. When she passed by the window, sunshine fell on her face and gave her skin a light, golden glow.

His first thought when he saw her was that he wanted to walk over and remove the large amethyst from the hollow of her throat and kiss her there. He wanted to feel the beat of her pulse against his lips, and then slowly let his mouth find her nipple and pull it into his mouth.

His lower body felt thick and throbbing just thinking about wanting her. And he hadn't been able to forget how eager she was for his touch, how responsive she was to his loving.

It was difficult to understand Olivia. She seemed as sane as he, yet she continued to talk about a ghost. That troubled him. He didn't believe in ghosts, and he didn't want his wife thinking one was entering her bedchamber. Maybe he should talk to her about it and find out if there was more to this ghost story than Olivia was willing to tell.

When that damned pike fell, he saw in her eyes that she was worried about him even though he'd just made a biting remark to her which he had immediately regretted. He'd just started to apologize when the iron pike crashed against his shoulder.

"Something tells me your thoughts have been some-where else and you haven't heard a word of what I've been saying," Arabelle murmured seductively as she lifted her arm to the back of the settee behind him and softly let her fingers thread through the back of his hair.

"Not true," he lied without compunction and only to spare her feelings. "It sounds like you had a lovely time in Bath."

"Yes. It was good to have some time to myself for a while, but now I plan to settle here in London for a long time."

"There's no place in the world like London," he said, knowing that it was time for him to go, knowing there wasn't anything he wanted from her.

She smiled at him while her fingers continued a leisurely pattern of massage at the back of his head.

"I was delighted when Mr. Haversham told me you wanted to see me. We used to enjoy each other, Andrew. We can again."

Andrew had thought they would, but now it was clear that even though she was still a woman of great beauty, he had no desire to renew their once torrid affair. He should have let bygones be bygones and not have attempted to recommence a relationship that had long since passed.

"Why do I suddenly feel like I'm talking to myself?" she asked when he remained quiet after her last comment.

"It's been good seeing you, Arabelle, but I should be going," he said.

Arabelle's eyes registered shock at his words, but she quickly recovered and said, "No, not yet, Andrew." She removed her arm from behind him and picked up his glass from the small table in front of them. "Let's have another drink before you go."

She extended the glass toward him. The crystal caught the lamplight and sparkled invitingly. For a moment, the ruby red wine seemed to be pulling at him as eagerly as her painted lips, but only for a moment.

He shook his head, declining another drink. Another glass of wine was not going to make him want her.

Arabelle placed it back on the table and moved closer to him, laying her hand on his inner thigh and pressing her body against his relaxed arm. Her dark golden-colored gown was cut low, revealing the full, fleshy swell of her ample breasts. Andrew couldn't help but compare them to Olivia's smaller, firmer breasts.

"Please don't go yet, Andrew. The night is just beginning," she whispered softly and so close to his ear he felt her warm breath tingle against his skin. "We know each other so well. I know how to please you. And I've learned a few more delicious things since we were last together."

He had no doubt about that.

"Let me show you. Let me give you the pleasure you deserve."

Her eyes were hot with desire; her lips formed a provocative pout. No doubt, like him, she was remembering the passionate nights they'd shared.

Arabelle's hand slid over to the junction of his thighs and cupped him with just the right amount of strength to elicit an immediate hardness.

She is good at her job.

"You are big and very hard, my lord." She laughed softly, huskily, sensuously. "You want me, my darling, and I want you now. Take me here on the settee and satisfy yourself."

She reached up and placed her dark pink lips on his and tried to evoke a reaction from him. Her hand did its work on him and he swelled with need. For a moment he gave in to her wine-coated kiss and returned her passion. She moaned her pleasure at his slight response.

Andrew's body told him he wanted a woman to sink deeply into. His body desperately wanted release. But after only moments of her wrapped in his arms he knew she was not the woman he wanted.

He drew away from her and said, "I'm sorry, Arabelle. I have to go."

"Wait," she said and pulled on his arm as he tried to rise. "If you don't want a permanent arrangement with me, that's all right. I'll find another. But don't cheat us out of tonight, Andrew. It won't cost you anything but your time, and I promise you won't regret losing that."

Her eyes implored him. They looked glassy with desire. Her chest heaved with the fear of losing him. And Andrew realized he wasn't even tempted by her anymore. She didn't feel right in his arms.

There had been a time he didn't care who the woman was as long as his body was satisfied. Now it mattered. If he just wanted a woman to satisfy him, this one would be fine.

He took hold of her wrists and pulled her hands away from him.

"It was good to see you, Arabelle. You are as beautiful as ever, but . . ." He hesitated, hoping to find the right words to soothe her, but realized there was nothing else he could say.

"But you won't be back, will you?" she finished for him with a resigned note in her voice and an acceptance in her dark eyes.

"No."

Andrew walked out.

$\mathcal{I}$T WAS DARK in the sitting room and it took Olivia a few moments to realize that the reason she could no longer see the account books laid out before her was because night had fallen and she hadn't lit a lamp. She had become so engrossed in what she was doing that she hadn't realized the afternoon had turned to evening.

After Andrew left that morning she had a great desire to go to her aunt, fling herself into Agatha's comforting arms, and beg her to take her back into her home. But Olivia had forced herself to stay put. If she went running to Agatha for any reason the first full day she was married she'd be setting a precedent from which she might never recover.

Olivia was a married lady whether or not she felt like one. She had to accept that and adjust to her new life.

She had to trust her own judgment. And her judgment was telling her she must hold her tongue and let Andrew see her softer side, her confident side, her helpful side. Not the shrew she had been that morning. She must have sounded awful, not allowing him to read his paper in peace as he'd done for so many years, and insisting he had invaded her room after he'd made it clear he hadn't.

Starting today she would be a new woman.

By midafternoon she felt light-headed and realized that she'd eaten very little in the last twenty-four hours. So she sat quietly in the dining room and ate alone while she stared at Lord Truefitt's gossip column. The tittle-tattle confirmed Andrew's claim that he'd been out of the house all night and couldn't possibly have been the shadow of a man she saw in her room.

That left her wondering again if maybe she had really seen Lord Pinkwater's ghost.

And if she had, should she tell her aunt that her deceased beau did truly live in Lord Dugdale's house?

No, she decided after much agonizing thought. She would remain quiet for now and wait to see if the man or ghost made another appearance before she said anything to Agatha.

Her meeting with Whibbs and the staff went very well. She had spent more time than she'd wanted to with Ellie, explaining what duties she expected of her during the day. After the debacle with the vase and the pike, which Olivia assumed was Ellie's fault although Whibbs hadn't come right out and said so, Olivia wanted to make sure the maid knew that she wasn't to touch anything in the house unless Olivia asked her to.

She also told Ellie that she didn't want her to be her shadow. Olivia was too independent to want anyone constantly anticipating her needs.

From all she could tell, Whibbs's account books looked in perfect order. He certainly had a knack for hiring reliable, capable servants who kept everything in tip-top shape. Andrew was lucky to have such a competent butler.

She looked up at the clock on the mantel and realized she had to go upstairs and dress for the evening. She hadn't heard Andrew come in, but he'd said he would be back in time to take her to the first party of the evening.

When she entered her room she saw that Ellie had laid out the right gown, undergarments, shoes, wrap, and reticule. The pale young maid might not know how to accomplish household duties, but she certainly knew how to dress a lady.

Olivia started changing and realized she kept hearing something that sounded like loud whispered voices, so she stopped undressing and listened. She couldn't make out any words that were said, but she was certain she heard a man and a woman talking.

She looked around the room and wondered where the voices could possibly be coming from. There was only one other room on this floor, and that was her husband's.

Suddenly Olivia gasped.

Andrew wouldn't have brought a woman, his mistress, into this house, into his room?

Would he?

He had stayed out all night on their wedding night. She couldn't put anything past him.

Without thinking about what she was going to do, Olivia grabbed her white lawn dressing gown and threw it on over her lace-trimmed chemise. Rather than taking time to belt it she simply held it together at her chest as she padded barefoot down the hallway to Andrew's room.

She knocked loudly.

Seconds later the door opened and there stood Andrew just as he'd been last night, dressed only in his low-slung trousers, showing far more of his beautiful body than she needed to see. For a moment she forgot why she was there and allowed her gaze to sweep over his broad shoulders, flat stomach, and narrow hips.

No man should be that tempting.

"I had a feeling it was you," he said in an almost cavalier way.

"Is that because you have a guilty conscience?" She tried to look past him into the room but the door wasn't opened wide enough.

His honey-colored eyes darkened as a flash of surprise showed in his handsome features, and for a moment she thought he might answer yes.

"No," he said. "What can I do for you?"

Suddenly she didn't feel so courageous.

"I heard voices," she said, a little breathless from her mad dash down the corridor, from seeing his splendid, naked chest once again gleaming like a beckoning beacon in the pale lamplight.

Andrew's brows drew together in a frown as he studied her face. "And?"

He certainly didn't seem to have a guilty look about him now. If he was hiding anyone in his room he didn't seem nervous or concerned about it.

"And I thought they must be coming from your room."

"These voices you heard?"

She nodded.

"What would be the problem if you heard me talking to Whibbs?"

"Nothing, but it was a female's voice I heard—talking with you."

"With me?" Andrew swung the door wider and stepped back. He bowed and bid her entrance with his outstretched arm. "There's no female in my room for me to talk to and I don't make a habit of talking to myself in a falsetto voice."

Olivia stepped inside and glanced around before settling her gaze on his face. Too many strange things she didn't understand were going on inside this house.

"But I'm sure I heard a man and a woman whispering."

She knew he could read her face and knew exactly what she was thinking. There was nothing for her to do now but stand her ground.

"Perhaps you heard the housekeeper or a maid, perhaps even your own maid, but the voice did not come from my room."

Olivia cringed inside.

What was wrong with her? How many mistakes was she going to make before she learned her lesson? She was a sensible person. At least she used to be before she met Andrew. Now she seemed to be constantly saying and doing the wrong thing. Of course, a maid could have been standing at the top of the stairs, or perhaps the voices drifted up from the lower floor.

Why had she immediately thought the worst about Andrew? Was it because he'd stayed out all night?

He folded his arms across his chest. "Last night you thought you saw someone in your room."

"I'm sure I did," she said, more to reassure herself that she wasn't going crazy than to convince Andrew. "It wasn't a ghost."

"And tonight you think you're hearing voices."

"Yes, I—know it sounds crazy, but . . ." She stopped and took a deep breath. She had to reclaim her wits and stop sounding insane. "But perhaps I'm overreacting to being in a strange house."

"Olivia, I think you are taking your ghost stories a little too far. If you were ever really searching for one, he's not here. And if it is just a ruse to enter my room, you don't have to make up an excuse. I told you. You're always welcome in here."

She sighed. Was it better for him to believe she thought she heard ghosts than think he had brought his mistress into their home?

Olivia let go of her robe and her hands fell to her sides. Had Agatha succeeded in making her think she was seeing ghosts and now she was hearing them as well? She looked up at Andrew and had a sudden urge to tell him about Agatha's search for Lord Pinkwater and make him understand that she wasn't crazy. She was just trying to help her aunt.

But she couldn't tell him. Agatha was so happy now that she'd returned and had been welcomed back into London's Society as if she'd never left. She had to stay quiet and let Andrew think what he wanted to about her.

She looked up at her husband. "I'm sorry I disturbed you again."

"Are you not feeling well?" he asked.

For the first time since they had met she saw real concern in his eyes and she found that comforting. "No, no, I'm fine. I do believe I'm taking my search for Lord Pinkwater a little too seriously."

He gently took hold of her arm and said, "Come in and I'll get you some water."

She allowed him to walk her over to a chest where he poured water from a pitcher into a glass and gave it to her. She sipped it and handed the glass back to him.

"Thank you," she whispered. "I'm sure my imagination is playing tricks on me. Perhaps it's because the vase fell the first evening I was here, and then this morning the pike, and now the voices."

"Both incidents were disturbing, but nothing to worry about. A ghost didn't cause either one. I spoke to Whibbs about the vase and he told me he believes it happened because a careless maid dusted it and left it too close to the edge. He was going to dismiss her but decided she could have one more chance. No doubt she's the one who dusted the suit of armor as well and was careless and left the pike loose."

An odd feeling assailed Olivia. So Whibbs hadn't told Andrew that she was the one who insisted that Ellie stay as her maid. Her respect for the butler grew.

Her eyes swept over Andrew's face. She was drawn to this softer side of him. "That was kind of Whibbs to allow her another chance."

"He's always been fair."

"Well, I should go back to my room and let you finish dressing."

One step took her so close to him their bodies were almost touching. Soft lamplight danced on his rumpled hair and sliced attractively across his freshly shaven face. She wanted to step into his embrace and bury her nose in his neck and breathe in his scent.

"Do you really want to go back to your room right now?" he asked huskily.

Had he read her mind? Were her feelings written on her face for him to see?

"Yes," she said, but a little voice inside her challenged her statement, and she made no move to leave.

He lowered his face closer to hers, his gaze intent on hers. In a softer voice he said, "Did you really hear voices or was it just another ploy to enter my room and watch me dress?"

Olivia stiffened. "After last night, how could you think I'd do that?" she argued. "You've made it clear you don't want me."

He ran the backs of his fingers down her cheek. His touch was warm, thrilling even though she didn't want it to be, and still she made no effort to leave.

"Oh, no, Olivia, I made it clear last night I do want you. Make no mistake, I want you."

His gaze left her eyes and traveled down to her lips, lingering for a moment before sliding down the length of her body and back up again to her eyes.

Suddenly Olivia's dressing gown was too hot and her chemise too thin. Her stomach felt as if it were tied in knots of desire. Anticipation of his kiss was so strong inside her she could barely keep from reaching for him.

Why did the thought of being his wife in every sense of the word excite her so?

He kept his face close to hers, his voice low as he said,

"I simply insist on picking the date, the place, and the time."

She was outraged that he would admit he wanted her but not right now.

Her shoulders flew back and she lifted her chin. "I refuse to be a chattel just waiting around for you to call me as if you were my master."

"You do like to issue challenges, don't you?"

"That was a promise, not a challenge. You said you wanted me. I never said I wanted you."

"But you do, Olivia. I see it in your eyes."

"You fool yourself, my lord."

"Shall I prove it?"

She started to turn away but he grabbed the lapels on her robe and pulled her to him. She willingly gave in to his irreverent tug, putting up no fight as his lips slowly descended to hers. She kept her eyes open, but his were closed. She saw the smoothness of his brow, the long length of his lashes. He took his time with the kiss, and though she loved the touch of his moist lips on hers, she made no effort to respond to him.

Without letting his lips leave her skin, he gave her short, sweet kisses that moved agonizingly slow to the side of her mouth, below her jawbone and back up to her cheek just below her eye.

It was the most sensual kiss he had ever given her and she melted over it. Her breath trembled in her throat. His touch was trained and skilled to elicit the most passionate of feelings from her. All her senses were tuned to this man.

He made her weak with a wanting she didn't understand and couldn't resist.

She couldn't deny to herself that she wanted so much more from him, but she wouldn't admit it to him.

His eyes opened and he saw her watching him.

"Have you changed your mind?" he whispered into her mouth.

"No," she answered, before surrendering to him as his lips claimed hers in a hungry kiss, taking and giving as much as she received.

There was suddenly a desperate urgency in the way he circled her in his arms and held her close, in the way he plundered her mouth. His tongue swirled and skimmed along the lining of her lips, sending chills of excitement to pebble her skin.

Andrew's hands slid up to her shoulders and he raked her robe off her arms and let it fall to the floor.

He lifted his head a little but their breaths still mingled as he whispered, "I love the taste of you. I love the feel of your soft skin."

Olivia's stomach flipped with delicious curls of passion. She hadn't forgotten the taste or the feel of him, either.

He peppered her lips with several soft sensuous kisses.

Heated with the sweet rush of desire, she lifted her lips to him again, and this time the gentle, sensuous kiss had been replaced with eagerness. There was demanding pressure in the meeting of their mouths.

Olivia felt a hunger inside Andrew that matched her own. His lips left hers and burned a hot trail of moisture all the way down the column of her neck to the hollow of her throat. There he stopped and tasted her skin with his tongue.

She gasped with pleasure. Olivia's arms slid around his neck. Her hands found the back of his head and her fingers wove through his hair before moving down to his back to caress the rock-hard muscles of his naked skin.

Andrew's hand slowly yet firmly moved up her rib cage and cupped her breast with a possessive hold that was firm but not hurting. His other hand slid around to her buttocks. He pressed her womanhood against the hard shaft beneath his trousers.

Olivia melted against his heat. Once again she welcomed the enticing pressure of him nestled convincingly against her softness.

"Olivia, tell me you want me right now. Let me hear you say it."

Her body wanted to say yes, yes, a thousand times yes, but her mind rejected that idea. He said he would pick the time and the place. He must pursue her.

"No," she whispered against his lips.

"Do you want me?"

She almost smiled at this game of words they were playing while her body felt as if it was being tortured with one amazing sensation after the other.

"It's none of your concern what I want," she managed to murmur into his mouth.

"I'm making progress. That doesn't mean no."

He deepened the kiss, thrusting his tongue in and out of her mouth, driving her wild with wanting. His hand slid down her hip and grasped the hem of her chemise and yanked it up to her chest. With ease his hand slipped over and caressed her bare breasts one after the other and back again.

Olivia gasped at the sheer pleasure of his hand on her skin. With his thumb and finger he softly rolled one nipple back and forth. She squeezed her legs together to try to stop the building tension inside her.

"Tell me you want me, Olivia," he whispered again.

"No," she managed to say again, even though her body cried out yes.

"Then stop me, Olivia. Stop me."

Thirteen

SHE HAD SURPRISED the hell out of him again.

Just when he thought he had Olivia where he wanted her, she pushed out of his arms and calmly walked out of his bedchamber, leaving him frustrated and irritated.

It was hours later and Andrew stood with a group of men who were discussing the capabilities of their latest prize-winning horses and hounds. Ordinarily he would be very interested in both, as hunting and racing were two of his favorite things to do, but not tonight. He couldn't keep his eyes or his thoughts off his wife or off her unexpected visit to his room a few hours ago.

Had she really heard voices or was it part of her continued plan to try to get into his bed? And if she wanted to get there so badly why wouldn't she have admitted to him that she wanted him as he had tried to get her to do?

And why was he fighting so hard against taking her to his bed? It wasn't that he didn't want her. He did. Desperately.

What he didn't like was the thought of her manipulating him again.

A hand clapped Andrew on the back and he turned to face John.

"I'm glad to see you decided to spend the evening with your wife."

"The evening but not the night," Andrew said in a surly voice.

"That doesn't sound promising, my friend. Come on, let's get a drink."

Andrew and John left the group Andrew had been standing with and threaded their way through the crowd of fashionably dressed men and beautifully gowned women. They made their way to the other side of the room not too far from where Olivia stood with her aunt, Lady Lynette, and Lady Colebrooke.

John picked up two glasses of amber liquid from a servant and gave one to Andrew as he said, "Something tells me you aren't taking to marriage very well."

Andrew looked at his friend. He was actually having a hell of a time with it. How could he explain he wanted his wife yet he didn't? He'd never been in a dilemma like that before.

"Would you take to marriage well if you were forced into it?"

"Probably not," John said.

"Then tell me how the hell do you think I'm supposed to feel?"

John looked uncomfortable for a moment, and then his gaze strayed over to where Olivia stood. "Look at it like this, it could have been worse."

"How?"

"Well, you could have been forced to marry someone like Miss Bardwell."

John's words reminded Andrew of the young lady they had once considered as cold and unattractive as a fish. His name had been romantically linked to Miss Bardwell's a couple of years ago simply because her dowry was heavy and his pockets were light.

"I would have shot myself before I would have married her," Andrew said with a light chuckle on his lips.

"My point exactly. At least Olivia is beautiful, shapely, and from the short time I spoke to her after the wedding she seemed quite intelligent."

Much too clever for her own good, Andrew thought as his gaze drifted over to look at her for at least the fiftieth time since they arrived at the ball and parted ways. She didn't appear the least bothered by their passionate embrace in his room. His mood was black. She was laughing and talking cheerfully with the ladies as if nothing had happened between them while he still bore the remnants of interrupted passion.

John was right. She was exceptionally beautiful, especially when she smiled and laughed.

"She still hasn't smiled for me."

"Maybe you've never given her reason to."

Andrew's attention jerked back to his friend. He hadn't realized he'd spoken those last words aloud until John answered him.

Could John's observation be right? Andrew had seen passion, concern, and shock in her delicate features but he hadn't seen laughter, contentment, or any happiness in her face when they had been alone. He supposed John was right. He hadn't given her a reason to smile at him. For some reason he suddenly felt a great need to see her beautiful smile directed at him.

"Is Truefitt's column right?" John asked. "Did you spend your entire wedding night at the club?"

Andrew didn't answer. He took another drink from his almost empty glass.

"You did, didn't you? You left her bed and went straight to the club to spend the night drinking and gaming. I can't believe you did that."

"I didn't take her to bed," Andrew muttered.

John's dark eyes rounded, and then suddenly blinked rapidly. "You didn't—you didn't?"

"Right. I didn't." Andrew turned up his glass and emptied it. He then winced as the strong liquor burned his throat and continued into his stomach.

John was clearly stunned, and Andrew didn't like admitting he'd failed to consummate his marriage on his wedding night. He was surprised he'd admitted it. That wasn't something a man would be proud of and certainly not something he'd tell just anybody, but he and John had been friends since they were fifteen.

"It's complicated," Andrew felt compelled to say.

"Complicated?" John asked as he glanced over at Olivia again. "What the devil makes it complicated?"

Andrew knew John was seeing exactly what he saw: a beautiful and vibrant young woman whom any man in his right mind would bed if he had the chance.

Andrew felt annoyed as hell. He had returned from Derbyshire thinking to pick up with his unencumbered life in London as the *ton*'s most notorious bachelor, the last of the Terrible Threesome and the one that hadn't been caught. He hadn't planned on getting trapped into marriage three weeks after returning home.

"Just trust me on this, my friend."

"All right, I guess I understand," John said, giving his full attention back to Andrew.

"No, you don't," Andrew said tightly.

"No, hell I don't. You're right. I don't understand not bedding your wife on your wedding night."

"Damnation, John, keep your voice down before someone hears you," Andrew said, looking around to the room to see if anyone was watching them. Thankfully everyone nearby seemed too interested in their own conversations to be listening to others.

John glanced around the room, too. He looked as exasperated as Andrew.

"I'm sorry. I didn't expect to hear anything so outrageous. What in bloody hell is going on with you?"

"Nothing I want to talk about. And don't press me about this, John. It's not something I can or want to explain."

"You're damned right you can't explain it."

"John, drop it."

His friend looked as if he was going to say more, but stopped himself and let out a troubled sigh. He stared uncomfortably at Andrew.

Finally he said, "So tell me, what's the latest word on Hawkins?"

Andrew let out a scattered breath before saying, "The Runner thinks Hawkins must have left Derbyshire for a safer place. Now that I've had time to consider it, I think that's probably true."

"Even though Derbyshire is where his family lives?"

"Yes. The bastard probably left town the very night he shot at me and gave the Magistrate the slip. Thompson thinks it was worth the time he spent there waiting to see if anyone was hiding Hawkins, but there's been no sign of him."

"You know, I have an idea," John said. "After the Season is over why don't we take a ride over to Derbyshire and have a look for him. We talked about that possibility with Chandler, remember?"

Yes, Andrew remembered, and his friends had quickly axed the idea when he'd mentioned it. Andrew was smart enough to know that John was just feeling sorry for him. He appreciated that, but in another way he hated it, too.

He could handle Hawkins and Olivia by himself.

"We'll talk about it after the Season," Andrew said, knowing they would never go. He wouldn't take his friends away from their wives, not even for a short adventure to Derbyshire.

OLIVIA WATCHED HER aunt talk, laugh, and gossip with Lady Lynette and Lady Colebrooke and she had to smile. Coming to London was the best thing that could have happened to Agatha. She hadn't looked so young, so healthy, and so happy in years, but Olivia couldn't say the same thing about herself.

London, with its people, its parties, and its excitement, was very different from the quiet life they lived in Kent. This was obviously the life Agatha was born to live. And Olivia found herself happy that her aunt was back where she belonged. But Olivia knew she was a long way from finding her own happiness.

She had decided not to mention to Agatha that someone or something had entered her room and that a pike had mysteriously fallen from a suit of armor. She was sure Agatha would insist it was Lord Pinkwater's ghost trying to get a message to her. Olivia wasn't ready to admit that it might possibly be a ghost creating mischief in Lord Dugdale's home.

While she had no trouble believing Ellie might be behind the pike and vase, there was no way the maid could have been the person in her bedchamber. She was much too small for the person Olivia saw. But was the man's form Lord Pinkwater's ghost? Olivia needed more proof. The only thing she was really sure of was that someone had entered her room.

Under the guise of turning her head to cough, Olivia glanced across the room to where Andrew stood talking with his friend John. They seemed to be in a deep conversation about something.

Olivia's heart ached just looking at him.

She didn't know where she'd found the strength to push out of his arms and leave his room rather than simply admit she wanted him to make love to her. It had taken all her willpower because it had felt so right to be circled in his warm embrace, pressed against his hard chest, his moist lips on hers.

It must have been the fear that he would reject her once again if she admitted she wanted him to make her his wife in every sense of the word. And that gave her the strength to walk away from him.

But she'd learned her lesson about walking into his room no matter what she thought might be going on in there. Twice she'd stepped inside and twice she'd regretted it. If he ever decided he wanted her, he would have to come to her room, to her bed.

"Olivia," Lady Lynette said softly, as she turned away from the other two ladies and faced Olivia directly. "Before I go, I wanted you to know that I've been thinking about what you said about that new apothecary."

"I hope my mentioning that hasn't caused you any duress."

Lynette smiled. "Not at all. I was wondering if you would have time to go with me tomorrow after we're finished with our reading group?"

"Of course, we'll plan on it," Olivia said, feeling excitement for her friend.

Olivia watched Lynette walk away and immediately started looking for Andrew's Aunt Claudette. She needed to find her and ask the address of the new apothecary.

"Olivia, dear," Agatha said. "Lady Colebrooke is talking to you."

"Oh, I'm sorry," Olivia said, looking at the beautiful blonde woman who stood in front of her with such calm and poise that Olivia had liked her the moment they'd met. "I must have been daydreaming. What did you say?"

Lady Colebrooke laughed and then said, "No doubt your thoughts were on your husband. I understand perfectly. I still find myself daydreaming about Daniel and we've been married over a year. I just wanted to say good-bye and I'll see you at our reading group tomorrow afternoon."

"Yes, I'll be there. Thank you for the invitation, Lady Colebrooke."

"You must remember to call me Isabella."

Olivia smiled, suddenly feeling better than she had in a days. She had made another friend. "I will."

When Isabella was gone Olivia reached over and gave her aunt a hug.

Agatha looked a little surprised but flattered. "What was that for?" she asked.

"I just wanted you to know that I'm happy to see you."

"You just saw me yesterday."

"I know, but keep in mind you have been my constant

companion for the past twelve years. It's only natural I miss you."

Agatha smiled. "What a sweet thing to say. I miss having you around the house, too, but I'm staying busy."

"I'm sure you are. Tell me, do you know the name of the apothecary that Andrew's Aunt Claudette mentioned that first night were at his house?"

An unusual frown flashed across Agatha's face. "Yes, indeed I do, but not because I asked. She told me I needed to pay him a visit. Imagine, her suggesting such a thing."

Olivia tried not to smile that a certain rivalry existed even though the ladies had been apart for twelve years.

"Would you like for me to send the name and address over to you? I certainly have no use of it."

"Early tomorrow, if you would. I'm going out and would love to stop by and see what he has."

Olivia glanced in Andrew's direction again and caught site of the Marquis of Musgrove Glenn. He was leaving a group of gentlemen he had been talking to. Perhaps this would be a good time to talk with him about Lady Lynette. Olivia wasn't having any success with her own marriage, but perhaps she could help her friend with the love of her life.

"Would you excuse me, Auntie, I see someone I want to speak to."

"Of course, Livy. You run along and I'll see you get the information first thing in the morning."

Olivia followed the Marquis and caught up with him just before he left the room.

"How are you tonight, Marquis?" she said, coming up from behind him.

He stopped and smiled when he saw her. "Quite well, Lady Dugdale. My best wishes to you on your marriage."

"Thank you, my lord."

"Matrimony obviously agrees with you. You look lovely tonight."

"That's very kind of you to say so, sir." She smiled at him, took a deep breath and said, "I was talking to Lady Lynette earlier and she was telling me how you two have known each other for a long time."

"Yes, I see her each Season, of course, and our families have gone to the same house parties for years."

"I suppose that's how she knew the names of your children."

"She knows my children?" he asked.

Olivia could see by the expression on his face that he was a bit confused as to why she would be talking with him about Lynette and his children.

As far as Olivia was concerned, if the Marquis was looking for his third wife there was no reason he shouldn't consider a woman who already loved him and cared about his children. And since he didn't know that, Olivia had decided to make it her business to enlighten him.

"Yes, I remember a few days ago when we were all talking together that she asked about your children and called each of them by name."

He seemed to ponder that a moment. "You know, you're right, she did. I do recall that now, but I've never taken my children to a house party. They're much too young. Perhaps she heard their mothers talk about them."

"I'm sure that's how she knew, but how lovely of Lynette to remember and to ask about them."

Olivia watched the Marquis's gaze look around the room until his gaze found Lynette. She was talking to an older lady whom Olivia didn't recognize. Lynette's rose-colored gown flattered her full figure. The red birthmark on her cheek couldn't be seen from the profile facing them.

All they saw was a tall, lovely, self-confident woman talking easily to her companion.

"The truth is, she's always been around, but I've never paid too much attention to Lynette," the Marquis admitted honestly.

Obviously not.

"But it was kind of her to take an interest in my children."

"Very kind," Olivia said. "And not only does she love children and is kind hearted, she's really quite intelligent."

"Oh, I don't doubt it." He turned back to Olivia. "It's a pity she's never married."

"Too true. I'm sure she would make some gentleman an honorable wife, and I know she would be a splendid mother."

He smiled indulgently at Olivia again, as if he was catching on to her ploy. "No doubt you are right about her."

"There you are, my darling," Andrew said, coming up to Olivia and slipping his arm around her waist. "I've been looking for you."

Olivia knew that couldn't be true. They had been in each other's sight since arriving at the party.

He squeezed her waist gently with his hand as he said, "Thank you, Marquis, for keeping her company, but she promised the next dance to me and it's about to begin."

Olivia mumbled a hasty good-bye as Andrew ushered her to the outer rim of the dance floor. They got in position and at the right downbeat took the first step that led them into the flow of all the others crowding the floor to waltz.

Andrew's frame was strong, firm, and secure as he guided her through the steps. She loved the feeling of being so close to him, if only for a short time.

"You looked as if you were enjoying your discussion with the Marquis."

"Hmm, I was. Is that the reason you decided we must dance?"

"Yes. You looked like you were enjoying yourself too much. Do you think a married woman should take so much pleasure in another man?"

She eyed him with a curious stare as they moved among the other dancers. "My pleasure came from the topic of our conversation, not from the man I was with."

"And what subject were you discussing?" he asked as he led her in a turn.

For a moment Olivia wondered if Andrew could be a little bit jealous and a spark of hope ignited inside her as she said, "Lady Lynette."

"The Duke of Knightington's daughter?" he asked. "Why?"

"Because she's my friend."

"In what way were you discussing her?"

"In a flattering way."

Andrew's brow wrinkled and his eyes darkened as they swept effortlessly across the dance floor in time with the music.

"What you just said told me nothing, Olivia."

"Quite the contrary, my lord, it tells you Lynette is my friend and the Marquis and I were having a friendly chat about her."

"I think your daily amusement comes from tormenting me, my dear wife."

"And I think you should trust that I wasn't discussing anything inappropriate with the Marquis."

"I didn't think you were." His words contradicted the wrinkle between his brows.

"Then why question me?"

"I was merely curious, and I might add, you still haven't told me what the two of you were talking about."

"I thought I did. We were discussing Lady Lynette."

"You are impossible."

You are impossible.

His words floated over her like a warmed blanket on a cold night. It wasn't what he said but how he said it. He voice was low and sensual as if he were trying to seduce her. His gaze penetrated hers and she felt connected to him in a way she hadn't before.

"I could say the same thing about you."

Andrew smiled at her and Olivia felt like her heart flipped in her chest. She wanted to wrap her arms around him and breathe in his scent. She wanted to feel his warm breath on her neck, behind her ear, but all she could do was continue the complicated back steps of the waltz as Andrew guided her.

"But would it be true?" he asked.

"Most definitely, my lord."

"I'm glad Lady Lynette is your friend," he said, lifting his arm for her to walk under.

"I think she's the only young lady who's not angry with me for taking you off the marriage mart."

Andrew chuckled. "I just realized that you have very effectively taken the conversation off what you and the Marquis were taking about."

"Not really. I told you we were discussing Lynette and so are you and I."

"So what were you doing, telling the Marquis all about Lady Lynette's many attributes?"

She looked at him with surprise in her eyes. "Yes, that is exactly what I was doing. How did you know?"

"I didn't. I was guessing."

"Well, he is looking for a wife, a mother for his children, and I think Lady Lynette would be perfect for him."

He twirled her under his arm again and as she faced him once more he said, "Really?"

"You don't?" she threw back at him.

"Well, I don't think I've ever thought about Lady Lynette getting married."

"Do you think because of her blemish no man would want to marry her?"

"No. I've just never had a reason for the subject to cross my mind."

"I suppose most gentlemen might consider her a spinster now. She is past the age most young ladies marry. But perhaps it's time the Marquis looked at a woman who would not only be a good wife but a good mother to his children."

The wrinkle returned to Andrew's brow. "And you told him this?"

"No, of course not. Not directly, anyway. I only hinted at it. I just planted a seed and perhaps got him to thinking about her in that way."

Andrew's eyes darkened again and the corners of his mouth tightened. "So setting a snare for me wasn't enough. Now you want to try to catch the Marquis in one as well."

Olivia's breath caught in her throat as the dance ended. "No," she whispered. "You've got it all wrong. That's not my intention at all."

Her husband let go of her as if she were a hot poker.

Why hadn't it dawned on her that Andrew would have thought her desire to help Lady Lynette was only meant to entrap the Marquis?

Fourteen

※⟡※

ANDREW HEADED FOR the breakfast room not knowing whether or not Olivia would be joining him. Their conversation had come to an abrupt halt several nights ago when he realized she was trying to leg-shackle the Marquis, and he hadn't had a detailed conversation with her since.

For the past three days Andrew had spent more time at his club than at his home. He had only seen Olivia for short periods of time during the past seventy-two hours. He left without seeing her in the mornings and would arrive at home in the evenings with just enough time to dress and escort her to the parties. Once there they parted ways and he wouldn't see her again until it was time to take her home.

He'd tried to enjoy the drinking, gambling, and the late night races in Hyde Park. He found himself going from White's to three and four other clubs in one night before heading home at dawn. For some reason a life that was once so important to him now held little fascination.

Just when he was beginning to think Olivia might not be as devious as he first believed, her true intentions were revealed to him again. He'd thought on it a lot the past few days as he played cards, and for the life of him, he couldn't figure out why she would want to entrap the Marquis for Lady Lynette.

He wondered if either of them knew what Olivia had in mind. The Marquis had danced with Lynette the past couple of nights but he'd danced with other ladies, too, including an older, wealthy widow.

Andrew had known both the Marquis's wives and they had been beautiful women, not that Lynette wasn't in her own way. Andrew enjoyed being around Lynette and he considered her lovely despite her birthmark. She was cheerful and had never let the discoloration on her cheek keep her out of sight of Society. He'd always admired her for that. As far as he knew Lynette had never even had a beau court her.

If the Marquis was interested in Lynette he would pursue her. He didn't need Olivia's help.

The first thing Andrew noticed when he walked in the dining room was that candles were lit. In the ten years he'd lived at this house he couldn't remember candles ever being lit at breakfast no matter how gray and dreary the day. He knew the light had to be Olivia's idea and for some reason he liked that. He found it almost comforting.

The *Times* was beside his plate as usual and just like all other mornings there was a place setting for Olivia. He had wondered since he'd not been to the dining room in several mornings if she might have decided to have breakfast in her chamber.

He sat down in his chair, opened the paper, and started to read. Whibbs came in and quietly poured his coffee.

Andrew was deep into a story about a murder in the hells when suddenly he was aware that Olivia was in the room with him. He hadn't heard her come in but he knew she was there. He slowly lowered the paper and saw her standing at the buffet table pouring tea with her back to him.

Desire for her stirred inside him. No matter what she did, he couldn't shake the fact that he wanted her. He'd wanted her since the first night he saw her in his room.

She was beautiful even from the back. Her hair was up, showing a long and slender neck. He wanted to rise, go over and kiss her nape. He wanted to bury his nose in her warm skin and breathe in her soft womanly scent.

Her shoulders were high and her back straight but not rigid. And even though the fashion of her dress hid her womanly figure, he knew her waist was small, her hips slightly rounded, and her breasts full and firm. He swallowed hard, remembering how their weight had felt in his hands as he massaged her, how satisfying her nipples had been in his mouth as he'd sucked. Her breasts were just the right size to bring him immense pleasure.

As he looked at her he wondered why he desired her so desperately. It had to be that he'd just been too long without a woman in his bed. He expected to remedy that this afternoon. He had an appointment with a lady named Alice Thunderberry. He hoped she would be so beautiful and desirable that all thoughts of his wife would vanish from his mind.

Olivia turned and caught him staring at her.

"Good morning," she said softly.

"Good morning," he returned.

Andrew stood up and helped her with her chair and when he sat back down he picked up his paper and noticed she had brought a book with her. Without looking at him, she opened it and started to read.

He put the paper back in front of his face and returned to the story he'd been reading but soon found he wasn't nearly as interested in it as he had been before Olivia entered the room.

Andrew kept expecting Olivia to interrupt him as she had before when they were at the breakfast table, but the minutes slowly ticked by. The only thing he heard was a small tinkling sound when she lifted her cup from the saucer and replaced it and the light rustle of a page turning in a book.

The silence grew.

It didn't take Andrew long to realize he'd rather Olivia talk to him than completely ignore him. He lowered the paper just enough to look at her over the top. His lower body tightened when he saw her lovely profile in the candlelight.

Her lashes were dark, long, and slightly curled on the tips. She had a small, narrow nose that seemed the perfect size for her face. Her cheeks looked soft and delicate and her lips were beautifully shaped and ever so tempting.

She seemed so completely engrossed in what she was reading, so serene, that she was oblivious to his concentrated scrutiny.

Olivia was a passionate woman. It was only natural for him to want her. But he didn't want to give in to his desire for her. He wanted to take one look at Alice Thunderberry and immediately want to take her to bed.

It struck him as odd that it had been his habit for years to read the paper at the table each morning but for some reason Olivia's reading a book and disregarding him bothered him.

Had she known it would irritate the devil out of him

for her to be so quiet? Is that why she brought the book with her?

He lifted his paper again and tried to concentrate on an article written about the latest antics from several members of Parliament but found Olivia was the only thing on his mind, even though she didn't seem to know he was in the room.

He lowered the paper again and said, "You're very quiet this morning."

She looked up at him. "I didn't want to disturb you."

An elephant trampling through the dining room couldn't have disturbed him as much as her quietness had.

He asked, "Were you safe in your room last night?"

Olivia's shapely eyebrows drew together. He could see she was confused by his question and didn't know how to answer.

"Did you have any unwanted visitors to your room in the middle of the night?"

Understanding showed in her bright blue eyes. "Oh, no, no. Nothing disturbed me. I slept soundly all night," she said and immediately went back to her reading.

He couldn't see the title of the book, but it must have been more interesting than the news he was reading. If he had to guess he'd say she was reading some of that romantic poetry nonsense that Byron published.

Finally he asked, "What are you reading?"

"Murder on the Thames," she said without looking up at him.

So much for thinking she might be reading poetry.

"That sounds like one of those horrid novels."

This time she looked at him. "It is. Thankfully I found it on your bookshelf. You don't mind if I read it, do you?"

"No, of course not."

"Good."

"But there are other types of books on the shelves. Some of them are more literary than such as that."

Olivia looked up at him and a sweet, genuine smile of amusement lifted the corners of her lovely lips. Andrew's shaft jumped to life beneath his trousers. It was the first time she'd smiled at him when it wasn't forced or deliberate, and damn if it wasn't worth the wait.

"I know. I looked your shelves over carefully. You have many books I will enjoy reading, but this is the book that Lady Colebrooke's reading society is reading right now. I've joined their group. I'm a few chapters behind so I need to catch up before I meet with them again this afternoon."

"I didn't know Isabella still had her reading society since she married last year."

"Yes, from what I understand it's very well attended each year during the Season."

"Odd. If I'm remembering correctly that group was once referred to as the Wallflower Society."

"Really? Why is that? No, I'm sorry. Forget I asked. I didn't mean to disturb you again and draw you into conversation. Please go back to your paper. I'll ask Lynette to fill me in on the group's history."

She immediately looked down at her book and started reading again.

He must really have been like a wild boar to Olivia a few mornings ago when he didn't want her interrupting him while he was reading the paper. She was determined not to bother him now, but today for some reason that was exactly what he wanted. He wasn't interested in the news.

He was interested in Olivia and he wanted to talk to her.

A few minutes later Whibbs and a maid walked in with steaming plates of eggs and ham.

Olivia marked her place with a satin ribbon bookmark, closed her book, and laid it aside. He did the same with his paper.

As soon as the servants left, Olivia turned to Andrew and said, "About the other night. I want you to know I have no intentions of trying to trap the Marquis for Lynette. I wouldn't do that. I was merely speaking favorably of Lynette to the Marquis."

She seemed sincere but she had appeared sincere when she said she didn't intend to leg-shackle him. "You must have had a reason for doing that," he replied slowly.

"I did. A very good reason, but I don't know that I should tell you."

Was she indicating she couldn't trust him? Andrew didn't know much about what was expected in a marriage, but one thing he did know was that he wanted his wife to trust him.

"Why not?" he asked. "Is there something about the Marquis I don't know?"

"No, but there is something about Lynette you may not know and I must have your promise that you won't say a word to anyone before I tell you."

Andrew suddenly realized that he and Olivia were having a conversation where they weren't snipping at each other. And he was enjoying it. She really had his curiosity high.

"You have it."

"Lynette is in love with the Marquis and has been for years."

That got his attention. He never expected Olivia to say something like that, and he couldn't help but be suspicious.

"But you hardly know her, why would she have told you her intimate feelings?"

"Perhaps she told me because no one else has ever asked her. I've noticed that a lot of people enjoy talking to Lynette, but they talk about themselves or someone else. No one ever asks Lynette about Lynette."

Now that Olivia had pointed this out, Andrew was sure it must be true. The only thing he ever heard about Lynette was what a lovely person she was. Did everyone in the *ton* overlook Lynette's feelings?

"I observed the way she looked at him," Olivia said. "And the way she watched his every move even if he was on the other side of the room. I asked her about him and she freely admitted she has loved him since her first Season."

Lynette in love? He'd never considered the possibility.

"Has she told anyone else?"

"I have no idea, and I have told you only because you questioned my integrity."

With good reason.

"I only mentioned some of her attributes to the Marquis because sometimes we fail to see what is right before our eyes."

Was that true?

Andrew could tell by the expression on Olivia's face that she was imploring him to believe her and he realized he wanted to. He wanted to forget she'd trapped him into marriage and take her to bed.

But something held him back.

"Yes, sometimes we see too much and there are other times we don't see at all."

Their plates of food remained in front of them untouched. Andrew laid his napkin in his lap and picked up his fork. He was impressed with his wife. She'd seen what others had missed, that Lynette needed a friend, someone she could confide in, and Olivia had offered help.

He wasn't sure he wanted to soften his feelings about his wife. It was bad enough that he wanted to bed her. He didn't want to start caring for her as well. That would put him in a hell of a spot.

It was best for him to continue to see her as the woman who duped him into marriage.

Later that afternoon Olivia walked back inside the house feeling better than she'd felt since she'd come to London. Her second afternoon with the reading society had been challenging but wonderful.

While they had tea, Lynette had filled her in on why the group had once been called the Wallflower Society by a group of the confirmed bachelors.

Isabella had once been very shy. After she became confident in herself she wanted to help other young ladies who were shy or reticent for one reason or another. Today they had one young lady who was missing a front tooth and another who walked with a limp. There was a beautiful young lady who had no use of her left arm since birth. At the reading society all ladies were made to feel equal and special. Isabella talked to them about being confident in every aspect of life.

Olivia considered it a splendid thing to do for the young ladies and she had enjoyed every moment of the meeting.

After the meeting she and Lynette had made another trip to the apothecary. He was developing a cream for her to use that would cover her birthmark. The shade of the concoction was still too light, so he had asked her to come back in a day or two for another test.

Olivia was also feeling good because she and Andrew

had actually talked that morning. She saw a softening in him that she hadn't seen before. He was still wary of her. She saw it in his eyes and the way he held himself in check whenever he was with her, but a crack in his hardness had occurred.

She understood his feelings, but she had to hope that in time he would come to realize she had not tricked him into marrying her.

She stopped in the foyer and took off her wet bonnet, cape, and gloves.

"Good afternoon, Madame. I trust you had a pleasant time."

"Lovely, Whibbs, simply lovely. I didn't even mind the drenching rain."

He took her things from her and said, "That's good. I'm going out on an errand. Do you need anything before I go?"

"No, thank you. I had tea at Lady Colebrooke's. The only thing I need is to go up to my room and get out of these wet shoes."

Later, after donning a pair of dry slippers, Olivia walked to her wardrobe to put away her reticule. She laid the black velvet drawstring purse on a shelf and suddenly went still.

She heard voices again.

Whispered voices of a man and a woman.

Was she going mad? Had her aunt's talk of searching for Lord Pinkwater affected Olivia in some way?

She remained still for a moment and listened. Her mind was not playing tricks on her. She heard talking.

Whibbs was the only male servant who worked in the house and he had just told her he was on his way out to run an errand.

Perhaps he hadn't left. Perhaps Andrew was home.

Olivia moved to the center of the room, trying to

ascertain where the voices were coming from. They sounded as if they were coming from the walls, but that couldn't be. The people had to be belowstairs, or upstairs right down the hall. She slowly opened her bedroom door and stepped out into the corridor.

She heard nothing.

She walked over to the top of the stairs and listened below.

All was quiet.

Looking behind her she saw the door to Andrew's room. Dare she? A shiver shook her but it wasn't cold in the house. She'd go to his door and listen. But nothing would make her open that door and go inside his room again.

Feeling a little guilty, she quietly tiptoed down to Andrew's bedchamber. She put her ear to the door but heard nothing. The voices hadn't come from inside his room, either.

She shook her head in confusion. There had to be a reasonable explanation. Perhaps she was just hearing something that sounded like voices. She walked back into her bedchamber and all was quiet for a moment or two and then suddenly she heard the voices again.

A woman's voice and then a man's.

"This is ridiculous," she whispered to herself. "I am not a madwoman. I am not going insane, but I am going to find who in this house is behind those voices be they human or ghosts."

Olivia walked out her door with purpose. There was only one place left to look.

Upstairs.

She knew there were guest rooms directly above her. They had no guests in the house, so all of those rooms should be empty. She supposed she could be hearing voices from the servants' floor, but she had her doubts voices would carry that far. It didn't matter; she wasn't going to stop looking until she found them.

Olivia lifted the hem of her skirt and slowly climbed the steep stairs. It was darker than she expected at the top of the landing. There was only one small window and the gray late afternoon didn't offer much light. She thought about going back down for a light but admonished herself for being so apprehensive instead and kept climbing.

She told herself that she was a sensible woman and she was not going to come face to face with Lord Pinkwater's ghost. She must swallow her anxiety and open each door on the corridor and look inside.

The first door she opened very slowly so that it made no sound and peeked inside. It showed a small, plain room with only a bed, chest, and chair in it. The second and third rooms looked just like the first.

Her footfalls were silent in her slipper-shod feet as she made her way to the last door at the end of the corridor. She slowly turned the knob just as she had the other three. But it didn't move. She tried harder.

It was locked. She thought she heard a shuffling movement inside the room and put her ear to the door. There was the sound of feet on the floor and a woman's whisper.

Olivia knocked and said, "Hello. Is anyone in here?"

There was more moving around for a moment or two and then the door suddenly swung open.

"Ellie!" Olivia exclaimed.

The maid's face was as white as if she'd seen a ghost, except for her lips. They were a dark pink. Her eyes looked almost wild.

"What are you doing in here with the door locked?"

"I was cleaning," she said nervously.

Olivia knew that wasn't true. She had been told not to touch anything in the house. Her duties were limited to Olivia's comfort.

Gently pushing past Ellie, Olivia walked into the small chilly room and looked around. The only thing that appeared different from the other three rooms was the abundance of wrinkles in the bedcovers. This bed had the look of being hastily made.

Ellie saw Olivia's gaze and quickly said, "I was taking a nap, Lady Dugdale. I know I shouldn't have. I know it was wrong, but I was so tired I thought my eyes might close while I was standing up. It was just for a short time, and I didn't think you would need me as you were out for the afternoon."

"You were sleeping?"

Ellie didn't look sleepy. She looked frightened.

"I know I shouldn't have. If you'll give me another chance I promise I won't do it again. I promise."

Olivia stared at Ellie. It was quite clear the bed had been disturbed, but Olivia wasn't sure Ellie had been sleeping on it.

"I heard voices," Olivia said.

Ellie's eyes widened. Her hands held tight to the hem of her apron. "Not from here. Or maybe I might have been talking in my sleep. I do that sometimes."

"I heard a man's voice."

"Oh, no, my lady, not from this room. If you heard a man it must have been Mr. Whibbs."

"He's gone. I spoke to him just before he went out."

"It was only me here, Countess. Look around. There's no place for anyone to hide."

Olivia looked carefully around the room. There were no wardrobes and the bed was too low to the floor for anyone to fit underneath. There simply was no place for anyone, especially a man, to hide.

"Please don't dismiss me." Her bottom lip trembled. "I promise I won't ever do this again."

Olivia knew she'd heard a man's voice, but it was clear there was no one in this room other than Ellie. Was it possible the man had slipped down the servants' stairs when she went back into her room after leaving Andrew's door? But how would a man have slipped into the house without anyone seeing him in the first place?

A strange feeling washed over her. She was seeing and hearing a man who couldn't be explained.

Olivia knew she should dismiss Ellie on the spot, but something held her back, and it was more than just the distraught look on the girl's face and the nervous fists of her hands.

What if Ellie was telling the truth? Olivia knew what it felt like to be accused of something that wasn't true. Andrew thought she had trapped him into marriage. She could understand why he felt that way because her aunt had insisted on the marriage. But that didn't make it true.

She reasoned she had to give Ellie the benefit of the doubt about no man being in the room with her, but what was she going to do about the maid slipping off during the day to sleep?

"What you've done is not acceptable."

Ellie's eyes looked too large for her elfin face. She blinked back tears. "I know, Madame. Just give me one more chance. Please. I don't have anywhere else to go."

Olivia was conflicted. Should she allow Ellie another chance? Would she be doing great harm to the maid's mother and sister if she didn't keep Ellie?

"All right, Ellie, one more chance. Is that understood?"

She smiled gratefully and her tears spilled onto her white cheeks. "Bless you, Madame. Yes, I understand and I promise I won't let this happen again."

"All right. Now get the wrinkles out of those bedcovers before you leave this room. And, Ellie, think twice before you do something else that you are not supposed to do. This is your last chance."

Olivia turned and walked out of the room. She was mistress of this house and it was her place to make the right decisions. She just didn't know if she had. She only knew that she wanted Andrew to give her a second chance to show him she was not the manipulator he thought her to be.

*H*E WAS IN a hell of a mess.

He wasn't interested in her.

Damnation! Had Olivia ruined him for all other women?

Andrew stepped out of the small house into the gray late-afternoon rain. He placed his hat on his head but didn't bother with his gloves as he headed for his carriage on the other side of the street.

He had just spent the better part of an hour with a beautiful young woman who knew all the ways to make a man groan with pleasure, and he was walking away from her. If he had any sense he'd be in her bed right now straddling her, buried so deep in her he'd never want to leave.

But no.

He was leaving with that same frustrated feeling he'd had since he first found Olivia in his room. No other woman commanded his attention like Olivia.

Within minutes of seeing Arabelle Woodward again he knew he'd made a mistake in going to see her. He didn't want to renew their relationship. Similarly, within moments of arriving at Alice Thunderberry's house he knew he didn't want to be there.

He wanted Olivia. Despite all her trickery, he wanted only Olivia.

Andrew lifted his collar against the rain and stepped off the curb to cross the street when suddenly he heard the pounding of horses' hooves on hard-packed ground. He heard the jingle of a harness and the rattle of a carriage. He heard a man yell as he looked up and saw two large brown horses and a phaeton bearing down on him.

In an instant, Andrew dove for the other side of the street and felt a horse's hoof clip his ankle as he landed on the cobblestones with a grunt and a roll. The horses and carriage thundered on past him, splattering mud and water all over him.

The carriage didn't slow down.

He lay in a muddy puddle for a moment, his heart pounding with the knowledge of how close he had come to dying. He would have sworn to anyone that he felt the horses' hot breath on his neck and the chilling wind from the carriage wheels on his face. A sharp pain shot through his ankle when he stood up, but he could put weight on the foot so, thankfully, it wasn't broken.

"Are you all right, my lord?" his coachman asked as he ran over to Andrew and tried to help him stand.

"Fine, fine," Andrew said, brushing off the man's assistance.

"That cowhanded fool didn't even stop to see if you were hurt."

"Did you get a look at him?" Andrew asked as he tested his ankle again for weight.

"No, sir. The rain's too heavy. Everything's a blur. My

thoughts are he was one of them reckless youth, who hasn't learned how to control his cattle. Should I try to find him?"

"No, no need. It was my fault. I wasn't looking where I was going. Thankfully my ankle seems fine and there was no harm done. Let's go."

"Where to?" the coachman asked.

Andrew had planned to swing by White's and have a drink or two before picking Olivia up for the evening's parties.

"Home," he answered.

Fifteen

As soon as Ellie had helped Olivia fasten her pale blue gown Olivia dismissed her. Olivia sat down at her dressing table and with jeweled combs arranged her hair on top of her head. Lastly, she pulled the choker of pearls with the large sapphire in the center out of her jewelry box and fastened it around her neck.

The more she thought about the maid the more she wondered if she should have given her a second chance. In truth, Ellie had been given a second chance when Olivia allowed her to stay on as her maid. As mistress of her husband's house she wanted to be fair and compassionate with the staff, but she had to set limits.

One thing was certain, no matter Ellie's pleading eyes or promises to do better, Olivia would not allow her to stay if she made another misstep. She would go immediately.

A knock sounded on Olivia's door and without thinking about who it might be she said, "Come in."

The door opened and Andrew stepped inside. He was handsomely dressed in his evening attire of coat with tails, beige brocade waistcoat, and buckled shoes. The only thing about him that didn't look absolutely splendid was the expression on his face.

She rose from her stool and asked, "Is something wrong?"

His gaze swept down her face and slowly took in the length of her before meeting her stare. He quietly said, "Yes."

Olivia walked to the foot of her bed. She felt heaviness in her chest. "What? You look distressed."

"Is that how I look?" A half laugh rumbled past his lips. "Yes, I'm sure I do. I am, and it's all because of you, my dear wife."

She should have known she was the cause of the wrinkle between his brows. She had done nothing but make mistakes since she first stepped foot in this house. She had hoped one day to be loved by her husband and not be left alone like her mother, but she was beginning to think that wasn't going to happen.

Olivia took a deep breath before asking, "What have I done now that has displeased you so?"

He reached behind him, closed the door, and then turned the key in the lock. "Did I say you displeased me?"

Olivia's chest tightened. Something in the way he looked made her want to back away from him but she forced herself to remain calm and still by the bed. She would not allow him to scare her away.

She cleared her throat. "No, but you said I had caused you distress. Are you going to tell me what the problem is?"

"I narrowly missed being trampled by two horses and a carriage this afternoon."

All concern for herself fled and fear for Andrew's safety struck her. She took a step toward him. "Are you all right?" she asked.

He nodded. "A bruised ankle is all, but that isn't what's bothering me."

"Then what?" she asked, feeling very thankful he wasn't injured or worse.

His expression relaxed a little, but the intensity stayed in his eyes. "I want you, Olivia."

Her pulse quickened and her heartbeat raced. That was not what she had expected him to say. "You told me this on our wedding night, yet you left me," she challenged him. "What has changed?"

"The timing. I want you now."

Olivia felt as if her stomach flipped. She had been waiting for him to come to her and make her his wife, but why now?

"Your timing is not good. We're expected to attend three parties tonight."

"To hell with the parties."

"You think I deliberately tricked you into marriage. You believe I was trying to trap the Marquis for Lynette. How can you want me?"

"The answer is simple. You have tempted me beyond my endurance. After I was almost run down this afternoon the only thing I could think about was how much I wanted you and what a fool I was to deny myself."

"No matter what kind of person you believe me to be?"

"No matter," he answered. "I have tasted you. I can't forget you and now I must have you."

Olivia felt as if her heart stopped beating. Wasn't this what she wanted, to be a wife to her husband in every way possible?

His gaze never left her face as he walked close enough to her to reach out and run the backs of his fingers lightly across her cheek. The lace from his cuff tickled her bare shoulder, causing her nipples to harden. She remembered how wonderful she'd felt when he'd taken her breast into his mouth.

"We're not going anywhere tonight, Olivia. We're not even going to leave this room to eat. I'm going to make love to you lying down, standing up, and sitting on the bed. We're going to make love on the floor and on our knees. I'm going to make love to you all night long. And when I'm through, you will have forgotten every man's name but mine."

His eyes were like glowing amber orbs, mesmerizing her. His face seemed relaxed and intense at the same time. With his penetrating gaze and seductive voice, he seduced her and she believed every word he spoke.

"I think of no man but you," she answered honestly.

One corner of his mouth lifted in a delicious-looking half smile. "That's the way I want it."

With the pads of his fingers he outlined her lips as his gaze swept down her face. She smelled that wonderful musky mint scent of his soap on his hand and her chest tightened.

"I'm going to take you fast the first time. It's been too long since I've been with a woman. My desire for you is great, and I won't be able to take it slow and wait. But after the first time, I'll give you pleasure beyond your wildest dreams. Do you understand what I'm saying?"

Oh, yes!

Andrew's fingertips still lay softly on her lips, so rather than speak, she nodded. She knew that the first time a woman mated with a man that there was discomfort, but Olivia was not worried. With Andrew there was no fear.

"It's going to be a long night. I'm not stopping until I've had my fill of you."

Her eyes searched his face for some deeper emotion than desire. What would happen to her when he had all he wanted from her? Did it mean he would send her away when he was satisfied?

Olivia closed her heart to such thoughts. They were for another day. She wouldn't let those concerns ruin tonight.

His fingertips left her lips and traveled down her chin, her neck, over her necklace to rest on the swell of her breasts that showed from beneath the neckline of her gown.

"You don't look frightened," he said.

"I'm not," she freely admitted.

"Good. I'll try not to hurt you."

You could only hurt me by sending me away.

He reached up and gently took the combs from her hair and let them fall to the floor as her hair fell past her shoulders, down her back. He pulled the length of it into his hands and threaded his fingers through it. Lifting the strands up to his nose, he breathed in deeply.

"It looks like golden silk. You're even more beautiful with your hair down, Olivia."

"Thank you," she whispered.

"I've tried so hard not to want you. You know that, don't you."

She nodded. He couldn't have made that any plainer over the last few days.

"I've tried to forget the times I've held you, touched you, and kissed you. But I can't. I'm desperate to make you mine."

"I haven't forgotten your touch, either."

"After tonight, you never will."

He let go of her hair and placed his hands onto her waist

and lifted her up on the bed and sat her down. Olivia had no idea what he was going to do and it didn't matter. She knew that too much had happened between them. He didn't trust her.

But she trusted him.

Andrew took hold of her shoulders and gently leaned her back on the bed, leaving her feet and legs hanging off the side. He remained standing, looking down at her. His gaze swept up and down her.

Olivia remembered that first night in his room when she'd watched him undress and show off his magnificent body. To her surprise, this time he didn't even take off his coat or neckcloth.

He reached down and slowly ran his hand over the bare part of her chest, letting his fingers glide lightly over her breasts and then up to the necklace at the base of her throat. He fingered the pearls a moment before skimming her skin all the way back down to her waist, stopping long enough to feel the indention before continuing along the flare of her hips, down her thighs.

Softly, slowly he let his palm graze over her most womanly part. Olivia felt such a shock of pleasure that she sucked in her breath. Her gaze flew up to his.

"You'll get used to my touch," he said. "Do you want me to turn out the lamp, or are you all right with it on?"

That would mean she couldn't see his magnificent body. She didn't like that idea. "I want to watch you," she said.

A hint of a smile played at his lips. "Good. I want to look at you, too."

Andrew reached down and pulled her blue gown up past her knees, past her thighs, past her waist to bunch just beneath her breasts. A shiver of anticipation shook her but she wasn't frightened. She was enthralled.

He reached beneath her to her back and untied the drawstring that held her drawers on and gently stripped them down her legs and off over her shoes. He pushed her chemise up with her gown, parted her knees, and stepped between them.

Olivia watched his eyes as he looked down at that part of her no one had seen since she was a babe. Olivia was surprised that she felt no shame or embarrassment as he devoured her body with his eyes. All she felt was expectancy. She had been waiting for this.

"The length of your golden hair is not the only beautiful thing about you that I haven't seen before. Your body is lovely, Olivia."

"I'm glad you are satisfied with me."

"Very. No woman has ever tempted me greater than you."

"Is that a good thing or bad?"

A half chuckle sounded in his throat. "I haven't decided. All I know is that even when I'm out at night gambling, drinking, or racing, I can't stop thinking about you being here waiting for me to come home."

Olivia smiled at him, showing that his words pleased her.

He reached down and cupped her waist, almost encircling it in his manly hands before letting his open hands plane softly down her stomach, down her thighs to the top of her stockings and back up to her innermost part.

Olivia's abdomen contracted crazily at his gentle touch. She gasped and slightly lifted her hips off the bed as he parted the folds of her womanhood and touched her core with tender strokes of his fingers.

His eyes darted back to her face. "Are you all right?" he whispered huskily.

"I'm not sure," she said a little breathlessly.

"Am I hurting you?"

"No. I don't know what you're doing, but I've never felt anything so, so wonderful, so heavenly."

"I'm only touching you. Relax and enjoy what is about to happen."

Olivia felt her body lifting to meet the motions of his fingers. Delicious spirals of sensations she'd never felt before had her gasping for breath. She heard soft moaning sounds and knew they must be coming from her lips.

Slowly Andrew dropped to his knees in front of her and removed his fingers and replaced them with his mouth and his tongue. They played on her center.

Olivia was horrified and glorified at the same time. She gasped again and tried to rise.

Andrew's hand flew to her chest and gently pressed her back down on the bed as he continued to caress her with his tongue. Within moments she realized she didn't want to rise and stop him, she didn't want to understand. She only wanted the amazing feelings to go on forever.

She didn't care what he was doing to her. What mattered was the way he was making her feel with his hot mouth and his quick tongue.

The tension and the vibrations quickly built deeply inside her. She picked up his hand from her chest and carried it to her lips. She purred and moaned into his palm while his tongue tormented her with a pleasure she had never experienced before. She arched her hips up to meet his mouth, not knowing any other way to respond to the new sensations wracking her body.

She didn't know what was happening. She only knew it was building fast. If this madness of pleasure didn't stop soon she felt she would burst with joy.

Suddenly she felt as if all the sensations that were bubbling inside her exploded.

"Andrew, Andrew," she whispered into his palm before her arms fell limp at her sides.

The immensity of her pleasure was so overwhelming she suddenly wanted to laugh about how good she felt.

The pleasure he had given her saturated her heart, her body, and her mind, and she knew without a doubt that she loved her husband with all that she was.

Andrew rose up over her again, his honey-colored eyes dark with desire. She watched as his strong hands, his manly fingers, unbuttoned his trousers, releasing his long, thick, and pulsing shaft to her view.

The large size of him surprised her but didn't frighten her. She was contented and ready for whatever came next.

Her legs remained off the bed. He remained standing over her for a moment longer, giving her more time to look at him before he bent over her and placed his manhood at her center. He held himself above her with one arm resting on the bed. She felt the hard push of him at her core. It was uncomfortable but not painful.

"You're too big," she whispered up at him.

He glanced down into her eyes and though his lips remained in a determined set, his eyes smiled at her as he said, "Oh, no Olivia, watch me. It will fit."

Suddenly his manhood broke through her barrier and slid inside her. She moaned from the unexpected pain and grabbed his shoulders. His hands circled her waist as he continued to push harder and further inside her.

"Hold on to me, Olivia."

She wrapped her arms around his strong back and buried her face in his crisp neckcloth as he continued to thrust his hips up and down and submerge himself deeper inside her. She heard his labored breaths, as if he were running with all his might. His hands slid from her waist up to her back and he cupped her to him.

A moment or two later his body went still and slowly he let his body press down on top of her, giving her all his weight.

"Damn, Olivia, oh damn," he whispered through heaving breaths as he rested his forehead on her shoulder.

She continued to hold him tight and said, "Did I displease you?"

He raised his head and looked down into her eyes. "No, no. What makes you think that?"

"You were cursing me."

Andrew smiled and grunted a laugh. "I was not cursing you. Sometimes men swear when they feel good as well as when they are angry."

She moistened her lips. "Does that mean I did all right?"

His burning, golden gaze held fast to hers. "You were perfect."

Olivia smiled a little shyly at him and said, "So were you."

Andrew lifted his head and looked down at his wife. He had given her pleasure before he entered her but didn't know if that would be enough to blunt the pain of losing her virginity. But he hadn't even kissed her on the lips. He knew he had to have release before he could love her as he wanted to, as she deserved to be loved.

"No, Olivia, I wasn't perfect. Far from it. I should have been gentler. I should have but I couldn't. I wanted you too badly."

"I meant you were the perfect size."

Andrew laughed and her arms tightened on his back and

he realized he loved the way her womanly arms felt around him. He loved the way she felt cuddled beneath him.

"And it was only painful for a moment or two," she added.

"It shouldn't hurt at all next time."

"I've never felt so, so many sensations at one time. There's nothing I can compare it to."

He smiled down at her, grateful that he had the good sense to see to her release before he grabbed his own.

"Nothing like it in the world," Andrew said as his thoughts drifted for a moment.

He'd tried to get interested in two different women since he had married Olivia, but he hadn't been able to. Both had left him feeling completely uninterested in taking them to his bed. He didn't understand it, but Olivia was the only woman he wanted right now and he wasn't going to fight his desire for her any longer.

She reached up and touched his lips with her fingertips. "I never imagined you could . . . do what you did with your mouth."

Oh, damn. Her words, her touch, had him growing inside her again.

He caught her fingertips into his mouth and sucked them for a moment before releasing them and saying, "I have many things to show you about my mouth and about yours."

She looked at him with innocent eyes that told him she wanted to know more. He took a deep breath and he grew bigger. He pressed into her with his hips. He hadn't been wrong about her. She was passionate.

Very, very passionate.

He lowered his head and his mouth met hers in a gentle kiss, sipping lightly from her until he felt her lips part. His

tongue slid between them and sank into the sweet hollow
of her mouth, dipping in and out again several times, teasing them both with playful strokes.

This intimacy with her felt so right. He wondered why
he had resisted her. His hand slid up to her breasts and he
opened his eyes and looked down. They were still fully
clothed.

Damnation, he had been in such a hurry he hadn't taken
one article of clothing off either of them.

He wanted to see her naked, completely naked, where
he could have the freedom to touch her and taste her wherever he pleased. But she was too alluring and he was too
settled inside her right now to bother with removing their
clothing.

Their evening had just started. There was plenty of time
for that later tonight. He wasn't ready to withdraw from her.

With eager hands he slipped her dress off her shoulders
and dragged down her bodice and her undergarment, freeing her breasts to his gaze and for his touch. He loved the
purring sound she made softly in her throat as his hands
skimmed over her nipples.

They grew hard and erect against his palm.

Andrew grew harder, too.

He took one nipple into his mouth and gently sucked its
sweetness before moving to the next. Her whole body was
delicious to him. He loved the way her nipples puckered
for him as he gently sucked them into his mouth and
played with them. He loved the full swell of her breasts.
They were plump but firm.

No woman had ever tasted sweeter.

When he kissed her again it was with desperation. An
unexpected urgency to take his pleasure from her once
again burned inside him.

He slanted his lips over hers and he felt her shudder with desire. He felt her sudden intake of breath as he slowly started moving again. He loved the feel of his manhood cradled at the center of her womanhood.

They lay thighs to thighs, stomach to stomach, and chest to breasts. Hungrily his lips moved over hers. His hand continued to skim her breasts and he thought he might lose himself inside her again before he got her ready to join him.

He slid one of his hands between them down to her womanly mound; her hair was soft. With ease he slipped one finger to her core and massaged her. She lifted her hips in satisfaction. His stomach tightened. She was moist and throbbing. He smiled against her lips.

"Oh God, I want you as if I'd never had you."

"I'm ready," she whispered and lifted her legs and wrapped them around his back.

He withdrew and then penetrated her wet silkiness with one long push, going in as deeply as he could with the first thrust. Her muscles tightened around him and he thought he might lose himself in her again with one stroke, but he held off.

He had to move slowly, very slowly so as not to end too fast. She moved with him, intensifying his pleasure. He groaned with a pleasure that superceded all that came before Olivia.

"Move with me. Stay with me," he murmured against her lips.

"I'm feeling it again," she whispered.

"Yes, Olivia, let it come. Take it."

He kissed her more tenderly than he ever had, wanting her to feel the way he felt.

She cried out her release at the same time he spilled himself into her for the second time.

Andrew slipped his arms under her back and pulled her tightly to him. He'd never felt more satisfied, more gratified by a woman.

In that moment he knew he didn't give a damn about what she had done to marry him. He only knew that no other woman had ever made him feel as complete and contented as Olivia had, and she was his.

No woman had ever touched his heart like she had.

Heart?

Andrew shook those thoughts away as he buried his nose in the crook of her neck and inhaled her womanly scent. He wasn't ready to think about anything having to do with feelings of the heart.

Sixteen

OLIVIA'S EYES FLUTTERED open. It was daylight. She immediately looked over at the other side of the bed.

Andrew was gone.

The pillow still had the indentation where his head lay. Had he been gone long? She reached over and touched the sheets.

They were cold.

When had she drifted to sleep? The last thing she remembered was Andrew stretched out beside her, cuddling her in his arms. Her cheek lay on his warm, strong chest and their bodies touched all the way down to her toes.

In a rush of memory all the kisses, touches, and mating of their bodies flooded her mind. She smiled contentedly. Had she really touched him with such abandon? Had he really moaned with such pleasure that her very soul felt connected to his?

Or had it all been just a wonderful dream?

Olivia looked over at the pillow again. He had definitely lain on it.

Last night was not a dream.

It was real.

Her husband had not only been skillful at pleasing her, he had been masterful at teaching her how to give him pleasure. Such undeniable pleasure.

And there was no doubt in her mind that she had pleased him.

Feeling languid, she stretched her arms up and over her head and suddenly realized she was naked beneath the covers. Suddenly, she put her hand to her throat. That is, she was completely nude except for her pearl necklace. That was the only thing Andrew hadn't taken off her during the night.

She sat up in bed and looked around the room. All her clothing had been draped over her slipper chair. Andrew must have picked up her clothes. She remembered him taking his time in disrobing her and throwing each piece to the floor.

Olivia lifted her hands up to her breasts. They were tender to her touch and there was a slight discomfort between her legs, but inside her heart she had never felt better in her life. She truly felt the happiness inside herself that Agatha had talked about.

But was Andrew happy?

She glanced at the clock on her dressing table and saw that it was half past one in the afternoon. She never slept past noon. But then she had never spent the night in a man's arms before.

Suddenly Olivia scrambled off the bed and over to her dressing table and poured cold water from the pitcher into the basin. If she hurried, maybe she could catch Andrew before he left for the day.

Within minutes she had washed, dressed, and put her hair in a neat chignon. After picking up her copy of *Murder on the Thames* she headed to the dining room, slowing down only as she approached the doorway.

She took in a deep breath, put a comfortable smile on her face, and walked inside. Her heart fluttered with the warm feeling of love.

Andrew sat at the table reading his paper. Clean shaven, hair neatly combed, neckcloth tied in a simple bow. He looked so handsome, so dashing. In that moment she knew that all the loving feelings she'd felt for him last night were still with her this afternoon and they were not going to go away. They had started the first night she'd seen him standing in the doorway of his home. Across the space they had connected.

He had captured her heart and it now belonged to him.

Andrew lowered the news paper when he heard her walk inside the room. Their eyes met.

She had an overwhelming desire to rush over and throw her arms around him and kiss him with all the passion she had discovered last night. She wanted to tell him how much she loved him and how much she wanted to be a good wife to him. All she needed were more opportunities like last night to show him.

"Good morning, Olivia."

His eyes had searched hers but his tone held no warmth and his lips had no smile.

She swallowed hard and her smile faded. There was no sign of the lover who'd been in her bed last night. A deep disappointment settled over her.

After all the lovemaking they had shared, she still wanted more from him. She wanted his love, his respect, his attention. She wanted him to believe that she hadn't trapped him into marriage. She wanted him to believe she wasn't trying to trick the Marquis into marrying Lynette.

Olivia wanted him to believe she was worthy of his love.

But if he didn't know that after the way she responded to him last night, a few more words from her would not change his mind.

"Good morning, Andrew," she said, sounding a little stiffer than she had intended.

She laid her book on the table and walked over to the buffet to pour tea.

Andrew rose and helped her with her chair but didn't touch her. She had expected more from him. Last night might have changed everything for her, but it was clear it had changed nothing for him.

An ache formed in her chest. Only Andrew could stop the pain.

Didn't he know that she could have never responded to him as she did if she didn't love him? How could he not know how she felt about him? Could it be that he knew and didn't care?

She immediately opened her book and started reading, but after only a few words, her gaze stayed on the page but didn't move. Her mind replayed the intimacies she and Andrew had shared last night.

How could *Murder on the Thames* compete with memories of her night in bed with Andrew?

Her thoughts tortured her with remembrance of his mouth on her lips, her breasts, and her most womanly part. She remembered the full feeling of his body throbbing inside hers.

"Olivia?"

Olivia jumped and looked up at Andrew. "Oh, did you say something?"

He gave her a half smile and her heart fluttered again, offering a little hope. "I called your name three times."

"I'm sorry, I didn't hear you."

"That must be a very interesting book you're reading."

"Yes, it is." She glanced down at the pages for a moment, feeling a bit guilty about her prevarication. "Did you want something?"

She looked into his eyes and for a moment thought just maybe he might be thinking about last night, too.

But he made no mention of it when he folded his paper and said, "I have several things to do today and I'm getting a late start."

"I'll have Whibbs get your breakfast right away," she said and started to rise.

"No, don't get up. I've already eaten. I was just waiting until you came down before I left."

For the first time she looked down at his plate. "Oh, I see. Then don't let me keep you," she said coolly. "I'm sure you have a lot of things to do."

"I probably won't be back until it's time to go to the first party."

He sounded so formal she had no choice but to answer in the same tone. "I shall be ready at the usual time. I hope you have a good day."

He rose and asked, "Will you go to your reading group today?"

"No, that was yesterday. I think I'll visit my aunt later."

"Give her my regards," he said and walked out of the room.

Olivia's heart sank to the floor. Andrew had made her his wife, but now she wanted to be a part of his life, too. She wanted him to love her and want to be with her. Would he ever forgive her for the forced marriage?

After a walk in the garden, Olivia ate breakfast and went upstairs to change into a carriage dress. But before she made it out of the house Ellie announced that Lady Lynette was in the parlor and wanted to see her if she was available.

A few minutes later Olivia walked into the parlor. "Lynette, I'm so glad you came by. I was just thinking about stopping by to see you after visiting Aunt Agatha."

Lynette rose from the settee and turned toward Olivia.

Olivia gasped in surprise as a smile stretched across her face. Lynette was wearing the flesh-colored paste from the apothecary over her birthmark and the dark red skin hardly showed at all. From a distance it looked as if the birthmark had disappeared. How wonderful for her friend.

"You look beautiful," Olivia said sincerely as she stood in front of her friend.

Lynette laughed. "I do, don't I," she said.

"Yes, you do. Absolutely lovely. Your birthmark is gone."

"Just hidden," Lynette said. "I had a note from the apothecary waiting for me when I rose. He asked me to come at once. It was much too early to call on you so I went with just my maid. He put the cream on and when I saw myself in the looking glass I started crying."

"Oh, Lynette, I hope they were tears of happiness."

"Of course. I can't thank you enough for all your help. Long ago I gave up hope there was anything that could make this disappear." She lightly touched her cheek. "But look what a few years have done."

Lynette reached over and gave Olivia an unexpected hug.

Touched by her friend's show of warmth, Olivia embraced her with enthusiasm and patted her affectionately on the back.

"I'm just so happy you have the confidence to wear the

concoction outside your house where others can see you. It really covers the birthmark very well."

"I think it's miraculous," Lynette said as they parted and sat down on the settee.

"Has your father seen you?"

"Yes, and all the servants, too, though none of them has had the courage to say a word to me," she said and then finished with a girlish giggle.

"What did your father say?"

"What you would expect a father to say. That I'm beautiful just as I am and I don't need anything to cover what God saw fit to give me."

"Your father is right. You are beautiful inside and out and you always have been," Olivia assured her.

"But I told him I want to do this. For the first time in my life I want people looking at me and not seeing my birthmark. I told my father that I'm going to wear the cream tonight."

Now that Lynette actually was going to do it, Olivia felt apprehensive for her. "Are you sure you're ready for that?"

"I was ready fifteen years ago."

"You know people will question you about it and talk about you, and I just don't want you to be upset by any of their comments."

"No one could question me more than my father. I'm confident this is what I want to do. I'm ready for their comments. I want to know what they think about me without my birthmark."

"Which party are you going to first? I want to be there in case you need a friend."

"That would be lovely of you, Olivia. I'll go to the Great Hall first. I might as well shock as many people as possible the first time I'm out."

Lynette laughed and Olivia joined her.

"But speaking of parties, what happened to you last night? I never saw you at any of the parties."

"I know. I—I, Andrew and I, well, we—" Olivia felt heat rise in her cheeks. She couldn't believe how dreadfully she was stumbling over her words.

Lynette laughed again. "You don't have to say anything more. I can see that you and your husband decided to spend the evening alone."

"Yes," Olivia said, quite happy to get off that subject. "How was your evening?"

"Oh, lovely. Simply perfect," she said with a teasing smile.

"And what made it perfect?" Olivia asked, though she had a feeling she knew.

"The Marquis of Musgrove Glenn asked me to dance again."

"Lynette, how wonderful."

"Yes, it was wonderful, magnificent, and breathtaking." Her eyes turned dreamy. "It was heavenly. I don't think I dance when I'm with him. I think I float on air the entire time we're together. After the dance we talked about his children. He told me he was impressed I remembered their names."

Olivia smiled. "Did he? How very nice of him to tell you."

"And he's very fond of my father, you know." She stopped and sighed. "But he danced with several other ladies last night. All of them much younger and prettier than I, and two of them are absolutely beautiful."

"I say nonsense to any of them being more beautiful than you. That is simply not true. And they certainly are not more knowledgeable of life and people and managing a house than you. They may be younger than you, but youth is not what the Marquis needs to take on the responsibilities of children. Besides, you are younger than the Marquis, are you not?"

"By four years. I think the dances I've had with him the last few nights are what made me decide I want to wear this cream tonight." She pointed to her cheek. "I want the Marquis more than anyone to see me as I would be without this mark on my face."

Olivia's heart swelled for her friend. They both wanted the love of a man who wasn't prepared to give it.

"I pray he will see you as the beautiful woman you are."

Lynette took in a deep breath. "Before his other two marriages I never tried to gain his attention. I couldn't compete with either of them. But I'm not going to lose this opportunity to let him know that I would make him a good wife and a good mother to his children. It's now or never."

"That's the spirit. But speaking of attention, what will you do if you are written about in Lord Truefitt's column?"

Lynette looked stunned for a moment. "Why would I write about—?" She stopped speaking abruptly, paused, and cleared her throat before saying, "Why would he want to write about me?"

Olivia looked closely at Lynette. She suddenly looked a little flustered and Olivia wasn't sure why.

"Lord Truefitt will write about you because of the change in your appearance, of course. This will be the biggest news of the Season. You must be prepared for the gossip you will stir. Or, perhaps you shouldn't read the gossip columns for a few days if it will upset you. I'm sure you will be mentioned."

Suddenly a cunning smile spread across Lynette's face that Olivia didn't understand. "Oh yes, maybe I will show up in Lord Truefitt's column, at least once. And don't worry about me being upset about it. I think it would be wonderful after all these years to have a little gossip written about me."

Half an hour after Lynette left, Olivia hurried upstairs to get her bonnet, pelisse, and reticule so she could go to her aunt's house. Before she could gather her things together Ellie came up and told her that her aunt had stopped by to see her.

Olivia walked into the parlor and saw Agatha sitting on the settee. Her shoulders and back were straight, her eyes were closed, and her face had that serene expression that she always wore when she was thinking about Lord Pinkwater.

Something stirred inside Olivia, and for the first time she could truly relate to what her aunt must be feeling when she thought about Lord Pinkwater. Olivia would be devastated if Andrew abandoned her for another. She could also feel and understand what her mother must have felt. It would be unbearable to be sent to the country to live while Andrew stayed in London.

What would she do?

Exactly what her mother and aunt had done. Spend her days reliving past love, knowing there was never going to be a future.

Olivia closed her eyes for a moment and silently vowed that she would not let that happen to her. She would not be cast aside by her husband.

"How are you, Auntie?" Olivia said, putting a smile on her face and walking over to the settee. Agatha's lashes fluttered open. Her sharp gaze centered on Olivia's face.

"Livy, dear, I was worried about you when I didn't see you at any of the parties last evening. You're not ill, are you?"

Olivia bent down and kissed her aunt on the cheek. "I am fine." A calming peace settled over Olivia as she sat down beside her aunt. "Andrew and I decided to stay home last night and get to know each other better."

Her aunt looked surprised. "Well, that's nice, dearie. You look happier than I've seen you since we arrived in London."

"I'm finally getting used to London, to my husband, and to marriage."

"That's what I wanted to hear. I know they are all big adjustments for you." She reached over and patted Olivia's hand. "I was so hoping you would find happiness here with the earl. I couldn't help but think there might be something developing between the two of you that first night you met him."

Her aunt was intuitive. If there hadn't been some kind of draw to Andrew Olivia would never have allowed him to kiss her that night. Olivia was sure she hadn't obtained happiness quite yet, but she definitely knew she would if she could change Andrew's opinion of her.

"Now tell me, Livy, I came over because I was thinking about Lord Pinkwater today and I wanted to know if he'd made contact with you yet."

Olivia's heart constricted. Though she had no reasonable explanation for the identity of the man she saw in her room on her wedding night, or the man's voice she heard, she couldn't tell her aunt she thought Lord Pinkwater's ghost was in the house.

"No, Auntie," she said, feeling comfortable with her answer.

"Have you felt his presence at all?"

"I don't think so," Olivia said, not knowing who or what

she had seen and heard in the house. "Has he visited you again or called to you since you've been in London?"

Agatha shook her head. "He's been quiet since I arrived. Except for the first night we came to this house." Her face looked pained for a moment. "I know he's here. Sometimes I feel him so strongly I can hardly bear it, but he won't speak to me. He remains silent, as if waiting for the right moment to speak."

Olivia wished she knew how to help her aunt, how to take away the pain of loss she'd lived with for so many years. In a way she would like for Lord Pinkwater to be a real ghost so he could come to Agatha and put her mind to rest.

"Why do you think he has stopped calling to you now that you are in London where he could reach you?"

"I don't know. I'm confused about that. He must be waiting for what he considers the right time. I think he has always liked the idea of me waiting for him."

And she was still waiting for him, but Olivia knew what Agatha didn't. Lord Pinkwater was never coming back.

"Would you like to walk around the house? Perhaps if you are alone he will speak to you again."

Agatha smiled and patted Olivia's hand again. "I think that is exactly what I'll do."

An hour later, Agatha made more excuses for Lord Pinkwater not showing himself to her and said it was time for her to leave. Olivia said good-bye to her and shut the front door. She turned to see Ellie standing right behind her.

Startled, she said, "Ellie, I didn't know you were be-hind me."

Her big pale blue eyes widened. "I'm sorry, Countess, I didn't mean to frighten you."

"I wasn't exactly frightened," Olivia said, though she wasn't sure that was a true statement. It wasn't like her to be spooked by anything, but all the talk of ghosts must have put her on edge. "Just please announce yourself next time."

"Yes, Countess."

"What did you want?"

"I was going upstairs to prepare your clothes for the evening and wondered if you had a special dress you wanted to wear tonight."

Olivia thought for a moment. "Perhaps the pale yellow one with the three flounces."

"I'll make sure your gloves and everything else match perfectly," Ellie said and then hurried to the rear of the house and up the servants' stairs.

Olivia rubbed her arms as if she were chilled. She tried to shake off the unsettled feeling she had when she saw Ellie standing behind her. Ever since she'd found the maid in the upstairs room she'd felt that something wasn't quite right.

Perhaps her unsettled feeling was simply inspired by Agatha's talk of Lord Pinkwater, or maybe there really were strange things going on in this house.

*T*HERE WAS A horse race in Hyde Park, so activity in various rooms at White's was slow. Andrew didn't even hear the smack of a billiard ball coming from the next room. Any other time he would have been out at the race himself.

Today he just didn't have the desire to go. That was unusual for him. But what was even more unusual was the fact that ever since he'd left his house he'd wanted to turn around and go back and be with his wife.

All he had been doing since he left was think about last night and how good Olivia had made him feel during those hours he'd spent with her. He'd had some idea how she would react to his touch, but she had responded to him beyond his dreams.

He desperately wanted to be with her again.

When he decided to marry Olivia he vowed she wouldn't disrupt his life. He planned to go about his daily and nightly routine as if he wasn't married, he planned to get a mistress, but none of those things were happening as easily as he thought they would.

Olivia kept getting in the way of his returning to his old life.

He hadn't been able to find a mistress because Olivia was the only woman he wanted to take to bed. He had lost his desire to spend the entire night at the clubs gambling, drinking, and gaming because he knew Olivia was at home and he wanted to be there with her. Now he couldn't even enjoy a horse race during the afternoon because he was thinking about Olivia.

She had bewitched him with her quiet presence. He told her he didn't want to talk at breakfast so she brought a book to read. That was damn irritating. He found out quickly that if she was going to be in the room he wanted her attention.

He laughed to himself and picked up his ale. He knew she'd captivated him the moment he saw her in his room, smelling his soap, but a lot of beautiful women had captivated him over the years. He didn't know how or why, but he knew Olivia was different from the rest.

Last night had proved that to him.

"Good Lord, I can't believe you're here. I thought you would have been out at the big race."

Andrew looked up to see Chandler Prestwick walking up to his table.

"You can't believe I'm here? I think it's more of a shock that you are here than I. Didn't you give up coming to White's after you married?"

Chandler chuckled. "Well, not completely. I still come in once in a while as you well know." He pulled out a chair and joined Andrew at the table.

"Obviously, as you are here."

"Today I'm meeting a gentleman who wants to talk with me about that new steam engine that everyone is talking about. He wants me to invest in its development."

Andrew motioned for the waiter to bring Chandler a tankard of ale. "Hmm. I should have known you weren't here in the middle of the afternoon just for drink and entertainment, but there's no reason you can't enjoy ale while you're here."

Chandler looked around the club room. "I see only three other people in this room and they're talking quietly. I don't think you're going to find much gaiety here today. It's all out at Hyde Park."

A good time is not what I'm looking for today.

"Sometimes quiet is good."

The waiter placed a tankard in front of Chandler. He moved it in a circular motion for a moment or two before saying, "John told me about you and Olivia."

Damn.

"Told you what?" Andrew said, hoping he might be wrong about Chandler's meaning.

"That you haven't made love to your wife."

Andrew swore under his breath. "I should have known he'd run right over and tell you."

"We're all three still best friends, Andrew. Our marriages haven't changed that."

"Well, it's no longer true."

Chandler leaned back as if Andrew had tried to strike him. "You don't think we're your best friends? Bloody hell, have we been that distant to you?"

"Hell no. I mean yes. No. We're friends, of course. I meant it's no longer true that I haven't been with my wife."

"Oh—so you've—"

"Yes. Not that it's any of your damn business or John's."

"Of course it is. I was beginning to worry about you. It's not natural not to take your wife to bed."

Andrew chuckled under his breath. He would have loved to have heard the conversation about this between John and Chandler. They probably had a jolly good time at his expense. He wasn't as irritated with them as he should be.

"My relationship with my wife is not something you two should be discussing, and I don't need any lectures from you or John about Olivia."

"Hell, I know that. It's why I've remained quiet. We know she forced you into marriage, but Olivia is still a beautiful woman. You needed to consummate your marriage."

Did Olivia force him into marriage? He used to think that but he wasn't so sure anymore. He could have gotten out of it if he'd tried. There were a couple of other choices.

"How did you know you were falling in love with Millicent?" Andrew asked his friend.

Chandler put down his ale without having sipped it and eyed Andrew curiously. "Is this a trick question?"

"No, damnation, I'm serious."

"All right. I guess the first thing was that I knew I wanted to kiss her the moment I saw her."

Andrew remembered wanting to kiss Olivia, too.

"And then I couldn't stop thinking about her. It was as if nothing mattered except Millicent."

Olivia was just about the only thing he thought about anymore. Even finding the bastard Hawkins was a distant second.

"When I was away from her I wanted to be with her. Whenever I was near her I wanted to touch her. I wanted to take her to my bed and—"

"All right, I understand," Andrew said, holding up his hand to stop Chandler before he told more than Andrew wanted to know.

"I didn't want anyone else to touch her even when dancing. Does any of this sound familiar?"

"No, no." Andrew denied what he knew to be true, but quickly corrected himself and said, "Maybe. Yes."

A knowing grin lifted one side of Chandler's lips. "Are you falling in love with your wife?"

"Oh, damn, I hope not," he whispered under his breath. "That's the last thing I want to do."

Seventeen

❦

$\mathcal{L}$IGHTS FROM THE Great Hall were gleaming, jubilant music played, and the chattering of the crowd rumbled out through the doors as Olivia and Andrew walked up the steps to the ballroom.

Olivia had taken special care with her appearance, wearing a pale yellow gown that was banded by satin ribbon on the capped sleeves, the high waistline, and the tiered hem of her skirt. Around her neck she wore a gold chain studded with dark and light amber-colored gemstones.

Andrew looked handsome in his evening attire of black evening coat, finely pleated waistcoat, and intricately tied neckcloth. As she had dressed for the party, Olivia had wondered if she and Andrew might have a repeat of the night before and never make it out of the bedroom, but Andrew had remained as aloof when he returned as he had been at breakfast.

The minute they stepped into the crowded ballroom,

Olivia knew something was different. There was an almost frenetic energy to the chattering that could be heard like a roar above the lively music. Olivia's stomach churned with apprehension. Lynette had to be the cause. Olivia wanted to find her quickly and see if she needed support or comfort.

She turned to Andrew and said, "There's someone I need to speak to right away. Would you excuse me?"

Without waiting for his answer or even looking back to see the expression on his face, Olivia waded her way through the crush of people in search of Lynette. She smiled at a trio of gentlemen she passed, bumped the elbow of a disgruntled dowager, and scowled at a group of ladies who were whispering behind their fans.

She walked the perimeter of the room but didn't see Lynette. In a far corner she caught a glimpse of her aunt, and Andrew's Aunt Claudette and the brusque Mrs. Farebrother. Olivia winced. The Lord Mayor's wife could try anyone's patience.

Olivia slowed her steps and calmed her breathing as she neared the ladies. "Good evening, everyone," she said brightly to the three of them.

The two aunts greeted her with smiles and hellos but Mrs. Farebrother lifted her sharp chin and immediately asked, "Have you seen Lady Lynette tonight?"

"No," Olivia said cautiously, hoping she didn't sound eager. "I just arrived."

"Well, look over there." Mrs. Farebrother pointed to the dance floor. "She's dancing with the Marquis of Musgrove Glenn again, but he's not her first partner of the evening. She's been dancing since I arrived."

Olivia caught sight of Lynette and the Marquis and she smiled with satisfaction. Both of them were tall and they looked splendid together; regal and happy. Yes, they looked happy together. How wonderful for Lynette that the Marquis was dancing with her again.

"Why is that a problem?" Olivia asked.

"She's never danced so much in one evening and I think it's because she looks very different," Mrs. Farebrother said with what sounded a little like disparagement.

"Really," Olivia tried to look innocently from one lady to the other. "In what way?"

Mrs. Farebrother's brows lifted and wrinkled into a frown. "After all these years she has decided to try to hide the birthmark on her cheek with some sort of flesh-colored cream or paste. Good Lord! Why bother? Everyone knows it's there."

"Perhaps she doesn't want to hide it but just make it less noticeable," Olivia said, a bit more defensively than she should have.

"That's a nice way to say it, Livy, and probably true," Agatha said.

"But I do have to wonder why she decided to do something about covering her disfigurement after all these years," Claudette said, a wrinkle of confusion between her brows, too.

"Especially now that she has passed the age to make a match," Mrs. Farebrother said.

"What do you mean passed the age?" Olivia asked, bristling. "She's still young. She's not yet thirty, is she?"

"Well, if not, she's very close," Mrs. Farebrother said as if she were speaking gospel.

"Surely a woman can get married at any age she desires," Olivia challenged. "A lady is never too old to marry."

"I hope not," Claudette said with a grin on her lips. "I should like to try my hand at marriage one more time before I die."

"Will that be your fourth or fifth marriage, Claudette?" Agatha asked.

"Fourth, not that I'm counting."

Agatha and Claudette laughed, but Mrs. Farebrother sniffed haughtily and said, "Laugh if you want, but a lady's prospects of a match diminish considerably after her third Season, and I think Lynette has seen more than ten Seasons pass."

"Perhaps her covering the birthmark has nothing to do with a man at all. I think she just decided to do something about her appearance for herself, and I for one think that's admirable," Agatha countered.

"I think you are right, Aunt Agatha," Olivia said, even though she knew for a fact her aunt wasn't right.

"I agree, too," Claudette said. "I use creams that I get from the apothecary on my face every day. That's why I look as youthful as I do."

Mrs. Farebrother screwed up her face even more at Claudette's comment. "I still think she did it because of a gentleman, and I wish I knew which one. But the poor girl, I don't think it will help. Every man knows she has the birthmark and no amount of creams or covering will change that fact. When she removes the cream the horrid red mark will still be there."

Olivia, Claudette, and Agatha gasped in unison.

"That's a dreadful thing to say, Mrs. Farebrother," Olivia admonished.

"It's not dreadful, my dear. It's true."

"If doing this makes her feel better about herself, everyone in the *ton* should support her as she's supported all of you these many years."

"Well said, Olivia," Agatha remarked with a beaming

smile on her face, obviously very proud of her niece's courageous stand for her friend.

"Balderdash," Mrs. Farebrother said. "Everyone has always accepted her as she is. She is, after all, a duke's daughter. Who would dare say anything against her to her face?"

"Good evening, ladies," Lady Lynette said as she stopped beside them. "I hope you are enjoying yourselves tonight. I seem to have caused quite a stir among the attendees."

A smile spread across Olivia's face. Lynette's face glowed with confidence; her eyes sparkled with a happiness Olivia had never seen in her before.

"Lynette, you are beautiful."

"Thank you, Olivia. For the first time in my life I feel beautiful. I don't think I've ever danced as much as I have tonight. I think it's because all the confirmed bachelors want to get close to me to see if they can tell what I've done to change my appearance."

"I hope you are denying some of them a dance just to keep them guessing," Olivia teased.

"Oh, I wouldn't. I'm having too much fun to do that. Tonight might be the only night I'm the belle of the ball, and I'm going to enjoy every minute of it."

"You know, it is quite remarkable how different you look," Mrs. Farebrother said as she leaned closer to Lynette and eyed her without censure to get a better look at Lynette's face. "I don't know why you didn't do something to cover your birthmark before now."

"Heaven's bells, Dorothy, must you always be so rude?" Agatha said.

"Me, rude? I am not," she said with outraged indignation. "I would never be disrespectful to another person."

Olivia, Lady Lynette, Agatha, and Claudette looked at each other and they all started laughing.

*A*NDREW STOOD WITH a group of men who were listening to Lord Windham talk about the latest scandal in Parliament, but his gaze and his thoughts were on Olivia. She was across the ballroom laughing with their aunts, Mrs. Farebrother, and Lady Lynette.

She had left his side the minute they walked through the door. It was as if she couldn't wait to get away from him. Maybe he couldn't blame her. He had been glum, but only because he was trying to figure out what he was feeling for her.

He could see she was having a good time, but he certainly wasn't. And it wasn't because he hadn't tried. It seemed that trying to have a good time was all he had done since he married Olivia. But it was becoming clear that the things that once held his interest—a mistress, gambling, racing, and drinking until dawn—no longer entertained him.

Olivia was stunning when she opened up and laughed without reserve. He wanted to see her that free, that uninhibited, and that happy when she looked at him.

Right now, watching her look so beautiful enjoying herself, the only thing he wanted to do was go over and take her by the hand and say, "Let's go home and go to bed."

That is all he had wanted to do since he'd left her side early that morning. He wanted to run his hands over her silky body and taste her skin, sink inside her, and . . .

"Lord Dugdale."

Andrew turned to see one of the servants standing beside

him holding a small silver tray with a folded sheet of paper on it.

"Excuse me, my lord, but I was asked to give you this. The man outside said it was urgent."

"Thank you."

Andrew took the paper and opened it. His gaze went immediately to the signature. It was Thompson. A quick scan of the short note told him the Runner was outside and wanted to talk to him. Maybe his luck was turning and Thompson had found Hawkins.

Andrew excused himself and walked outside the Great Hall. The night was clear of clouds and fog. There was a lingering chill in the air. Lamps glared a harsh light up and down the street, but Andrew saw Thompson standing on the far side of the road and walked over to him.

"What do you have for me?" he asked while still walking up to the Runner.

"Good evening, Lord Dugdale. I'm sorry to disturb you."

"Do you have good news?"

"I have news, but I don't know if you will consider it good."

"Out with it."

"I have reason to believe Hawkins is here in London."

"You mentioned this possibility before. What makes you think this?"

"I learned a lot about him and his habits by asking around when we were in Derbyshire. He likes to gamble, but he has a nasty habit of not knowing when to quit. He often wins big and he loses big. He seldom walks away when he's winning."

"I know this," Andrew said, trying not to let his frustration show. He wanted to hear that Thompson had found the man, not that he knew his habits.

"We've asked around and found out that a newcomer who fits Hawkins's physical description and his gambling preference has been at three different clubs in the area. I have agents at all three places as we speak. I think he's here in Town and it's only a matter of time before we grab him."

"London is a big city. There are a lot of men who fit that description."

"Yes, sir, but everybody is an individual. And this man stands out in the places he goes because his speech is better than that of most of the crowd around him and he acts as if he's a man born to a title."

That sounded like Hawkins. "All right, Thompson, keep looking."

"One more thing before you go, my lord."

"Yes?"

"Be watchful. He tried to shoot you the last time he saw you. He might try again."

"Just find the man."

Thompson nodded and Andrew turned and headed back into the Great Hall. He had to give some thought to Thompson's warning. Not for himself, but he did have Olivia now to worry about. He certainly didn't want the man shooting at him with Olivia anywhere close by.

As he entered the ballroom again one of the young bachelors walked up to him and said, "Dugdale, isn't The General the horse Westerland won off your friend Fines last year?"

A scowl eased across Andrew's face as he looked at the man and tried to remember his name. Westerland didn't win The General. Andrew's friend John had given the gelding to the Marquis of Westerland when he failed to follow through with a bet, but Andrew didn't want to get into that with the gentleman whose name he couldn't even remember.

He simply said, "Fines gave Westerland The General."

"Yes, that's the one. Westerland has The General up against a black stallion tonight at Rotten Row. Word has it that the stallion has never lost a race."

"Is that right?" Andrew said.

"That's what we're being told. Some of us are heading over that way to put down our wagers and watch the race. Come join us."

For a moment Andrew was mildly intrigued, but only for a moment. "Thanks for letting me know, ole chap, but I can't make it."

Andrew walked off.

They had only been at the party a little over an hour but he was ready to find Olivia and take her home. To bed.

He stopped halfway up the steps and chuckled to himself.

"Damnation," he whispered.

What was wrong with him? He was sounding just like Chandler and John. He was beginning to understand why they would rather be home with their wives than at a party with over two hundred people or at gentlemen's club with half-drunk gamblers, or at a horse race.

He didn't know what made Olivia different from all the other women he'd pursued. What was it about her that had him more interested in being alone with her than with a group of men watching horses race or with a well-paid mistress?

When had he changed? And what caused it?

It couldn't just be taking her to bed. He'd never let the enjoyment of a mistress's bed keep him from a horse race.

Olivia was different from every other woman, be she mistress, lady, or doxy. He'd known that the moment he saw her standing in his room. Just thinking of how she looked that evening caused a rise in his lower body.

He bounded up the steps and strode into the large room. A quick glance around told him Olivia was not nearby. He perused the perimeter of the dance floor, passing giddy young ladies, gossiping dowagers, and hopeful bachelors on his search for Olivia.

He steered clear of his Aunt Claude, Miss Loudermilk, and Mrs. Farebrother, who were motioning for him to join them. Pretending he didn't notice, he waved and kept on walking. He didn't want to get caught up in a conversation with the three of them ever again. He'd rather have a burr in his drawers than listen to them bicker.

When he passed the balcony doors he looked out and saw Olivia standing outside with Lady Lynette and the Marquis of Musgrove Glenn.

He stiffened.

Was Olivia still trying to match Lynette and the Marquis? The two ladies were listening intently to something the Marquis was saying. Suddenly both ladies laughed and Andrew realized there was nothing sinister about the two ladies. They were simply conversing as friends with the Marquis.

His gaze strayed to Lynette. Something was different about her. She had never looked more beautiful. No, maybe it was that she'd never looked happier. The Marquis was smiling, too, and at Lynette.

He thought back to what Olivia had told him that morning at breakfast. Watching them now, he realized that if Olivia was trying to play matchmaker between Lynette and the Marquis it *was* because she'd seen something between the two of them that no one else had seen.

The Marquis and the duke's daughter certainly looked enchanted with each other. He believed Olivia was truthful when she'd said she wasn't trying to trap the Marquis for

Lynette. And the man actually looked interested in Lynette.

Andrew's attention drifted back to his wife, who was still conversing with the two. A warm feeling settled over him and he felt a desperate need to touch her. He didn't want to resist the way she made him feel any longer. He wanted her.

He walked over to the three of them and slipped his arm around Olivia's slender waist and pulled her up firmly to his side.

"I've been looking for you," he whispered close to her ear before greeting Lynette and the Marquis.

When Lynette faced him Andrew saw immediately that the birthmark he'd always seen on her face had disappeared. He blinked rapidly, trying to hide his surprise.

"Lynette, you look lovely tonight," he managed to say.

Her smile to him was like a ray of sunshine. "Thank you, my lord."

"I was just telling the ladies about the gardens at Musgrove Glenn. You've been there, haven't you, Dugdale?" the Marquis asked.

"Yes. For a fox hunt a couple of years ago, I believe," Andrew said, still trying to take in the new Lynette with her birthmark covered. "The grounds and gardens are tremendous."

"Well, perhaps I'll host another hunt this October or," the Marquis turned toward Lynette, "if my marriage status changes by then maybe a house party would be the better event."

"If you are married by then, my lord, I'm sure your wife will help you make the right decision," Olivia said.

"Excuse me, my lords, ladies," said a gentleman Andrew didn't recognize. "Lady Lynette, I believe you promised the next dance to me."

"Oh, Mr. Peabody, you're right, I did. I'm sorry, I didn't realize it was about to start."

Lynette excused herself and Andrew watched a scowl form on the Marquis's brow as she walked away. Was the Marquis the reason for the sudden change in Lynette's appearance? Lynette had never married, but as kind as she was to everyone, she'd probably be a wonderful mother to his children.

Olivia had been trying to help these two people see that they would be good for each other. And since he was a betting man, he'd be willing to wager the family home that Olivia had something to do with Lynette's new look.

His admiration for Olivia grew.

Andrew looked down at his wife and he liked what he saw. He liked the fact that Olivia cared enough about Lynette to want to help her. He liked the fact that she brought a book to the breakfast table so she wouldn't be tempted to interrupt him when he was reading the paper. But he was going to tell her he was wrong to be ill-tempered about that. It didn't take him long to realize he'd rather talk to her than read the paper. He could do that later in the day.

But more than anything, he liked the fact that she belonged to him.

Andrew gently squeezed Olivia's waist to get her attention.

When she looked up at him, he said, "It's late. Let's go home."

Eighteen

ANDREW HELPED OLIVIA into the carriage and instead of sitting opposite her, he sat down beside her. He could tell it surprised her, and she scooted on the cushion to give him room.

That wasn't his intention.

He wanted to be close to her. He wanted to feel her body next to his and he deliberately let his thigh touch her leg so he could feel her warmth. There was something indefinably satisfying about just being in contact with her.

As soon as the door was shut behind them the phaeton took off with a bounce and a jerk. There was little light inside the carriage, but enough for him to see how delicately beautiful her profile was. He liked the way her long, dark lashes curled slightly on the ends. Her small nose had a soft and feminine slope to it. But her lips were most tempting of all, full and beautifully shaped. Even the proud tilt to her chin was lovely.

He said, "I knew there was something different about Lynette tonight, but it took me a few moments to figure out what it was."

Olivia faced him and he felt a rush of passionate heat sear through him, giving him an instant arousal. He had a sudden urge to lay her back in the seat, lift her skirts, and take her quickly and ease the pain of wanting in his loins, but Andrew forced that image from his mind.

Olivia was his wife. Not a doxy who was willing to let a man satisfy himself in a carriage for a few coins.

He could wait until they arrived home. But in order to wait he had to put his mind on other things.

"What did you think about her covering her birthmark?"

In the dim light he watched Olivia's lips move as she spoke and tried to concentrate on her words, not on how much he wanted to bend his head down and kiss her lips, kiss the hollow at the base of her throat, and then take her breast into his mouth.

He blinked away the image of her eagerly responding to his touch.

"I thought it made it easier to see how pretty her face is and how lovely her green eyes are."

"I'm glad you saw her that way. That's what she wanted, for people to look at her face for once and not see the birthmark. She's tried various creams and potions in the past but finally something was developed that covered the red and looked natural."

"I have enjoyed Lynette's companionship at parties for years. I like her for who she is. Not for what she may or may not look like."

"I'm sure a lot of people feel that way, yet she has always felt she was at a disadvantage where making a match was concerned."

"I can understand her thinking that."

"Were you ever attracted to her?" Olivia asked.

The only attraction Andrew could think about right now was the one he had for his wife. It was difficult for him to carry on a conversation about Lady Lynette when all he could think about was the anticipation of getting Olivia home, undressed, and beneath him.

Andrew cleared his throat, but he was really trying to clear his mind of pictures of Olivia stretched nude on her bed beckoning him to come sate her and himself.

"If you mean attracted as if I were going to be her beau? No. I've always thought that if I'd had a sister I would have wanted her to be like Lady Lynette. She's friendly, confident, steady, and dependable."

"That's a very nice compliment. I see her that way, too."

It was usually a short ride from the Great Hall to his house, but tonight it seemed to be taking hours.

"I don't exactly know why, but something tells me you might have had a hand in the change in Lynette's appearance," he said.

Olivia looked away for a moment, and when she turned toward him again in the shadowed moonlight that drifted inside the carriage through the small windows he saw that her eyes implored him to understand her.

She said, "If that were true, would it make you angry with me?"

Her words struck him hard. Is that the way she saw him, as always angry? Was he?

Yes, at times. He had felt trapped into a life he didn't intend by two cunning women. But he didn't feel that way anymore. He was beginning to believe that Olivia hadn't set out to trick him into marriage as he first thought. He had been angry, but wasn't now.

Andrew looked down into her eyes, wishing she could see him more clearly so she would know how he was feeling. "I'm not angry with you about anything, Olivia."

"I'm glad. I wanted Lynette to see and believe that she is a beautiful person on the outside as well as inside. I don't want you or anyone thinking I am trying to help Lynette trick any man into marriage. I wouldn't do that."

"At one time I thought exactly that, but I've changed my mind."

Her lovely eyes widened. "Does that mean you believe I wasn't trying to be a matchmaker?"

He could no longer bear not touching her. He reached over and caressed her cheek with his fingertips, letting them slowly trace the outline of her lips. Just touching her face caused his lower stomach to tighten and a surge of hardness between his legs.

Andrew smiled mischievously and said, "Yes. I've been thinking and I've decided that there are some people who need a little nudge from friends, enemies, fate, or maybe even a ghost to help them see that they are meant for each other."

He could see in her face that his words surprised her as their meaning sank in, but just as quickly a flash of doubt shone in her eyes.

Her breath quickened. "Don't tease me, Andrew."

"I'm not. I'm speaking the truth."

His fingertips traveled over her chin and down the slender column of her throat to rest in the hollow at the base of her neck, where he felt the fast pump of her heart. He liked the feel of her excitement.

Anticipation ran wild inside him. He loved the feeling.

Olivia's hand fell to his thigh and she leaned toward him. Andrew knew she didn't realize she was touching him very close to the center of his desire, but oh, he did. The heat from her small gloved hand seared him with eagerness to possess her.

"Tell me what you mean," she said.

"It was a ghost that brought us together, wasn't it? You did tell me you were looking for a ghost in my room."

Olivia's brows drew together in a frown. "Yes, but I—I suppose I never adequately explained that, did I? And I should."

He shook his head. "You can explain it again to me sometime, but not now. The only thing I want to hear from your lips is, 'Kiss me, Andrew, kiss me.'"

She continued to look cautiously at him for a moment or two. She was wary of him and he didn't blame her. He had accused her of trapping him into marriage. There wasn't anything romantic about the way he'd behaved since their marriage.

"Must I ask again?" he questioned her with his eyes as much as his words.

Suddenly a smile broke across her face, a beautiful, glowing smile that showed just how gorgeous she was, and she whispered, "Kiss me, Andrew, kiss me."

He lifted her chin with his fingers, bent his head, and slanted his lips over hers in a slow, tender kiss. The longing and the passion inside him were too intense to go softly or slowly. When her lips parted and she leaned sensually into him, he deepened the kiss.

Her hand on his thigh slipped closer to the throbbing shaft between his legs. That sent a slow spreading of delicious, languorous warmth sizzling through him and he lifted his hips toward her.

His tongue swept inside her mouth, slowly, delicately,

so he could enjoy the sweet taste of her. His uneven breaths quickened and so did hers. That was all the confirmation he needed. She wanted him as much as he wanted her, and that gave him immense satisfaction.

With quickness his arms slid around her back and he pulled her up to him as his mouth ravished hers. He felt her firm breasts against his chest and tightened his arms around her. His lips left hers and he brought his tongue down the long sweep of her neck, tasting her, devouring her.

Olivia arched her back, giving him greater access to her throat and chest, and he took full advantage of her offering.

His mouth found her breast and searched for her nipple hidden beneath the thin material of her gown. Through the silky fabric, he found the tight bud peeking above her undergarment and gently tugged on it, nipping it with his teeth. Her nipple grew harder under his playful touch.

He felt her tremble with desire. Immense pleasure surged inside him to know that he could make her feel so wonderful.

Amid the sexual fog that had enveloped him, some sixth sense kicked in and Andrew realized the carriage had stopped and so did he, groaning as he pulled away from her.

A small involuntary whimper of reluctance swept past her throat.

"We're home," he whispered.

Trying to gather his wits and slow his breathing, Andrew opened the door and jumped down and then took Olivia's hand and helped her out of the phaeton. They remained quiet as they walked up the steps and into the house.

While Andrew was helping her with her wrap Whibbs came in and took their cloaks, along with their gloves and other things. Andrew said a few words to the butler but he really didn't know what. All he could think about was getting Olivia upstairs.

When Whibbs turned away, Andrew took Olivia's warm hand in his and led her up the stairs.

At the top step he turned to her and said, "My room or yours?"

She smiled and said, "Mine's closer."

And with that Andrew pulled her into his arms as his lips came down on hers in a punishing kiss that she accepted with eagerness that pleased him and aroused him.

He kissed her harshly, madly, and Olivia matched his fierce hunger. Andrew was desperate to touch every inch of her beautiful body and sink his shaft deeply into her. His body commanded him to take her quickly and satisfy himself, but he knew he couldn't give into that wanton urge. He wanted to give Olivia all the pleasure she had experienced last night and more.

While their mouths continued to mate he backed her up until his hands found the door knob. He didn't know how but he managed to open it without letting go of her or without breaking their kiss.

Once inside he kicked the door closed behind them. He shoved his hands between them and slipped her gown far enough down her arms that he could free her breasts from her undergarments. A whisper of satisfaction eased past his lips and into her mouth as he cupped, lifted, and firmly squeezed each breast, feeding his insatiable desire to touch her with all the hunger he was feeling.

In seconds, her nipples swelled and hardened beneath his gentle tug. The soft, feminine sounds of delight she made elated him and added to his own enjoyment.

"Does that pleasure you, Olivia?" he mumbled against

her lips, not wanting to stop kissing her long enough to speak clearly.

"Very much so. I don't understand why it feels so blissful, why I can hardly breathe, but I love the way you make me feel."

He chuckled into her mouth. "I can hardly breathe myself," he whispered.

He continued to massage her breasts, loving the feel of their soft, firm weight in his hands. Just touching her helped ease the intense hunger inside him and gave him such pleasure that he never wanted to stop. A burning heat surged through his loins and a longing filled his heart. He wanted to completely possess her as his wife without any doubts or reservations.

"My sweet Olivia. There is so much more about loving to teach you than what you've experienced so far."

"Teach me, my lord, teach me."

With eager hands he took hold of her gown and with a few pulls lifted it over her head and threw it aside. He reached around her and untied the stays, then raked the shift off her shoulders, down her arms, past her waist, leaving the flimsy material to glide down her legs and puddle at her feet. Taking great care, he untied her garters and rolled her silk stockings down her legs and off her slender feet.

Andrew quickly disposed of the rest of her undergarments in the same efficient way, and then he ran the palm of his hands and tips of his fingers over her naked shoulders and breasts, down to the slender curve of her waist and back up again. All the while he gazed at her gorgeously shaped body.

He took in her beauty knowing that she could see his great craving for her in his eyes. He wanted her to know just how deeply he ached for her.

"I want you so desperately I find it difficult to maintain control."

"Is that good or bad?" she asked and reached up and untied his neckcloth.

Huskily, he said, "Very good. I want you on the bed beneath me, but I'm going to wait and take my time at pleasing you first, God willing."

"Then you better help me undress you," she said with a smile.

Andrew helped her make short work of removing his clothing and shoes, dropping them near hers on the floor.

When he stood naked before her she reached out her hands and rubbed her palm tantalizingly slowly over his chest, lightly scraping his tight nipples, making him groan with enjoyment. Her gossamer-light caress teased him and offered no mercy to the pure torment she inflicted on him. Andrew trembled with wanting, willing her with his thoughts to go lower and touch his hardness, feel its thickness, its weight in her hands.

"Your body is magnificent," she said, "so big and strong."

"I fear you are stretching the truth, Olivia, but I do like hearing you say it."

"I speak with all honesty."

He smiled down at her. "And you, my wife, are more beautiful than Venus."

Andrew reached up and pulled the pins from her hair and dropped them to the floor. With gentle hands he slid his fingers into her hair and shook it free of the bun that held it off her neck. He crushed its lush length into the palm of his hands before he let it tumble down to her back. It was so long that it reached to her breasts. He quickly pushed it to her back so it wouldn't cover her beauty.

"I don't want anything hiding your loveliness from me, not even your glorious hair. I don't want to stop looking at you or touching you."

"I like looking at you, too," Olivia said as she let her open palms glide down his chest to his waist, to his abdomen, to his manhood.

Gently, she took hold of him. Andrew closed his eyes, threw back his head, and sucked in his breath at her tender, unexpected touch. His muscles contracted in sweet pain at her bold action.

His body ached to possess her, but he was determined to take their love making slower than his body wanted him to go so he could completely satisfy them both.

"You are so big and hard," she said as she stroked the length of his shaft.

"For you, yes," he whispered, enjoying her touch, yet hurting from having to hold himself in check.

Olivia leaned in close to him and kissed his chest, pulling his small nipple into her mouth. Andrew's legs went weak with need. One arm went around her and he cupped her head and helped guide her while she sucked his nipple into her mouth. His other arm snaked between them and he covered her hand with his and showed her how to hold him and stroke him to give him the most pleasure.

But he could only allow this foreplay for a few moments. It felt too good to continue.

"I want to feel your skin next to mine. I want to feel your body inside mine," she whispered as she reached up and pressed her lips to his.

She must have read his mind. He was slipping over the edge of his endurance. He gently took hold of her hand and moved it up to his chest.

With no thought of pillows or coverlet, he reached down

and scooped her up and laid her on top of the soft, luxuriously feminine bed. He stretched the length of his naked body on top of hers, and he groaned with indulgence from the sheer thrill of having her soft body beneath him once more.

Andrew wanted immediately to enter her, but knew if he did he would spill his seed before he had given her pleasure. He had no desire to leave her wanting. He wanted to fill her and satisfy her completely before he gave in to his own gratification.

His fingers feathered the outline of her face as he looked down at her and whispered, "I'm glad you're mine, Olivia."

"Always want me, Andrew. I need you to always want me to be with you," she whispered.

"I will, my love. You know I will," he answered with a deeper feeling than he thought possible.

He bent his head and kissed that warm soft spot behind her ear. For a moment he rested his face in the crook of her neck. He breathed deeply, drinking in her warm, womanly scent. He kissed her soft feminine skin. He inhaled the scent of freshly washed hair. She was so warm. With tenderness he kissed his way down her neck, down to her breasts, taking first one and then the other into his mouth, moving slowly as if he had all the time in the world.

For the first time in his life he wanted to do more than just satisfy a woman, he wanted to make Olivia feel treasured. He wanted her to know she was more important to him than any other woman had ever been. He didn't know why or what exactly he was feeling but he knew he wanted something more than just gratification from Olivia.

Leaving her breast moist from his tongue, he brushed

her lips with his, easing over them with the lightest contact. She opened her mouth and playfully caught his bottom lip with her teeth. His tongue thrust in deeply, sipping from her mouth. They teased each other with nips and kisses. With a loving hand, he raked his fingers down her breast, over her slim womanly hip and shapely inner thigh.

Andrew moved his hand back up and caressed the warm skin of her stomach and up to her breast again, before inching his hand lower until he found the softness between her legs. There, he cupped her gently for a moment before finding the center of her desire with his fingers. He caressed her with a soft, circular movement.

Within moments, she gasped and arched toward him. "Oh, yes, Andrew. That is where it feels best," she murmured, dragging her lips away from his.

"Tell me more."

She kissed his chin, his neck, and moved back up to his lips. "That is where I hunger for you."

She trembled beneath his loving caress.

Andrew smiled. There was immense satisfaction in the way she responded to him. He relished the sensations touching her gave him.

He didn't want her excitement to end too soon, so he stopped stroking her center and positioned himself at her opening and pushed to enter her.

Olivia was so tight his body trembled.

Her arms went around his back and she hugged him to her. Using easy thrusts he pushed himself in and out, going deeper each time.

"Open up and take all of me, Olivia. Move with me," he whispered into her ear as he kissed the warmth of her neck.

She raised her hips and matched his movement until

they were moving as one. As soon as she joined him their tempo increased until Olivia cried out in passion. Andrew felt her body relax beneath him.

Andrew allowed his body to release hold and he gasped with ecstasy as his body settled softly upon hers. He didn't know if he had ever felt so complete.

Lying with her, he realized he didn't give a damn if she had forced him into marriage. Not one damn. She was the woman he wanted forever in his life.

Forever?

Did that mean he loved her?

Andrew lay quiet and still on top of her as he thought about that possibility. He no longer had pleasure in the things that used to amuse him. He wanted to be home with Olivia. He enjoyed looking at her, talking to her, and just being with her.

He especially loved the way she challenged him at every turn.

Did all that equate to being in love with her?

He rose on his elbows and looked down at her. She smiled up at him and his heart fluttered. Could what he was feeling for her be love? He certainly hadn't planned on that happening.

Olivia opened her mouth as if she was going to say something but he put a finger to her lips and silenced her. He didn't want this time with her to end and he wasn't ready to talk about what he was feeling.

"I've not had enough of you, Olivia. Not nearly enough."

"Then kiss me, Andrew," she said from beneath his fingertips. "Kiss me and show me more of what you can teach me."

And he did.

*O*LIVIA'S EYES POPPED open to the semidarkness of her room and she blinked rapidly to adjust her sight. Something had awakened her. Andrew lay facing her, his arm thrown over her waist. His even breathing told her he was sleeping peacefully.

But her sixth sense told her there was something wrong.

She had that odd feeling again as if someone was in the room with her, watching her, yet she felt no sense of danger from the feeling.

She recognized it as the same feeling she had had her first night in Andrew's house. She listened but didn't hear anything other than Andrew's soft breathing and her own breath. Without moving Andrew's arm from her waist she rose slowly up on her elbows and looked toward the door and gasped.

The shadowy figure of a man was going out her door. The same man she had seen on her wedding night.

Olivia bolted up in bed.

Andrew stirred. "What's wrong?" he asked.

"I saw that man again. He just went out the door."

"What?" Andrew said, coming instantly awake. He sat up quickly and looked at the door.

Olivia scrambled off the bed and ran to her wardrobe for a wrap. "I saw him. It was the same man who was in my room before."

In one fluid motion Andrew rolled off the bed and picked up his trousers, stepping into them as he hurried to the door. Olivia met him there and he jerked it open.

They stepped out into the corridor. It was quiet, dark, and empty.

"Are you sure you saw someone?" Andrew asked as he buttoned the flap on his trousers.

"Yes, but—" Olivia hesitated as a chill swept over her. "Do you smell smoke?"

Andrew sniffed. His eyes widened. "Damnation! Get down the stairs."

Nineteen

❧

*A*NDREW GRABBED OLIVIA'S hand and they raced down
the stairs. The smell of something burning grew stronger
with each step they took. By the time they reached the bottom of the stairs Olivia saw a small plume of smoke floating out of the parlor. The fire couldn't be too big with so
little smoke.

"Get the servants and get out of the house!" Andrew exclaimed as he let go of her hand and quickly disappeared
into the smoke.

Olivia looked at the front door and then back at the entrance to the parlor. She didn't want to wake anyone until she
knew how big the fire was. And she certainly couldn't run
out of the house and leave Andrew to fight the fire alone.

With no idea what she would see or do once inside, she
entered the parlor. She immediately put her hand over her
mouth and nose to keep from breathing in the smoke.

The draperies covering one window were the only things

burning. No one in the house was in immediate danger so she didn't yell "fire." She watched Andrew yank the flaming fabric from the wall to fall on the floor. He turned to grab a pillow from the settee and saw her.

"I told you to get out," he shouted as flames shot up at him.

"No, I'm going to help you put out the fire," she insisted and looked around the room.

"Your hair and robe are too long. You'll catch fire," he said and began to beat the leaping flames with the pillow.

But Olivia was already racing toward the far wall where she saw a small tapestry. She jerked it down from the rod where it hung and hurried back over to the fire. Throwing her hair to her back and catching her robe between her legs, she helped Andrew smother the fire until all that remained was the smoldering fabric crumpled on the floor.

With labored breath and eyes and throat stinging from the swell of smoke, Olivia looked over at Andrew. Moonlight shone in from the bare window and bathed him in soft light. He was dressed in nothing but his half-buttoned trousers, his bare feet planted next to the charred remains of the draperies. His rumpled hair fell across the scowl etched in his forehead, but to her, he'd never looked more handsome.

And she'd never been more certain that she loved him with all her heart.

He coughed again and in a raspy voice said, "You shouldn't have stayed." Concern was etched in every line of his face. "You should have gotten everyone out of the house."

I couldn't leave you. You're my husband and I love you.

"When I saw that nothing but the draperies were burning I knew there was no immediate danger to anyone. I knew we could put out the fire," she said, wishing she could say so much more, but knowing now wasn't the time to profess her love.

"You are too brave for your own good."

His compliment pleased her, but rather than remark on it she said, "Do you think whoever did this is still in the house?"

Andrew shook his head. "Only a fool would remain in a house after he set it on fire. Whomever you saw leaving your room just tried to kill us."

"No, it couldn't have been the man I saw. There wasn't time for him to have made it downstairs and set the fire. We were at the door seconds after I saw him."

Andrew's expression remained dark. "The fire didn't start by itself. There's a half-burned candle on the floor. Someone lit the candle and opened the window so the breeze would blow the draperies into the flame. There's no way this could have been an accident."

"I agree. Whoever lit the candle probably left the house by going out the window, but it couldn't have been the man I saw." She stepped closer to Andrew. "I know you're going to think I'm crazy but I think—I think what I saw in my room was a ghost."

He coughed again and cleared his throat. "Olivia, this is not the time to start that."

"No, let me finish, Andrew. I think the spirit awakened me and wanted me to follow him to the door so I would smell the smoke. I think he wanted to warn me so no one would be injured."

Andrew's eyes searched hers again. "Olivia, that's preposterous. I have lived in this house for over ten years. If there was a ghost in this house, surely I would have seen him by now."

"Perhaps you have never seen the ghost because you don't believe. Nothing else explains how the man I saw disappeared so quickly."

"I don't even know that you saw anyone."

"I'm not lying," she said indignantly.

"I'm not accusing you of that, but maybe you were dreaming you saw a man, or maybe you just saw a shadow."

"No. I saw him as clearly as I saw him on our wedding night. It was the same ghost—ah—same man."

"Why do you think he came into your room that first night? What was he warning you of then?"

"I don't know. Maybe he wanted to warn me that someone was in the house placing the pike where it would fall on you with the least bit of jarring. I don't have all the answers, Andrew, but I know strange things are going on in this house that can't be explained."

"I agree with you. Strange things are going on inside this house and outside, too, and it's past time I got to the bottom of them. Too many things have happened for them to all be coincidence."

A shiver of fear raced through Olivia. "Are you thinking about a couple of days ago when you were crossing the street and a carriage almost ran you down? When you hurt your ankle?"

"Yes. The driver didn't stop to see if I was all right. At the time there was no reason to think it was anything other than a careless youth on a runaway carriage, but now I'm sure it wasn't."

She reached out and took hold of his arm as she said, "Why didn't you—"

Andrew winced and jerked his arm away from her.

Olivia gasped. "You're hurt." Even in the grayish

moonlight she saw a large red welt on the inside of his forearm. "You've been burned. Come to the kitchen and let me see to it."

"I'll be all right," he said.

She placed her open palm on the upper part of his arm, refusing to let him brush this injury off as not important. "Andrew, please, you can't take a chance on the burn turning putrid. Let me take care of you."

"All right."

He relented and followed her into the kitchen, where he sat down at the table and lit the lamp. Whibbs had told Olivia which cabinet held the assortment of salves and medicines her first day in the house. She found the basket of ointments and placed it on the table in front of Andrew. She then poured water from a pitcher into a basin and collected some clean cloths from the cupboard and sat down to wash the wound.

Olivia pushed her hair to her back before dipping the cloth into the pan. She squeezed the cloth, letting the water dribble over the burned area on his arm. The expression on Andrew's face told her the cool water was soothing.

They were silent for a few moments until Olivia said, "I was looking for the ghost for my aunt."

He looked up and his gaze met hers. "What?"

"That night you found me in your bedchamber I was there because of Agatha. The ghost is the reason we came to London."

"So you really are a ghost hunter?" he asked.

Olivia smiled at him as she continued to let the cool water wash over his wound. "It sounds so disturbing when you put it that way."

"No, Olivia, coming to London in search of a ghost is what sounds troubling."

"I suppose it is. It was disturbing for me, too, at first. I felt the same way you do when Aunt Agatha told me that Lord Pinkwater's ghost was calling to her from the grave."

"Your aunt?"

"Yes. Perhaps you don't know that she was once betrothed to Lord Pinkwater."

"I don't think I did hear that."

"Probably not. It was so long ago. My aunt was only eighteen at the time. Anyway, Lord Pinkwater broke the engagement, but Agatha never stopped loving him or hoping that he would return to her one day. Even after his death. A few weeks ago, she insisted his ghost called to her and told her to come to London and find him because he had something important to say to her."

"And you agreed to come to London and help her because you believe in ghosts."

"No." Olivia put down the wet cloth and picked up a dry one and lightly patted the burn. She liked taking care of Andrew. "At the time I was quite sure I didn't believe in ghosts, but I knew I had to help my aunt. She wanted to search private homes until she found the one where Lord Pinkwater's ghost resides."

"You think his ghost is in my house?" he asked incredulously.

"I didn't at the time, but now I'm beginning to wonder. Do you remember the first night we met? An urn fell from the stairwell landing."

"Even though I tried to drink myself into oblivion that night after you left, I remember every moment of it very well."

"When the urn fell Aunt Agatha considered it a sign to her from Lord Pinkwater letting her know that he was in this house."

"And that's why you were upstairs looking for him."

"Yes. She wanted to search your house, but I couldn't let her for fear someone would catch her. I was afraid she would tell them what she was doing and they would think she was a crazy old woman who should be kept locked away from Society. Her position in the *ton* has always been the most important thing in her life. I couldn't bear the thought of anyone finding out that she was looking for Lord Pinkwater's ghost."

"So you were protecting your aunt's reputation."

Olivia nodded as she lightly rubbed the salve on his arm. The burn was red and angry looking but Olivia considered it a good sign that no blister had formed.

"Even now she asks me if I have seen him or felt his presence in the house."

"And what do you tell her?"

Olivia wrapped his arm in strips of the white cloth.

"That I haven't seen him. I can't explain who or what I've seen in my room twice now, but I don't believe I was dreaming. What I saw was too real. I'm beginning to think a ghost is the only reasonable explanation."

"I don't believe in ghosts," Andrew said softly, "but I do believe in you. If you say you saw a man in your room, then I believe you."

"Thank you."

"But what I have to do now is find the man who started the fire, and I have a feeling I know who he is. I'm going to look for him as soon as I get you out of this house."

Olivia's hands went still. She felt as if her breath stalled in her chest. Her gaze flew to his. "What do you mean?"

"I'm going to make arrangements today to have you escorted to my house in Derbyshire until I get this settled. There are plenty of servants there to protect you."

Olivia's mind went blurry with thoughts and her head felt heavy. All she could think was that Andrew was sending her away to his country estate and he would be staying in London.

"No," she said in a hoarse whisper as she rose from the table and looked down at him. "I don't want to go."

Andrew rose, too. "You'll be safe there."

No, she would be abandoned. He would never come back for her. She would be forced to live a life of loneliness just like her mother.

Her stomach quaked. She felt as if her heart were breaking in two. "Don't send me away, Andrew," she whispered. "Don't."

"Olivia, someone is trying to kill me. I don't want you to be harmed. Go upstairs and start packing. I want you out of this house and on your way to Derbyshire before the sun is high in the sky," he said and turned toward the kitchen door.

For a moment she felt as if the world were spinning around her, leaving her dizzy. She grabbed hold of the table to steady herself. Her mind was a jumble of words but they all said the same thing. Andrew wanted her to leave. After their passionate love making, after he had her believing he might grow to love her and want to share his life with her, he was sending her to his country estate.

If she left, she would be giving in to her husband's command as her mother had given in to Olivia's father's demands. But Olivia was not her mother. This house was Olivia's home and she belonged by Andrew's side no matter the circumstances. If the possibility of a ghost hadn't frightened her away, she wasn't going to let anyone else scare her off. Andrew needed her.

She couldn't force him to love her, but danger or not, she wasn't leaving.

As he walked through the doorway she calmly said, "I'm not going anywhere."

Andrew stopped and turned around to look at her. His eyes searched her face. "Olivia, you can't stay here."

"Watch me, my husband."

His expression turned serious. "Don't you understand that your life is in danger if you remain here?"

"What about your life? If I am in danger in this house, so are you."

"I can take care of myself."

"And I can take care of myself. I have a ghost watching over me, remember."

Andrew leaned his shoulder against the door frame and crossed one bare foot over the other. "That does not amuse me, Olivia."

She took a deep breath and tried to calm the trembling she felt inside herself. "It wasn't meant to, but perhaps the truth will. My mother was sent to the country to live out her days while my father remained the carefree man in London. She waited day after day, week after week, month after month for him to come back to her, and he would for a day or two each year. Just long enough to keep her loving him and wanting him."

Olivia took a few steps toward Andrew and continued. She felt tears sting the back of her eyes, but she willed them not to spill onto her cheeks. She wouldn't allow herself to cry.

"I've watched my aunt live her life continuing to love a man who jilted her almost fifty years ago. She's never loved another because to this day she waits for his ghost to come back to her. I won't live my life waiting for you to return for me."

Andrew straightened. Concern etched its way across his

face and his eyes softened. "Olivia, I wouldn't do that to you."

"You are doing it. I am your wife. I love you and I will stay here with you. We'll face together whatever befalls us, be it danger or safety. I will not be frightened away by some coward who tried to burn down our house."

He walked over to her and gently took hold of her upper arms. "Do you mean that?"

She didn't take her eyes off his face. She was fighting for the man she loved, and she didn't intend to lose.

"Yes. I'm staying."

"No, that part I understood clearly. Did you mean it when you said you loved me?"

Olivia's heart quickened. Had she actually said those words out loud? She hadn't meant to tell him that she loved him right now. It didn't seem the right time, but now that she had said the words she couldn't deny them, even at the risk of his scorn.

"I mean it, Andrew," she whispered. "I love you with all that is inside me, and I can't bear the thought of being separated from you. Do not send me away."

Andrew's heart swelled with love as he looked at his beautiful wife professing her love for him. From the moment he'd met her he had known she was strong, capable, and not easily deterred. But until now he hadn't realized just how formidable she was, or just how lucky he was that she belonged to him.

He pulled her close and hugged her tightly. Olivia was in danger—not from a ghost, but from a real man named Willard Hawkins. Andrew had to make sure she was safe. Sending her to his country estate with Runners to protect her until Hawkins could be found was the right thing to do, but after her plea, there was no way he could do it.

He kissed her hair just above her ear and then whispered, "I love you, too, Olivia. It must be love that I'm feeling, for I've never felt this way about another woman before. I don't want to live without you."

Her arms circled his waist and she hid her face in his chest. "Please don't say that if you don't mean it."

Andrew lifted her head so he could look into her eyes. "I mean it. I don't know how it happened or why it happened. All I know is that I've fallen in love with you and I don't want you to leave my side."

"I can't believe you love me. You thought I trapped you in to marriage."

"I did for a long time. But not anymore. I now know you're not capable of that kind of trickery."

"Oh, Andrew, I'm so glad your no longer think the worst of me."

He kissed the tip of her nose. "It came as quite a shock to me when I finally realized it was love I was feeling for you. When I came down the stairs and saw the fire, I was truly frightened for the first time in my life. Not for myself but for you. At that moment I knew all these confusing feelings I had for you were love and devotion to you and no other."

"Andrew, you've made me so happy."

He laughed softly. "It does make you feel good inside, doesn't it?"

"Very much so." She reached up and placed her lips on his, but that one short kiss was not nearly enough.

Andrew bent his head and rained kisses on her lips, her cheeks, her eyes. Olivia leaned into him and he savored the taste of her. Admitting that he loved her made the taste of her all the sweeter and he wanted to kiss her everywhere. But he knew they were under time constraints.

When he lifted his head, he looked deeply into her eyes and said, "You're mine, my love. I can't let anything happen to you."

Olivia smiled up at him. "Nothing will as long as we're together. I know I'm safe with you."

He brushed her hair to the back of her shoulder. "Olivia, I have a great fear that you might be hurt if you remain in this house. There's a man who wants me dead and he obviously doesn't care who dies with me."

"Tell me who wants to kill you and why."

"I'm sure the man is Willard Hawkins. He once worked for me. I found out that he had been adjusting the account books and stealing from me for years. When I confronted him, he pulled a gun and shot me. The bullet grazed my arm and gave him enough time to get away."

"How can we find him?"

"We can't. I've had men trying to locate him for weeks now. I was told they had tracked him here to London."

"These men know he's in London but not where he's staying?"

"Right. He must have found a window open tonight, possibly the one in the parlor, and crawled inside to start the fire."

"What about the other unexplained things that have happened in the house?"

"My guess is that he probably bribed one of the servants to let him in and create mischief, hoping it would look like an accident. At the moment I have no idea which one that would be."

A curious expression came over Olivia's face and she looked at him and said, "I do."

Twenty

As THEY STOOD in the kitchen, with only a low burning lamp for light, Olivia told Andrew how Ellie came to be her personal maid, including the fact that Whibbs had already had doubts about her. Olivia admitted she had rehired Ellie to be her lady's maid because she felt sorry for her.

"Do you remember the evening I went to your room and told you I heard voices?" Olivia asked.

"Yes. You mean you actually heard voices? That wasn't just a ploy to come into my room and steal a few kisses from me?"

"Certainly not," she said indignantly before she noticed a teasing gleam in his eyes. "Andrew, this is not the time to amuse yourself at my expense."

He grinned and dropped a soft kiss onto her lips. "Sorry. I couldn't help myself. There are some things that are very easy to tease you about."

"And I will welcome it at a later time. But for now, I'll

continue my story. A few days later I heard voices again, and this time I knew you were not in the house so I went on a search to find where the voices were coming from. I found Ellie upstairs in the room directly above mine. She insisted there had been no one with her and that she had been napping."

"She admitted to sleeping while at work?" he asked. "And you didn't dismiss her at once?"

Olivia hated having to admit that she had not terminated Ellie's employment, especially now when she could see how wrong she had been to keep the maid on.

"No. I know I shouldn't have listened to her, but I was trying to be compassionate, so I agreed she could have another chance. I told her I would let the transgression pass, but if it ever happened again her employment would be terminated immediately."

Andrew looked down into her eyes. "I'm glad you are a kindhearted person, but if someone has more than one problem at work there is usually a valid reason as to why one's not up to the task."

"Are you thinking what I'm thinking?" she asked.

He nodded. "That somehow Ellie has been helping Willard Hawkins slip in and out of the house, and he is the one who has been creating the mischief, trying to get rid of me by way of an accident."

"But how did she get him in and out without anyone seeing him? Or perhaps she has been doing the things at his direction."

"That's what we have to find out," Andrew said.

"If we inspect the suit of armor I believe we'll find that it was tampered with in some way to make it fall. And the urn that narrowly missed hitting you when it fell from the landing? It may have been manipulated so it would crash to the floor. Whibbs put the armor in the attic. We can easily check that, but I'm sure the broken urn has long since been thrown out."

"Maybe not," Andrew said. "I remember Whibbs saying something about saving the pieces until someone he knew came back to town. He thought she might be able to put it back together so that no one would know it had ever been broken. There's a good chance it's in the attic, too."

"Let's go up and check for both."

"It will be daylight soon. Let's get dressed and see what we can discover before Whibbs and the rest of the servants begin to stir."

They hurried up the stairs to their rooms and quickly dressed. In the attic, they found the armor standing in a corner. Olivia held the lamp close to the hand where the pike usually rested. It was clear the fingers had been pried apart so wide that the pike wouldn't fit securely in the fist and the least bit of jarring or disturbance would make it fall.

Next they checked the attic over for the broken urn. They looked in trunks, baskets, bags, and drawers. Andrew hadn't seen half the stuff that was in the attic, as he'd never bothered to look at the things relatives before him had piled into the room. It was crammed full of possessions others had deemed too important or too sentimental to throw away.

Just as they were about to give up Olivia saw a wooden box sitting on top of a tall chest. Andrew stood on a chair and handed the box down to Olivia.

When they shined the lamp on the broken pieces of china they looked up at each other and laughed softly.

"What made us think there would be a clue in this?" Andrew asked as he picked up a couple of large pieces of the vase and looked at them.

"I think we're trying too hard," she said and glanced

down in the box again as she started to take the lamp away. Something caught her eye. She reached into the box and pulled out a single strand of white embroidery thread. It was attached to the broken handle of the urn.

"What's this?" Andrew said.

"A piece of thread tied to the handle. Look how long it is."

"I don't think Whibbs would have tied this to the handle of a broken urn."

"Me neither. Why do you suppose it is on there?"

He studied the string. "I can only guess, but my thoughts are that someone tied the string to the handle so they could hide on one side of the landing and pull the urn off the landing from the other side."

"And it could have been set up the night before. The thread is so fine it wouldn't have been seen unless someone was looking for it. Someone could have been hiding almost anywhere upstairs and pulled on that thread."

"And made the urn fall," Andrew finished.

"That's why no one was seen on the landing when it fell."

"It's a very clever idea."

Olivia wrinkled her forehead. "I don't think Ellie would have had time to do these things during the day without someone seeing her."

"You're right. It's possible she let Hawkins in the house. He could have accomplished these things while everyone in the house was sleeping."

"I don't like the idea of that man being in our house."

Concern etched its way across Andrew's features and Olivia knew he was thinking that it was too dangerous for her to be in the house as long as this man was free. But she wasn't leaving him.

"I don't, either. And I sure as hell don't like the thought that he might have been the man you saw in your room."

"It couldn't have been him. That first night my door was locked. That's why I thought it must have been you. I knew you would have a key. But tonight, I'm certain it wasn't you or Hawkins in my room."

"Believe what you will about your phantom, my love. I would rather a ghost be in your room than a real man."

Olivia smiled. He was going to allow her to believe she had seen a ghost. "I love you with all my heart, Andrew. I'm so happy no one has been hurt."

Olivia reached up and kissed him. She would have made it a quick kiss, but Andrew cupped the back of her head, allowing the kiss to linger. The sweetness of it touched Olivia to her soul.

"I love you, too," he whispered softly when the kiss ended. "I want to take you to my bed and show you just how much I love you, but right now we have more work to do."

"There will be time for loving later, but what can we do now?"

Andrew lifted his head. "Let's go up to the room where you found Ellie and see if we can find anything in there that will give us a clue."

They quietly left the attic and walked belowstairs to the guest room. It was small and contained only a bed, a chest, and a slipper chair. Andrew ran his hands up and down the walls looking for a crack in the wood that would indicate a secret door, but he didn't find anything.

"Where was she standing when you came in?" Andrew asked.

"By the bed. I remember thinking that the covers on the bed had been disturbed and wondered if she could have possibly had a man with her. I was sure I heard a man's voice, but when she was the only one in here I assumed I was wrong."

"Let's move the bed and have a look at the floor."

Olivia helped Andrew ease the bed to the other side of the room. They knelt on the wood floor with the lamp at their knees and quickly found a trap door. Andrew slowly opened it. Cold, dank air rose up to meet them as he shined the lamp into the hole.

"There's a ladder," he said. "It appears to be some kind of narrow shaft that's been built to run along the back wall of the house. Very clever. On this wall it makes it easier to hide the secret passageway with a fake outside wall."

Olivia shivered. "That means whoever built this house wanted to sneak out without being noticed."

"Or he wanted to sneak in," Andrew said and winked at her. She laughed softly.

"I love to hear you laugh," he said. "You need to do it more often."

"I have many reasons to be happy, my lord."

"So do I," he answered.

Olivia looked down at the opening again. "Where do you think this passage leads?" she asked.

"I don't know. My guess is that it's been here since the house was built. This fake wall isn't the kind of thing you can add later. Here, hold the lamp while I climb down. I'm going to find out where it goes."

"No, *we're* going to find out," she said. "I'm coming, too."

He put his hand on her shoulder. His touch was warm, strong, and comforting. "Olivia, I have no idea where this goes. It looks treacherous and I don't want to take any chances on you falling. Stay here and hold the lamp for me."

She looked down at the shaft. "We're in this together. Don't leave me out now."

He reached over and kissed her softly, briefly, on the lips. "You are an amazing woman, you know that?"

Olivia smiled at him and whispered, "I know that I love you."

Andrew returned her smile. He placed the lamp at the edge of the opening. "Hold your dress away from your feet and take your time following me. Be careful of the light when you step down. I'll go slowly in case you need help."

Andrew climbed down into the narrow shaft. Olivia grabbed the hem of her dress and started down the ladder. It was dark, cold, and damp inside the walls of the house. Within a couple of minutes her hands and feet were numb.

It seemed they climbed down for hours, but Olivia knew it couldn't have been more than a few minutes before Andrew whispered, "I've reached the bottom. Stay where you are until I find an opening to the outside."

Olivia tried to look down but she couldn't see anything but a little crack of light from some kind of opening in the wall. She was beginning to feel chilled all over when suddenly there was a creak of wood. She knew Andrew had opened a door.

"Come on down," he whispered.

A few steps farther and her foot hit the ground. She let go of the ladder, dropped to her knees, and crawled out the door Andrew held open for her. When she stood up she saw she was on the ground at the back of the house. There was a very narrow clearing between the house and a row of tall yew trees.

Sunrise was just beginning to break the sky, turning the horizon from midnight blue to dusty pink.

"I guess we now know how Hawkins got in and out of the house without being detected."

Olivia looked from the trap door to the yew trees. "How would he know about this secret shaft?"

"That's easy to explain," Andrew said, pulling her into

his arms. "He used to come to London twice a year to go over the account books with me. He always stayed in that room. He could have been looking under the bed for a stocking or a shoe and found the door."

"And Ellie hadn't been working for you long when I came. Hawkins must have had her apply for a job at your house."

"That's why she was begging you to let her stay when Whibbs was ready to turn her off. She had to stay so she could help Hawkins."

"Oh, I can't believe I fell for her lies."

"Olivia, don't worry about that. We've all made mistakes."

Olivia snuggled deeper into the comforting heat of Andrew's arms. She pressed her nose into the warmth of his neck and said, "What do we do now?"

Andrew kissed the top of her head as he held her tightly. "We go back inside and plan a trap for Willard Hawkins."

OLIVIA SAT RESTLESSLY in the parlor with her needlework in her lap. The room had been scrubbed clean and the scent of beeswax and lemon polish had replaced the smell of burned fabric. She had already sent the housekeeper out to purchase new fabric so more draperies could be made for the window.

The day was passing slowly. Olivia had done more pacing than sewing and reading put together. It was her job to spend the day at the house and keep an eye on Ellie.

It was Andrew's line of reasoning that Hawkins would know that the house didn't burn down last night and that he would come see Ellie to find out what was being said about the fire or possibly to plan other mischief. Andrew wanted everyone going about their day routinely, which meant he had to be away from the house, but not very far.

Andrew had a Runner hiding in the garden watching the outside trap door. Another man was stationed just outside their garden waiting to signal Andrew, who was waiting in a hired coach down the street, if Hawkins showed up.

Thompson had been stationed inside the house in Andrew's book room, pretending to be going over his account books, but Andrew made it clear to the man his only mission was to keep Olivia safe should Hawkins make it inside the house.

"Countess."

Olivia looked up from her sewing to see Ellie standing in the doorway. "Yes?"

"Lady Lynette is here and wondering if you might be available for her to visit."

Olivia studied over it for a moment. She started to say no, thinking there might be trouble if Hawkins showed up. But Andrew said for her to follow her routine as much as possible, so she decided not to send Lynette away.

"Yes, of course, show her in."

A few moments later Lynette walked into the parlor. The first thing Olivia noticed was that Lynette was wearing the facial cream that covered her birthmark.

"Lynette, how lovely of you to drop by," Olivia said, putting her sewing aside. She rose from the settee and the two ladies hugged.

"I'm sorry to stop by again without previous arrangement," Lynette said with a big smile on her face.

"Don't be silly. Have a seat. I'll have some tea brought in."

"No, none for me, thank you. I don't have the time today. I have so much to do, but first things first."

"All right," Olivia said, glad Lynette wouldn't be staying too long, but curious as to why she had come. She sat down beside Lynette.

"I came over to tell you that I won't be stopping by anymore."

Olivia stiffened at the shock of Lynette's words, yet she was confused by the smile on her friend's face. "I don't understand. Did I do something wrong?"

"No, no. You did everything right. I won't be stopping by because I won't be in London. This morning the Marquis of Musgrove Glenn asked my father for my hand and my father agreed. I'll be moving to Sussex with my husband."

Chills of excitement pebbled Olivia's skin as she grabbed Lynette in another tight hug. "I'm so happy for you. How wonderful. So very wonderful! Tell me how it all happened. Did you know he was going to ask for your hand?"

"No, no, of course not, but it is a dream come true. My father called me into the parlor this morning and the Marquis was there. Father told me that the Marquis had asked for my hand, and if I agreed, he would give me a few minutes alone with him so he could make a proper proposal."

"And he did?" Olivia asked with her smile as big as Lynette's.

"Yes! He told me he has always been fond of me. Can you believe that? He's always been fond of me."

"Of course he has, Lynette. You are special to many people."

"He asked if I would be happy married to him and taking care of his children. I told him of course I would. I love children. And then he asked if we could marry without waiting so he could quit the Season and get back to his family. We'll be married next week."

Olivia took hold of Lynette's hands. "Lynette, I don't know what to say except to extend my very best wishes for a long and happy marriage."

"Thank you, Olivia, and thank you for helping me believe in myself."

"I didn't do anything. You just told me the Marquis has always been fond of you."

"He said that when he saw me last night with my birthmark covered it was like looking at a new woman, like he was seeing me for the first time. But this morning he realized that my birthmark is part of who I am and he has always been fond of me just the way I am. He said I should wear the cream to cover it if it made me feel better but he now considered my birthmark a beauty mark."

Olivia squeezed Lynette's hands. "It was so sweet of him to say such a lovely thing to you."

"He told me that when he saw so many men dancing with me last night he was worried one of them would ask for my hand before he could."

"I'm sure he was right, and he did the proper thing by coming to your father at once."

"Guess what he did after he told me that."

"What?"

Lynette bent close and whispered, "He kissed me on my lips. It felt so wonderful I thought I was going to faint."

Olivia laughed. "I agree that kissing the man you love makes you feel that way."

"I think I'm walking on air. My feet may never touch the ground again." Her expression turned more serious and she said, "There is one more thing I must tell you before I go, and I must hurry, as I have two other ladies to see this afternoon. In fact, they are married to the other two Terrible Threesomes."

"Do you mean Lady Dunraven and Lady Chatwin?"

"Yes, Millicent and Catherine. They both already know what I'm about to tell you and I felt it only right that you know, too." She stopped and took a deep breath. "I have been writing Lord Truefitt's column for two years now."

"Ohhh," Olivia whispered as a chill shook her. "Oh? You? You mean he's not a man? He's you?"

Lynette nodded as she opened her reticule and handed Olivia a sheet of vellum. "This will come out later today in the paper."

Olivia looked down at the vellum and read:

> The ghost of Hamlet's father couldn't be more popular than a certain duke's daughter who arrived at the Great Hall last evening as a diamond of the first water. She quickly became the belle of the ball, claiming dances from bachelors young and old. She was sought after so vigorously she was heard saying, "Unhand me gentlemen, by heavens! I'll make a ghost of him that lets me."
>
> *Lord Truefitt*
> *Society's Daily Column*

Stunned, Olivia looked back to her friend. "I had no idea."

"Very few people know, but I wanted you to know because you have given me a new life."

"You did that for yourself, Lynette. But tell me, how did you get started writing the column? Why did you do it?"

"The column has always been written by a lady. The name was made up to help protect the identity of the first lady to be Lord Truefitt. Since I took over I've tried to make the column fascinating for the readers. Millicent always used a quote from Shakespeare. That's why I wanted to end my last column with a line from Shakespeare."

"Lady Dunraven used to write as Truefitt, too?"

Lynette smiled. "Only for a very short time, and you must never tell anyone about any of this."

"Never," Olivia said.

"Millicent took over from her aunt, who had an accident and was unable to write the column any longer. The responsibility of writing the column has brought me tremendous satisfaction, but now I must give it up to be with my husband, and I do so with no reservations."

"So there will no longer be a Lord Truefitt's column?"

"That's up to the *Daily Reader*. Perhaps the owner will find someone to take my place. The only thing I know is that it will no longer be me. I'm changing my name from Lord Truefitt to Lady Musgrove Glenn and I shall be very happy leaving the gossip behind and taking care of my husband's children."

Olivia leaned back in the settee and smiled. "You will have a marvelous life, Lynette, and I shall look forward to seeing you after you become Lady Musgrove Glenn."

*A*NDREW WAS GOING crazy in the enclosed carriage. He didn't know why he thought he could stay in this small compartment all day and not drive himself insane. In the wee hours of the morning it had seemed like a good idea, but at that time he'd also been convinced that Hawkins would show up early in the day to find out what the servants were saying about the fire.

Obviously he was wrong. Noon had passed and so had tea time. In another hour it would be dark, but he still had hope Hawkins would appear. It was the time of day that Olivia had heard the voices in her room. But to be safe, he had to make plans in case Hawkins didn't show. It wasn't safe to let Olivia stay another night in the house until Hawkins had been caught.

Andrew was trying to decide if he should take Olivia to her aunt's house for the night and station a Runner outside for their protection or if they should go to an inn.

Suddenly the carriage door was jerked open and his groom said, "He's here."

"Let's go," Andrew said as he jumped from the carriage and ran down the street. As he neared the house he slowed down and lightened his steps, not wanting to make noise and alert Hawkins.

Andrew quietly walked up to the Runner who'd been hiding in the back garden. "He just went through the trap door, my lord," the burly Runner whispered as Andrew drew near.

Judging from the time it had taken Olivia and him to scale the shaft, Andrew figured Hawkins should be about halfway up to the maid's room.

He looked at the Runner and said, "Give me five minutes and then pull the tin plate from under the shrub and nail it over the door."

Andrew walked as quietly as he could. He wanted to get into the house with the least amount of noise. He didn't want Hawkins getting spooked and trying to rush down the shaft to the back garden.

He eased open the door and entered the foyer. Silently he walked down the corridor, past the parlor. He heard Olivia and Whibbs talking about menus in the dining room but he kept softly walking toward his book room. He stopped at the doorway. Thompson saw him and immediately rose from his chair. Andrew motioned for him to follow.

With stealth and calm they quietly climbed the stairs to the guest floor and slowly walked to the room with the trap door. Andrew listened for a moment. He heard shuffling noises from inside. He reached inside his coat and pulled out his loaded pistol. Thompson did the same.

As soon as he heard voices, Andrew turned the handle. The door was locked. He heard frantic whispering. He shoved his shoulder into the door and it burst open. Hawkins was trying to scramble back down into the shaft. Ellie stood beside him holding the trap door open.

Andrew and Thompson pointed their pistols on Hawkins and he straightened.

"Make any move I don't like and you're a dead man," Andrew said, and he meant every word.

Hawkins slowly lifted his arms into the air.

*F*ROM THE WINDOW, Olivia watched Ellie and Hawkins, hands tied behind their backs, being taken away by Thompson and his men. She closed her eyes and breathed a sigh of relief. From now on she would trust Whibbs judgment concerning the help.

"You can come away from the window now. It's over."

Olivia turned around and saw Andrew walking into the parlor. "Oh, Andrew."

She rushed into his arms and kissed him and held tightly to him. The day had been draining, and just being in his arms was heavenly.

"It's over," he said again as he kissed her lips, her cheeks, her eyes.

"I'm so glad no one was hurt."

"I just want to hold you, my love," Andrew whispered in her ear. "I just want to love you."

"Forever, Andrew, I will love you forever."

"Don't promise me that if you don't mean it."

She looked up into his eyes and smiled. "How can you doubt it? You've already tried to get rid of me and I wouldn't go, remember?"

Andrew laughed. "Yes. Never listen to me when I want to send you away."

"Andrew, I love you. I was heartbroken when you asked me to leave."

"I know. But now you understand I didn't want you to go away to live. I only wanted you out of danger."

"Yes, but to me it was my mother's story and Agatha's story all over again, always loving a man who kept them waiting for him."

"You will not have that problem, my love. In fact, I think I should take you upstairs right now and show you just how much I love you."

"Let's go," she said. He took her hand and as they walked into the foyer to head up the stairs, a knock sounded on the door.

Olivia tensed. Andrew motioned for her to stay by the stairs. He slowly opened the door and said, "Miss Loudermilk."

Agatha stepped into the foyer. "Afternoon, dearies, I hope I haven't called too late in the day."

"Not at all," Olivia said, even though Andrew was giving her the sign to tell her aunt it was a bad time. "Come into the parlor and have a cup of tea."

Olivia and Andrew followed Agatha into the parlor and Andrew kept trying to kiss Olivia and she playfully pushed him away.

Agatha took her usual seat on the settee and Olivia sat beside her.

"Can I get you something to drink, Miss Loudermilk?" Andrew asked.

"I'd love a little of that port Claudette is always talking about."

"All right. Perhaps you'd like to try it, too, Olivia," Andrew said.

She nodded to him and turned to Agatha and said, "Did you have a special reason for dropping by?"

"Yes, I wanted to tell you that Lord Pinkwater came to see me last night."

"He did?" Olivia looked from her aunt to Andrew, who jerked around to look at both of them when he heard Agatha's comment.

"I guess he got tired of me trying to find him and he found me."

"What did he say?" Olivia asked.

That faraway look came into Agatha's eyes and her bottom lip trembled. "He's not coming back. He told me to go on with my life. He's not coming back for me."

A lump of sadness grew in Olivia's throat. "How do you feel about that?"

"Well, last night I cried as I did that first night he left me."

Olivia took her hand. "I'm so sorry, Auntie. What can I do?"

Agatha took a deep breath and forced a smile. She took her hand out of Olivia's and said, "You can stop feeling sorry for me. I've thought about it all day and I decided that if Claudette is not too old to be looking for her fourth husband, I'm certainly not too old to look for my first."

Olivia gasped. "What?"

Agatha looked over at Andrew and said, "You don't think I'm too old to marry, do you?"

Andrew handed her a glass of port and one to Olivia and said, "Of course not. Once they know you are finally available, gentlemen of all ages will be seeking your attention."

"See, Livy," Agatha said, then sipped the port. "Mmm. Very nice. Claudette always had excellent taste."

"Auntie, you can give up Lord Pinkwater just like that?"

"What do you mean, just like that? It's taken me close to fifty years."

"Well, I—I'm happy for you."

"I'm not sure I understand it, but I know for the first time since I was eighteen I feel as if Lord Pinkwater has truly set me free."

"This calls for a celebration," Andrew said.

"Yes, it does," Olivia agreed. "We also found out that Lord Pinkwater's ghost did not cause the urn to fall the first night we were here."

Olivia and Andrew explained to Agatha what happened with Hawkins and Ellie.

Agatha smiled contentedly. "Your estate manager and maid might have caused the mischief here in the house, but it was Lord Pinkwater's ghost that brought you two together. Make no mistake about that."

Andrew winked at Olivia and said, "And I shall always be grateful to him for that."

A short time later Agatha left and Olivia and Andrew closed the door behind her.

Olivia turned to Andrew and said, "Do you really think she's going to look for a husband?"

Andrew smiled and pulled Olivia into his arms and hugged her tightly. "I think she might look, but whether or not she'll marry I have no idea. In any case, she and Aunt Claude will have a good time talking about it."

"Andrew, I do think it was Lord Pinkwater's ghost who came into my room."

"Do you really?" he asked with all sincerity.

"Yes, and I have this strange feeling I'll never see him again. Now that he has spoken to Aunt Agatha I think his mission here is done and he won't be coming back."

"I hope you are right, Olivia. I don't like the idea of you seeing any man in your chamber except me."

"You know, Aunt Agatha was right. Lord Pinkwater did bring us together."

"In that he brought you to London, yes. But I was drawn to you when I first saw you in the receiving line at my house. I think you must have felt the same way because you were certainly letting your gaze feast upon me."

"Feast!" she said in mock horror. "I was merely appreciating a handsome man."

He smiled. "And what was it that caused you to kiss me later when we met in my chamber?"

"I was merely curious about your room and your kisses."

"And if I'm remembering correctly I still haven't had you in my bed yet."

"I believe you are right."

"I suggest we go upstairs right now and change that."

Olivia looked up into his eyes and answered, "I agree, my love."

Andrew reached down and lifted Olivia up into his arms and started up the stairs with her.

Olivia thrilled to his touch.

Epilogue

THE LATE AFTERNOON crowd at White's was small as Andrew, John, and Chandler took their seats at a corner table in the club room.

"How long has it been since the three of us have been alone together?" John asked.

"At least a month," Andrew said.

"More like two," Chandler corrected him.

Maybe Chandler was right. Andrew was enjoying spending so much time at home with Olivia that he didn't seem to notice time anymore.

A server set a bottle of expensive port and three glasses on the table in front of them.

"Who ordered this?" Andrew asked.

"Me," Chandler said as he poured a splash into each glass. "I have news that calls for a celebration."

"Then out with it," Andrew said as he looked at John.

Chandler picked up his glass and said, "Millicent is with child. I should have a son by next spring."

"Congratulations," Andrew and John said at the same time.

They clinked their glasses together and all sipped their port.

John cleared his throat and said, "Well, I have a bit of news of my own."

Andrew and Chandler looked at him curiously.

"Well, I don't think you can top his news," Andrew said.

"No, but I can equal it," John said with a grin. "Catherine is expecting a babe next spring as well."

Cheers went up from all three of them and they toasted again. As they sat their glasses back down on the table Chandler and John looked at Andrew.

Laughing, Andrew held up both his hands. "No, no. Don't look at me. I have nothing to confess. There are no babes expected at my house."

"But you are—well, I mean, you are . . ."

"Yes, damnation, John, I am sleeping with my wife."

"Don't get icy. There was a time you weren't."

"A very short time, which I don't need to be reminded about. I happen to love Olivia very much."

"Good."

"Glad to hear it, old chap," Chandler said. "Now, I just had a thought. There's a very good chance, if you have a son soon after us, that our sons could be the second generation of the Terrible Threesome."

"I rather like that idea," John said.

Andrew looked at his two friends and remembered when they used to plan their own futures. Now they were planning their sons' futures. Life had changed for all of them.

"So what do you think about that idea, Andrew?" Chandler asked.

"I think you both will have daughters," Andrew said.

The friends looked at each other and laughed.

Dear Readers,

I hope you have enjoyed *A Taste of Temptation*, which is the last story in my Terrible Threesome Trilogy.

If you missed either of the first two books, don't despair. They are still available. Just go to your favorite local bookstore or Internet bookstore and order *A Dash of Scandal* and *A Hint of Seduction*.

I love hearing from you. Please contact me directly through my website at ameliagrey.com.

Enjoy,
Amelia Grey

Regency romance by
Amelia Grey

A Dash of Scandal
0-515-13401-5
A recipe for success...
Start with one village girl turned mysterious society
columnist. Add one aristocrat planning to expose her.
Mix in a cunning thief. And you'll have one
delicious Regency romance.

A Little Mischief
0-425-19277-6
An earl is at his wit's end when his marriageable sister
joins Miss Winslowe's Wallflower Society—and ends up
being accused of killing London's most eligible bachelor.

A Hint of Seduction
0-425-19802-2
Everyone thinks Catherine Reynolds has come to London
to make a match, but she's really come looking for her real
father. But when she does meet a handsome man, it turns
out her true love could actually be her half-brother.